MOON FLIGHT

GILL LEWIS

Illustrated by
Pippa Curnick

David Fickling Books

31 Beaumont Street
Oxford OX1 2NP, UK

Moonflight
is a
DAVID FICKLING BOOK

First published in Great Britain in 2023 by
David Fickling Books,
31 Beaumont Street,
Oxford, OX1 2NP

www.davidficklingbooks.com

Text © Gill Lewis, 2023

978-1-78845-257-1

Cover and inside art by Pippa Curnick

3 5 7 9 10 8 6 4 2

Papers used by David Fickling Books are from well-
managed forests and other responsible sources.

DAVID FICKLING BOOKS Reg. No. 8340307

A CIP catalogue record for this book is available from the British Library.

Typeset in Goudy Old Style by Falcon Oast Graphic Art Ltd,
www.falcon.uk.com
Printed and bound in Great Britain by Clays Ltd, Elcograf S.p.A.

For

Victoria Birkett,

my agent,

who has guided my little ship through stormy waters

and found a harbour for my own stories, in a world of so many stories.

Tilbury

Elberry

Nimble-Quick

Rose

Marfaire

Yersinia

Obsidian

Ship Rat

PROLOGUE

The Seventh, Seventh-Born

It is a truth universally acknowledged that the seventh-born rat of the seventh-born litter is a rat in want of adventure.

Tilbury Twitch-Whiskers was no exception.

He just didn't know it yet.

Mrs Twitch-Whiskers, upon the birth of the seventh rat baby of her seventh litter, looked at the little squirming infant and wept salt tears. For he was so much smaller than all the others. His skin was so pale and thin that she could see his little pink heart beating inside his chest. And she never wanted that little heart to stop. So she announced to anyone that would listen that Tilbury was actually her eighth-born ratling, and that her seventh-born had already been taken by a marauding crow. Indeed, a marauding crow had taken nearly all of Mrs Twitch-Whiskers' seventh litter, except for little Tilbury and his fierce sister, Nimble-Quick. Tilbury had entwined his tail around Nimble-Quick's, holding her tightly, as she fought back at the crow.

Maybe this was why Tilbury and his sister became so close, because they had clung to each other during this terrible moment and survived.

'Tilbury is my eighth-born ratling,' insisted Mrs Twitch-Whiskers. 'But he has a weak heart and a weak chest and must stay with me.'

No one challenged her on this, because it is also a truth universally acknowledged that a rat in want of adventure does not last very long in the world.

Piers Piccadilly, the seventh-born rat of the seventh-born litter of Peter and Penelope Piccadilly, was accidentally swallowed whole by a seagull when he chewed his way into a discarded ice-cream cone. Millicent Morden, the seventh-born rat of the seventh-born litter of Merry-Weather and Marylebone Morden, was struck by lightning when she tap-danced across the lead roof of St Paul's.

It was no surprise to find that Mrs Twitch-Whiskers forbade little Tilbury to venture to the outside world. In fact, she told him so many tales of all the terrible things that could befall him, that it was no surprise either that Tilbury grew up to be a nervous little rat, scared of his own shadow. So, he spent his days inside the chandlery of Tilbury Docks, and his little nose never smelled the outside air. He only ever saw the sky through the glass pane of a window.

But an adventurous spirit cannot be contained, for if adventuring cannot be undertaken in the outside world, then the curiosity and imaginings of such a mind are turned inwards and can be the beginning of some of the greatest adventures of all time.

PART ONE
THE
DOCKLANDS

A Tale of a Silk Wing, the
Cursed Night and a Gilded Cage

CHAPTER ONE

The Chandlery, Tilbury Docks

'Tilbury, sit still or this needle will pierce right through you.' Mrs Twitch-Whiskers held the needle deftly in her paw, but little Tilbury wriggled and fidgeted, impatient to leave. He had important things to do today. She pushed more featherdown into the lining of his jacket and stitched the pieces together, making sure it fitted him perfectly. 'Remember that weak bones need protection,' she fussed. 'If you tripped over your tail, you could break your little legs.'

Tilbury waited while his mother fastened the front of his jacket. It was made from soft brown velvet that she had traded from the Rubbish-Tip Rats. His little trousers were padded with featherdown too. Mrs Twitch-Whiskers had indulged in her love of bling, and had made them from silver sequined material, safe in the knowledge that no sharp-eyed magpies could reach him indoors. In fact, the only parts of Tilbury's body now exposed were his paws, his tail and his head.

'Don't forget your hat,' she said.

Tilbury picked up the padded hat and pulled it over his head, wriggling his ears free. The hat was made from a tough brown leather and lined with soft fleece. His mother tied the ribbons underneath his chin and patted his head, checking the padding was thick enough to protect him. She stood back and admired her work. Her tailoring skills were well known amongst the Dockland Rats, and she traded her magnificent sartorial creations at the monthly market. For it is also well known that rats have a good eye for neat needlework and can be a little vain when it comes to fashion.

'There now. Off you go and make sure you come to no harm. And stay inside,' she called after him as she did every day. 'For a rat with weak bones and a weak heart must not go seeking grand adventures of his own. You could catch your death of cold.'

And little Tilbury duly paid attention to his mother's words. For the world outside was vast and terrifying. And besides, the chandlery held everything little Tilbury could ever want to know.

Tilbury lived with his large, unruly extended family in the attic rooms above the chandlery at Tilbury Docks, where the city of London ends, and the Thames reaches out into the sea. Ma and Pa, his brother and sisters, and aunts and uncles and all his cousins lived there. The broken windowpane that had perilously let in the marauding crow had since been blocked with pieces of wood and old carpet. So, the attic rooms were now snug and dry, but most importantly, safe.

Aunt Swinney, Uncle Tubs and their children lived in the grand doll's house, Aunt Lily-Mae slept with her family in the old suitcase, Uncle Eddy and the cousins made their home in the wardrobe amongst the moth-eaten clothes, and Cousin Jak lived in the old trunk full of books.

Tilbury's ma and pa had taken up residence in an old saggy sofa. It was big enough for all the forty-two children from their seven litters, and yet small enough to feel cosy and like home. Being from the seventh-born litter, Tilbury and Nimble-Quick were the youngest and smallest in the family, but they quarrelled and played, fought and frolicked with their older brothers and sisters like any large family. The cushions of the saggy sofa were stuffed with goose feathers, and there, curled up with his sleeping siblings, was the warmest place Tilbury could be on a cold winter's day.

And today was one of those days, at the end of winter when the sky is the colour of forget-me-nots and ice crystals grow their own pattern of flowers on the windowpane.

But little Tilbury was not in bed with the others.

Tilbury had plans.

'Come on, Nimble-Quick,' he called. 'Today's the big day.'

Nimble-Quick raised her head from the sibling pile. 'Is it morning already?'

'Come on,' said Tilbury, impatiently. 'We're going to make rat history.'

Nimble-Quick yawned and stretched. 'Coming.'

Their mother insisted on dressing Nimble-Quick in a red

3

woollen smock with white lacing. She licked her paws and smoothed down her youngest daughter's fur. 'No ratling of mine leaves the attic ungroomed,' she scolded.

But Nimble-Quick had no interest in fashion and wriggled away as soon as she could. She grabbed her sewing bag and hurried after Tilbury.

'Where are you going with that bag?' called Ma.

'I have some embroidery to finish on a dress,' said Nimble-Quick.

Ma frowned. Nimble-Quick often neglected her sewing, even though she was deft with a needle. Ma couldn't help thinking there was some other purpose to the sewing bag today. The ratling was definitely up to no good. 'Look out for your brother,' Ma insisted. 'For the cold will snap his bones.'

Tilbury and Nimble-Quick set off, but then Tilbury turned back. 'I almost forgot,' he said. He pulled a large piece of cheese from the food store and put it in the rucksack too. 'I promised Marmalade Paws his favourite snack.'

The two siblings slipped through a gap in the wainscot, their feet pattering on the dusty wood. Then they squeezed through a crack in the chimney brickwork and scrambled down, their claws and tails gripping onto the uneven chimney walls.

Down,

down,

down,

down,

down . . .

Through the darkness.

All the way to the chandlery basement.

Tilbury sat still in the old basement fireplace and sniffed the air. The grate hadn't been used for over a hundred years and it was full of soot and sticks and feathers from ancient crows' nests.

It was always dusty and musty in the basement. The air was still, and shafts of sunlight sliced through the dust from the grille high above at ground level. Humans hardly ever came down to the basement. It was filled with wondrous things. There were nuts and bolts and fine wire. There were ball bearings, clips and screws, pins, spring barrels, cogs and wheels. It was an emporium of mechanical delights that offered Tilbury inventions of endless possibilities.

Today, he and Nimble-Quick would attempt something that hadn't been done in Dockland Rat history in nearly two hundred years.

'Come on,' Tilbury called to Nimble-Quick.

Tilbury stepped out into the basement, and as he did, a large ginger paw curled around his tail and lifted him high up in the air.

And little Tilbury found himself face to face with an extraordinarily large ginger tomcat, its smile showing yellowed, but very sharp, teeth.

CHAPTER TWO
Marmalade Paws

'Marmalade!' said Tilbury.

'I thought you weren't coming,' said the tomcat.

Tilbury tickled Marmalade under his chin and a great rumbling purr came from the large cat's throat.

Marmalade Paws was huge. He was kept by the chandlery owner to chase mice and rats, but the only running he ever did was to the sound of the tin-opener, opening his dinner. He loved to lie in the dust and catch the sun's rays.

'I've brought you some cheese,' said Tilbury, opening his rucksack.

Marmalade closed his eyes and sniffed. 'Mmm! Stinking Bishop, my favourite.'

'I'll bring more tomorrow,' said Tilbury.

'You're so very kind,' said Marmalade, taking the lump of cheese gently in his mouth.

Tilbury left Marmalade licking the cheese off his whiskers.

Nimble-Quick scuttled past Marmalade, keeping a wary eye on him. 'Ma wouldn't approve,' she said. 'That beast could bite your head off in a second.'

'Marmalade wouldn't do that,' said Tilbury. 'He's my friend.'

'Cats are no friend to us,' hissed Nimble-Quick. 'We are ancient enemies.'

Tilbury stopped beside the leg of a workbench. 'Marmalade says he doesn't like killing things. He says it makes him feel queasy.'

'It's their instinct to kill,' snapped Nimble-Quick. She looked back at Marmalade who had rolled on to his back to turn his fluffy tummy to the morning rays of sun. 'Besides, you shouldn't let anyone know you can speak Sphinx.' She lowered her voice to a whisper. 'Other rats will talk. It's just not normal.'

'I don't see why it's so bad to learn the language of cats,' said Tilbury. 'Maybe if we understood each other, we could get along better.'

'Right! Little brother,' said Nimble-Quick, rolling her eyes. 'I won't actually need a cosy chat with a cat before I'm its breakfast.'

'Besides,' continued Tilbury, 'Marmalade teaches me Olde Sphinx too, the language of the great king cats. He says lions and tigers are so big that they even eat humans. Imagine how big they must be!'

Nimble-Quick shuddered. 'I'd rather not imagine. Cats are quite big enough. And I still say you can never trust a cat, not even Marmalade.'

'Come on,' said Tilbury. 'We are about to make rat history. No rat has ever flown since the Great Bartholomew created his Silk Wing.'

'We're not technically flying,' said Nimble-Quick. 'We're gliding. We can't take off from the ground without something to launch ourselves upward. Bartholomew's Silk Wing could take off from the ground by itself.'

Tilbury sighed. He often dreamed of making such a machine. Legends were told about the Silk Wing, a flying machine that could take rats up into the air. Many stories had grown into myth and legend about its maker, for Bartholomew had been born nearly two hundred years ago, a long time for humans, and seemingly longer for rats whose lifespans are so much shorter than that of people. It was said that the Silk Wing and the detailed plans to build it had been destroyed by Bartholomew himself. And Bartholomew, being a seventh-born rat of a seventh-born litter, had come to a sticky end, at the very pointy end of a jewel-encrusted dagger.

Nimble-Quick reached into her sewing bag and pulled out the piece of sewing she had been working on. It was a garment made of fine sky-blue silk. It was gossamer thin, very light and strong, sewn together with gold thread. She took off her woollen smock and pulled on the garment, pushing her paws and feet through the sleeves and trouser legs. It clung close to her body, but two broad sheets of silk were attached from her paws to her feet, so that when she opened her arms wide, it looked like she had wings.

'I'm going to call it a bird-suit,' she said, flapping her arms.

'Do you think it will work?' asked Tilbury.

'Only one way to find out,' said Nimble-Quick. 'Come on, let's get on with it.'

Tilbury nodded and scuttled under the workbench. He came back out pushing the latest invention he had been working on. It was a large mechanical catapult, with a rachet system of cogs and wheels to pull a piece of rubber tubing back and stay taut. A small hook allowed the catapult to be released.

'You don't have to do it,' said Tilbury. 'Ma would be so mad at us if you got killed doing this.'

'I'll be fine,' said Nimble-Quick. 'Besides, we've put plenty of sacking down.'

Tilbury looked along the basement floor to the piles of sacking and sawdust that they had placed for a soft landing. He had experimented by catapulting a small block of wood into the air to estimate where Nimble-Quick might land. 'OK, let's do this.'

Tilbury turned the handle and the rachet system of the catapult pulled the rubber tubing back until it was fully stretched. He tested it for tautness and checked the angle, so that Nimble-Quick would be launched upwards. 'It's ready,' he said. He pulled off his tough leather hat. 'Have this just in case.'

Nimble-Quick put on the hat, climbed onto the platform and leaned back against the rubber tubing. She kept her paws by her side and focused on the soft landing.

'Ready?' said Tilbury.

Nimble-Quick took a deep breath. 'Ready.'

Three . . .

Two . . .

One . . .

Tilbury released the hook.

10

There was a moment of silence, then a gigantic . . .

PING!

. . . and Nimble-Quick shot like an arrow, into the air.

Higher and higher and higher went Nimble-Quick. Her paws were pressed against her sides, but as soon as she reached the top of her arc of trajectory, she spread her arms outwards, and the bird-suit's wings opened wide.

And she flew.

'It's worked,' yelled Tilbury.

'Woohoo!' called Nimble-Quick, soaring away from him.

He expected his sister to glide down to the pile of sacking, but the bird-suit caught a draught of air that wafted through the grilles at the top of the basement window, and Nimble-Quick soared on and on, past the soft landing, over the workshop counters and then down, down, down.

Tilbury heard a shriek of panic and he saw Nimble-Quick flapping like an injured bird before she dropped out of sight.

There was a yowl and a screech and then deathly hush, as Marmalade Paws streaked across the floor.

'Nimble-Quick!' called Tilbury, running to the place where she had come down. 'Are you all right?'

There was no answer. Nimble-Quick lay on her back, her eyes staring upwards.

'No, no, no, no, no!' shrieked Tilbury. 'Nimble-Quick, say something!'

But Nimble-Quick wasn't moving at all.

CHAPTER THREE

The Shape of a Feather

'Oh, Nimble-Quick!' wailed Tilbury. 'Don't be dead. This is all my fault.'

But when he bent down to his sister, a huge grin spread across her face.

'Nimble-Quick? Are you OK?' he said.

Nimble-Quick turned to look at him. 'Oh, Tilbury. That was the most wonderful feeling in the world. I flew! I really flew!'

'You're not hurt?' said Tilbury. 'You missed the soft landing I put out for you.'

Nimble-Quick got to her feet and rubbed her bottom. 'Luckily I landed on Marmalade's tummy instead. I gave him quite a shock.'

'We mustn't tell Mother,' whispered Tilbury.

Nimble-Quick took Tilbury by the paws. 'Definitely not. She would stop us at once. Oh, Tilbury. Come on.' Her whiskers quivered in excitement. 'Flying is the most wonderful feeling in the whole wide world. I want to do it all over again.'

Tilbury spent the morning catapulting Nimble-Quick into the air. Each time, Tilbury made small adjustments to the tension on the rubber band so that he could predict Nimble-Quick's landing.

Nimble-Quick found that she could steer herself with her tail, and also soften her landing by back-beating her arms at the last moment. She even learned that she could land on her feet rather than in a crumpled heap in the sacking and sawdust that Tilbury had laid out for her.

'It really is the most peculiar thing,' said Nimble-Quick, 'but if I angle my paws in such a way, I can feel the air catch under the wing to lift me upwards.'

Tilbury's whiskers quivered with excitement. 'With a few more adjustments, I think we may discover the secret of flight.'

Nimble-Quick's eyes shone. 'You must have a go. You have to feel what it is to be a bird.'

Tilbury shook his head. 'Ma says I've got weak bones and a weak heart. I don't think I would survive such excitement.'

'Have a go,' pleaded Nimble-Quick. She slipped out of the bird-suit and pulled on her woollen smock, passing the suit to Tilbury.

Tilbury ran his little paws across the fine silk and shook his head. 'It's too big for me anyway,' he said. He sighed. 'Imagine if Bartholomew had left his plans for the Silk Wing. I wonder how he flew from the ground without a catapult to help.'

'How do birds do it?' said Nimble-Quick. 'Some of them are heavier than us, but they fly.'

'They've got wings,' said Tilbury.

'I know,' said Nimble-Quick. 'But just now I had wings, but I couldn't take off from the ground, I could only glide.'

Tilbury opened his mouth to say something, then closed it again. Nimble-Quick had a point. He didn't know the answer to her question, and his mind began to spin and spin. Maybe if he studied the birds, the answer would hold the secret to the makings of the Silk Wing.

'Come on,' said Nimble-Quick. 'I'm starving, and Ma will be worrying where we are.'

Tilbury pushed his catapult invention under a workbench and glanced across the floor. Marmalade Paws had curled up in an old wicker basket, keeping well away from Tilbury and Nimble-Quick, just in case another flying rat should land on his tummy.

Tilbury followed Nimble-Quick back to the fireplace, where he picked up one of the old crow's feathers. It was a long primary feather from the tip of a wing, and totally covered in soot, but Tilbury held it in his teeth as he scrambled back up the chimney to the attic rooms.

'There you are,' said Ma. She looked at the musty feather that Tilbury carried. 'Don't go bringing that thing into our home.' She closed her eyes at the memory of the marauding crow that had taken some of her children. 'Take it away, Tilbury.'

Tilbury took it to his favourite place by the attic window where he loved to sit and watch the world. He was sheltered by a cardboard box so that passing crows and gulls couldn't spy him there. He held the crow's feather in front of him and studied it. It was so light, yet strong, and Tilbury marvelled that a bird could grow such a beautiful, intricate, yet simple piece of engineering. But it couldn't be just that it was light that helped birds to fly. He turned the feather over in his paws and noticed the feather didn't lie flat but was curved. He gently blew on the feather and noticed how the feather strained to lift from his paw, as if it wanted to rise into the air. Maybe the shape of the feather was important to flight too. And Tilbury's curious mind began thinking about the flow of air over the curved surface of the feather, and his imagination began to soar.

CHAPTER FOUR
The Cursed Night

'I've brought snacks,' said Nimble-Quick joining him.

Tilbury sniffed. 'Mmm! Smoked Cheddar, my favourite.'

Pa was a cheese merchant, and he collected and sold his cheeses at the monthly market, and so their stores of food always included cheeses of all sorts. Sometimes the ripest Camembert stank out the attic rooms. Aunt Swinney would often complain about the stink and keep a large clothes peg to put over her nose just to make a point.

From Tilbury's viewpoint at the attic window, he and Nimble-Quick could see up the Thames towards the sprawling city of London. Tilbury's family, and his aunts and uncles and cousins, were Dockland Rats that lived at Tilbury Docks. The river connected them to the other Dockland Rats upriver, past Canary Wharf and Tower Hamlets all the way to Walton-on-Thames. The Dockland Rats had grown with the ever-expanding city of London

throughout the centuries. Once a month, after a full moon, they traded their wares with each other on the shoreline of the Thames at low tide. Food, drink and clothes were bartered on the riverbanks. But above all else, Dockland Rats coveted jewels and precious stones for their hoardings, for a rat's standing and influence could be measured by the size and quality of their jewel collection. The trading ships that came to the Docklands provided rich pickings for jewels to be acquired from the human world.

Nimble-Quick sighed. 'There's such a big world out there, and I can't wait to explore. I've only been as far as Tower Bridge with Ma and Pa to the markets. Oh, I'd love to ride the London Eye. Imagine having a swim in the Serpentine or seeing the horses at Buckingham Palace.'

Little Tilbury stayed silent, for he felt his heart ache whenever Nimble-Quick spoke about leaving Tilbury Docks. He and Nimble-Quick were six months old, and when a ratling reached a year of age, he or she would set out on a full moon to seek their fortune. But Tilbury knew he would never leave the chandlery at Tilbury Docks. Ma said he would not live long in the outside world where there were dangers at every corner.

'You should come to the next market,' said Nimble-Quick. 'You'd love the cheeses, the fruits, the fine clothes. Why, last time we saw a travelling flea circus, called The Plague. And, oh . . .' she paused. 'You'd love the jewels. Ma said she wants an emerald for our hoarding, but Pa says he'd have to sell a year's cheese to buy it. He says he'll trade his Spanish cheese for a piece of turquoise stone instead.'

Tilbury listened to Nimble-Quick rattle off the precious stones and jewels she wanted to buy. All Dockland Rats kept their jewel hoardings safe, but the most precious gems of all were protected by the Elders in the Tower of London, high in the dusty attic rooms.

'Pa says he's seen the *Morning Star*,' said Nimble-Quick. 'He said he saw it when he delivered his vintage cheese hamper to the Elders.'

The *Morning Star* was a big diamond that had been captured by a rat many years ago from one of the many trader sailing ships from the Far Shores. The Elders kept other gems too, from the *Sacred Heart*, a large ruby, to the *Summer Sky*, a small, perfectly cut sapphire. It was the Elders who held the old knowledge and the Elders who ruled with wisdom and justice over the Dockland Rats.

But little Tilbury held no fascination for jewels or sparkly things. They did not excite his curious mind that yearned to find out how the world fitted together and how things worked.

But there was one exception, one jewel that he did want to know about.

It was a jewel that fascinated and connected all the Dockland Rats.

A black diamond.

The *Cursed Night*.

It was a diamond that had been seized by the Great Bartholomew on his travels to the Far Shores.

It was held within a gilded cage beneath the Tilbury Docks, a cage so intricately designed by Bartholomew himself that no rat since had been able to open it.

The cage was only exposed for one hour either side of the lowest of low tides, showing the mysterious black diamond inside.

The *Cursed Night* held both a curse and a prophecy.

And it was said, that to look into the cut surface of the diamond was to look into the deepest darkest reaches of your soul.

CHAPTER FIVE
The Gilded Cage

'Imagine seeing the *Cursed Night*,' said Tilbury. He frowned. 'Well, I wouldn't want to see the actual diamond.' He shuddered at the thought of seeing deep into his soul. 'But I'd like to see the Gilded Cage.'

Nimble-Quick took his paw. 'The black diamond holds the curse inside it.'

Tilbury shivered. The curse had hung like a storm cloud over the Dockland Rats ever since Bartholomew had taken the diamond one moonlit night and brought it back from the Far Shores. Legend told that the diamond cursed anyone who desired it. Its magic could summon enemies and turn friend to foe. Rats would fight for it and die for it. Its evil shadow cast such greed and treachery that it could darken even the kindest of hearts. It was said that the one who desired and possessed it held power over all. Bartholomew had bitterly regretted bringing the *Cursed Night* back

to the Docklands, and so he had made an elaborate gilded metal cage of puzzle-locks to keep the diamond safe within, so that no one could possess it for themselves.

'I've heard Ma and Pa say the curse is getting stronger, pulling evil closer,' whispered Nimble-Quick. 'They say our enemies are gathering. They seek the diamond too.'

'But we have no enemies,' squeaked Tilbury. 'Do we?'

Nimble-Quick pulled Tilbury closer. 'Oh, Tilbury, there is much talk at the market that the Underground Rats have been seen in daylight.'

Tilbury clutched his tail. 'But the Underground Rats were banished to the Everdark long ago, for trying to steal the Elders' gemstones.'

'They are getting bolder,' said Nimble-Quick gravely. 'They have been seen in the outside world. They are drawn to the power of the black diamond too. There is darkness inside the diamond. It's rising like the tide.'

Tilbury felt his chest tighten. 'But the *Cursed Night* is safe inside the Gilded Cage. Isn't it?'

'It still has the power to curse us,' whispered Nimble-Quick. 'Pa says a wave of its evil is washing over the city. Only last month three rats from Millwall Dock were so busy fighting over a diamond ring they found in the mud that they didn't hear a loose dog. It killed them all. And don't forget, Cousin Jak's wife was driven so

insane with greed that she saved her jewel hoardings instead of her ratlings when their home flooded in Tobacco Dock.'

Tilbury clutched his paws together. Cousin Jak had lived alone since that terrible day. 'But the prophecy says there will come a warrior rat to open the cage and return the diamond to the Far Shores. Only then will we be released from the curse.'

Nimble-Quick nodded. 'Bartholomew's design must be ever so clever if no rat has been able to open it in two hundred years.'

Tilbury sighed. 'I'd love to see it.' His paws twitched at the thought of seeing something made by Bartholomew himself.

Nimble-Quick was silent for a while, staring out of the window. Then she turned to him and lowered her voice. 'I've seen it,' she whispered. 'I've seen the Gilded Cage.'

Tilbury turned to her. It wasn't like Nimble-Quick to tell lies, but she could tell a good story and embellish the truth. 'When have you seen it?' he asked. 'We're not allowed to see it until we're a year old, and Pa says the only way into the Great Hall is along the mud of the shoreline at low tide to get beneath the old wharf.'

'I've seen it,' whispered Nimble-Quick. 'I've been in the Great Hall. The walls are green and dripping in slime, and the Gilded Cage is embedded in a stone pillar.' She leaned forward. 'I've seen it with my own eyes.'

'I don't believe you,' said Tilbury, shuffling away from her.

'The Keeper guards the entrance at low tide. You wouldn't get past the Keeper.'

But Nimble-Quick crept towards him. 'I've found another way in.'

'Impossible,' whispered Tilbury.

'I have,' said Nimble-Quick. 'There's a drain from the basement that leads beneath the wharf. And there are rotten wooden slats where you can see into the Great Hall. Candles burn in glass bottles that hang from the ceiling, and the Gilded Cage gleams with gold.'

'Really?' said Tilbury.

'Really!' said Nimble-Quick, her eyes shining.

Tilbury grasped Nimble-Quick's paws. 'Oh, Nimble-Quick. Tell me what it's like,' he urged. His mind spun with the excitement of hearing about one of Bartholomew's greatest inventions.

'You have to come with me,' she said.

Tilbury shook his head. 'And leave the chandlery? Oh, Nimble-Quick, Ma says I would surely die. You must tell me all about it. Describe it for me.'

Ma's voice rang out. 'NIMBLE-QUICK! TILBURY! Where are you?'

Tilbury's little heart sank, for the answer he so desperately wanted to hear would have to wait.

CHAPTER SIX
The Secret of Flight

'NIMBLE-QUICK! TILBURY!'

Ma found them next to the attic window. 'There you are. Come on, Nimble-Quick. It's foraging time.' She passed Nimble-Quick her travelling cloak and sack. 'There's a new delicatessen that's opened, and Pa thinks he knows a way in. He has his eyes on a piece of Bitto Storico, a cheese made from the milk of cows that graze the pastures of one single valley in Italy.'

Nimble-Quick pulled on the brown coat. It was unlike Ma's other dazzling needlework creations. It was unremarkable, and that is exactly what it was intended to be. For a rat in a travelling cloak goes unseen by human eyes. Rats can pass as shadows, as windblown paper or swirls of dust, and indeed never be seen at all by the human world.

Ma turned to Tilbury. 'We'll be back after sundown,' she said. 'Aunt Swinney and Uncle Tubs will be around if you need anything.'

Tilbury nodded, but he had no intention of going to see his aunt and uncle. Last time he went, Aunt Swinney had made Tilbury sweep the floors and tidy the beds, and all for a mouldy crust of bread. He curled up beneath his box by the window and stared out. Gulls were wheeling high against the crisp blue winter sky. He could hear their mewling calls. Their feathers looked impossibly white and bright in the strong sunshine. Then, far, far below, he could see his family spreading out across the dock on their foraging trip, tiny scurrying dots keeping to the dark shadows.

He sighed. He was used to being alone, but Nimble-Quick's description of the Gilded Cage in the Great Hall tugged at him. There would come a time, when Nimble-Quick reached a year of age, when she would go with all the year-old ratlings to see the *Cursed Night* at the Darkening Ceremony.

The Darkening Ceremony was an age-old tradition. Before leaving home, each young rat was given the chance to try to open the Gilded Cage, to see if they were the warrior rat that would release the *Cursed Night*. Some rats believed the Gilded Cage would never be opened. But the ceremony gave a chance to dress up in finery, eat and drink with friends and pay respects to the Elders who protected the prophecy. It was also a rite of passage for each young rat to say goodbye to their family as they ventured out on their own.

Tilbury sighed again and crawled from his box to stand at the window and press his face to the glass. This was the closest he would come to being outside. He closed his eyes and felt the coldness of the world beyond the chandlery press against his cheek.

The big wide world was waiting for Nimble-Quick, but not for him.

THUMP!

Tilbury's eyes snapped open. A huge herring gull had spied him and landed at the window ledge outside and was pecking at the glass, trying to get him.

Close up, it was much bigger than Tilbury had imagined. All feathers, beak and great big feet. It fixed Tilbury with its bright yellow eye, hitting its beak repeatedly at the window.

Peck. Peck. Peck.

It flapped its wings to balance on the narrow ledge. Tilbury could see all the way down its large open mouth. There was plenty of room in there for a small rat like him. But Tilbury didn't step away. He was watching the bird's wings. It wasn't just the feathers he was interested in, but the shape of the wing. The whole wing held the same shape as the flight feather. It curved upwards and then down. He walked along the window trying to get a different angle of the gull. He understood, then, that he needed to make a wing of silk with the same curve as the gull's wing. He stood on tiptoes trying to get a better view, and all the time the gull called and kept up its frenzied flapping attack at the window.

'TILBURY!'

Tilbury found himself knocked off his feet and dragged back into the attic room by his tail. Aunt Swinney had hold of him and pulled him into the shadows. 'For the love of Bartholomew,' she screeched, 'are you trying to get us all killed?'

'The answer's in the wing,' announced Tilbury. 'The secret of flight.'

Uncle Tubs peered at him and shook his head. 'Strange little ratling, aren't you! There's always one in every litter.'

'I need to go back and see the bird,' said Tilbury.

'Oh no you don't,' snapped Aunt Swinney, tightening her grip. 'Just wait till your ma and pa hear about this. You're staying here with me.' And she marched Tilbury inside the doll's house. 'Now, don't be idle. I need these floors mopped, and when you're done you can polish the crystals on the chandelier. I don't want to see a speck of dust.'

Tilbury's heart sank. Ma would be really cross. She might even forbid him from sitting in his favourite place by the window. For the first time in his life, Tilbury felt trapped. And worse still, he was now stuck in Aunt Swinney's house and had to mop the floors until sundown.

CHAPTER SEVEN

King of All Kings

It was fortunate for Tilbury that his family returned from their foraging trip in high spirits. When Aunt Swinney frogmarched him home, he received a quick telling-off from Ma and Pa, but their attention was swiftly drawn back to their bulging foraging sacks.

Aunt Swinney's whiskers quivered. 'No discipline,' she squeaked. 'It's no wonder Tilbury's turned out like he has.'

Ma narrowed her eyes at Aunt Swinney. 'There is nothing wrong with Tilbury.'

Aunt Swinney sniffed. 'If that bird had got through the window, we'd have all been in trouble. But it seems the Twitch-Whiskers family think they're better than everyone else.'

Ma showed her teeth. 'Well, that's rich coming from you, dear Swinney. It's only silver plates and bowls for your family.'

But Pa stepped between Ma and Aunt Swinney. He held out

a piece of chocolate wrapped in foil. 'For you, dear Swinney,' he said with his most winning smile. 'A cherry liqueur chocolate to say thank you for looking out for our Tilbury today.'

Aunt Swinney took the chocolate and headed back to her doll's house home, tutting loudly as she went.

Ma turned to Tilbury. 'Oh, Tilbury, what were you thinking? That gull could have eaten you whole.'

Tilbury wanted to describe the shape of the wings and the feathers and how they could hold the secret to flight, but he knew his mother wasn't looking for that answer. 'I'm sorry, Ma,' he said.

Pa put his paw around him. 'Come and look, Tilbury. Look what we've found. We shall have a foraging feast tonight.'

His brothers and sisters had found enough food to last a whole week. They had foraging sacks filled with cereals, biscuits and bread.

Elberry, the eldest of the first litter, had a bag full of chocolate raisins. 'I don't see why we have to give half our foraging to the Elders,' he grumbled.

'Because they keep us safe with their wisdom,' said Ma. 'And they are too old to forage for themselves.'

Elberry stuffed a raisin in his mouth. 'They do nothing but eat, sleep and drink wine all day.'

'Elberry!' scolded Ma. 'The Elders protect the prophecy and the ancient words of Bartholomew. When the time comes, when the Gilded Cage is opened, we'll need their guidance. So we must keep the Elders safe and well fed, so they can lead us in uncertain times.'

'The Elders are weak,' said Elberry, narrowing his eyes. 'I'm not the only one to think this. Some say the Elders don't want to find the warrior rat at all, because without the prophecy to protect, they would lose their fine foods and soft beds in the Tower of London.'

Ma stood in front of him and wagged her paw in his face. 'Be careful what you hear and what you say, Elberry. You never know who is listening. Words can be the most dangerous weapons.'

'But it's true,' said Elberry. 'And danger is coming ever closer. There is talk of an uprising of the rats in the Underground. The Underground Rats have always wanted the *Cursed Night*. They will fight us to get it.'

'As long as the *Cursed Night* is secure within the Gilded Cage, we are safe,' said Ma.

Elberry's whiskers bristled. 'There is other talk too,' he snarled. He paused, making sure his brothers and sisters were listening. 'It is said there have been sightings of the Golden Rats.'

'That's enough,' snapped Ma. 'Don't go scaring your brothers and sisters with fairy tales.'

'The Golden Rats will creep into our homes and kill us in our sleep,' hissed Elberry. 'They will drive their jewel-encrusted daggers deep into our hearts.'

'Elberry!' shrieked Ma, covering Tilbury's ears. 'Enough!'

'Come, come,' said Pa. 'Golden Rats belong to the old stories. The last of their kind were killed in the Battle of Bakerloo over a hundred years ago. Indeed, some say they are myth and legend and never existed at all. The *Cursed Night* is safe inside the Gilded Cage. Let's not argue, it gives me indigestion. And indigestion is

31

the worst thing when there is much feasting to be done.' Pa was especially happy with the foraging trip, as not only had he returned with a large piece of Bitto Storico, but he had managed to secure a lump of Pule, a rare Serbian cheese made from the milk of the Balkan donkey. 'Oh, Ma,' he smiled. 'I may be able to trade in the markets for that emerald you so desire.'

Ma smiled. 'I have had a good foraging trip too.' She reached into her sack and pulled out materials of all colours. She had threads and new needles and another small bag of buttons. Ma's button tin held myriad curiosities and Tilbury and Nimble-Quick had spent many a rainy afternoon playing with the buttons.

But all Tilbury could think about now was the Gilded Cage and the talk of Golden Rats.

When they were stuffed full of chocolate raisins and cheese, he curled up next to Nimble-Quick and shivered, spying over his shoulder. 'Do you think there really are Golden Rats alive now?'

Nimble-Quick shook her head. 'If there were any around, we'd have seen them by now.'

Tilbury sighed. 'Tell me about the Gilded Cage,' he said. 'I would so like to imagine what it looks like.'

'No words can describe it,' said Nimble-Quick.

'Please try,' said Tilbury.

Nimble-Quick shook her head firmly. 'If you want to know what it looks like, you'll have to come with me and see it for yourself.'

Nimble-Quick could be infuriating, Tilbury thought. The more he asked about the Gilded Cage, the more she would stay silent on the matter. But the thought of venturing further than the chandlery filled Tilbury with deep fear.

Back in the basement, they worked on the design of Nimble-Quick's bird-suit. Tilbury made parts of the wing more curved, inspired by the shape of the gull's wing, while Nimble-Quick sewed pleats and tucks to help channel the air beneath the wing to give lift.

With each adjustment, Nimble-Quick could soar further, and she could control her turns and lands too.

'We should go outside and test it in the wind,' said Nimble-Quick.

Tilbury shook his head. 'You know Ma says I'm not allowed outside.'

'We won't go far,' said Nimble-Quick.

Tilbury sighed. 'Ma says I'm not to.'

Nimble-Quick frowned. 'Do you really want to spend your whole life in here?'

Tilbury felt little tears prick in his eyes. He didn't know what he wanted. Nimble-Quick was so brave and unafraid of anything.

'I'm safe here,' he whispered.

'What about me?' said Nimble-Quick.

'Well, you're safe here too,' said Tilbury.

Nimble-Quick stood up and swished her tail in anger. 'One day, when I reach a year of age, I'll leave Tilbury Docks, but if you won't come, I'll have to leave without you.'

Tilbury grabbed her paws. 'Then stay,' he pleaded. 'Stay with me. We'll be safe here. Together, forever.'

Tears fell from Nimble-Quick's eyes. 'I want to live, Tilbury. I want to see the world. I want adventures of my own.'

'But it's so scary out there,' said Tilbury. 'Anything could happen.'

Nimble-Quick pulled her paws away from Tilbury's. 'I couldn't live like this. Life without adventure is no life at all.'

'But what if you die?' asked Tilbury.

Nimble-Quick stuffed her bird-suit into her sewing bag. She marched across the basement floor to the chimney breast. She turned to face Tilbury. 'But if I stay here, I will never live.'

And with that, she scuttled up and away towards the attic rooms.

Tilbury sat down and watched his tears make big fat splotches in the dust. Marmalade came to sit beside him, curling his fluffy tail around him.

'Greetings, great king,' said Marmalade in the language of Olde Sphinx.

Tilbury smiled through his tears. Marmalade was trying to cheer him up, teaching him the ancient language of the kings of his kind, the language of lions and tigers.

'Can you remember what to say to a king?' asked Marmalade. 'It could make the difference between being *at* the dinner table, not *on* the dinner table.'

'Greetings, great king,' said Tilbury bowing low. 'I offer you my life as your humble servant. For you are the king of all kings. The

34

king of all kingdoms.'

'Very good,' said Marmalade. 'Did I ever tell you the legend of the great tiger-king who ruled the Sundarbans? It was said his roar could even turn the tides.'

Tilbury leaned into Marmalade's soft fur. There would have been a time when Marmalade's stories would have comforted him. But now he felt no comfort at all. These were just stories, legends of old. They held no place in the real world and weren't useful at all.

'Don't you ever want to leave the chandlery?' asked Tilbury.

'Why would I?' said Marmalade. 'I have everything I need here.'

'But haven't you ever wanted to see the world?'

Marmalade stretched out. 'Why bother, when I can sleep in the sun.'

Tilbury sighed. Soon the eldest of his brothers and sisters would be leaving the family home, then all the others would follow.

One day, it would only be Tilbury left.

And the thought of that made him feel so utterly alone.

CHAPTER EIGHT

The Darkening

The day that the children of Mr and Mrs Twitch-Whiskers' first-born litter were to leave home crept closer and closer.

Ma had been busy all month sewing their travelling bags and new clothes for their adventures ahead. She had made fine new clothes for herself and Pa too. The Darkening Ceremony was an occasion like no other, a time to dress up, a time to present young ratlings into the world. It was a time to show off one's jewel hoardings as a sign of wealth, health and happiness, and standing in society.

While their brothers and sisters in the first-born litter prepared themselves, Tilbury sat with Nimble-Quick, and watched a full moon rise above the city, casting ghost-light across the river.

'It's just not fair,' sighed Nimble-Quick. She glanced back at their mother who was combing the fur of Elberry, the first-born son of her first litter. 'I don't see why we can't go to the Darkening too.'

'I wouldn't want to,' said Tilbury with a shiver.

'We'll have to one day,' said Nimble-Quick. 'When it's our turn, when we're one year old too.'

'That's if I live to be a year old,' said Tilbury. 'Ma says I won't make old bones. Besides, she wants me here. She says I won't survive in the outside world.' He watched Ma fastening silver buttons to Elberry's coat.

Ma kept wiping tears from her eyes. 'Oh, my little babies. You all grow up too quickly.'

'Careful, Ma,' said Pa. He put his paw on her shoulder and dabbed her face with the end of his silk scarf. 'You don't want Elberry's coat all wet. Everyone knows our children will be the best dressed for the Darkening Ceremony. They will all say, "Oh, there goes Mrs Twitch-Whiskers with her elegantly dressed children. So fine, that needlework. So delicate. Such style. Such grace."'

'Oh, but must they leave tonight?' wailed Mrs Twitch-Whiskers, sinking down to her knees and sobbing.

Ola, the second-born of the first litter, put his paws around his mother. 'We'll come back and visit you, Ma. But the world is big and wide and waiting for us.'

Kayla, the third-born of the first litter, sat down beside her mother. 'We are a year old now, Ma. It is time we leave and seek our own fortunes.'

'But I will lose you all,' sobbed Ma. She threw herself to the floor. 'You will all leave me one day.'

'Tilbury won't,' said Ola. 'You'll always have Tilbury.'

'Yes,' sighed Ma, sniffing. 'Maybe there is some comfort in that.'

Pa helped to fold new clothes for the leaving packs for their first-born litter. Ma had made each of them a travelling coat, a rucksack with a set of spare clothes and a silk map of the Thames and all the docklands that stretched from Walton-on-Thames to the sea. Pa put in a lump of cave-aged Cheddar and a piece of chocolate wrapped in shiny paper for emergencies.

'Come on, Ma,' said Pa gently, pulling her to her feet. 'We don't want to be late for the Darkening. It's the honour of every Dockland Rat before he or she leaves the family home.'

'You're right,' sniffed Ma. 'We must do our children proud.' She dressed herself in a gown of rose taffeta with a ribbon of pearl beads. She wore a hat festooned with semi-precious stones: tourmaline, lapis lazuli and topaz. She fastened Pa's jacket, smoothed down the frills and patted his large tummy. 'Honestly, Mr Twitch-Whiskers, I think you have been eating all the cheese at the cheese market, not selling it.'

'I have to sample it first, my dear,' chuckled Pa. 'And after all, my own father always said that a fat rat will survive a lean winter.'

'As long as he does not get so fat he gets stuck in a drainpipe, like Uncle Harold,' said Ma. She sighed, tears welling up again at the thought of all the dangers of the big wide world.

Pa kissed Ma on the nose. 'Do not fret, my dear, for you and I were young rats once and yearning for our futures. Why, if I had not been seeking my place in the world aboard the barge from Brentford, I would not have met you.'

Ma dried her tears and smiled. 'You are always right, dear-heart.' Then she called to all her other children. 'Come, my dears. Come and say goodbye to your brothers and sisters of the first-born litter. Wish them well, good luck and much cheese upon their travels.'

Tilbury and Nimble-Quick joined the others in a line to give their oldest siblings a hug and a kiss goodbye.

'Come back and see us,' said Tilbury.

'Of course,' said Ola.

Nimble-Quick held Ola's paw. 'I wish we could come to the Darkening too. Are you going to look into the *Cursed Night*?'

Ola fell silent and glanced back at Ma and Pa. 'I think I will shut my eyes. I don't think I am brave enough.'

'Is it true,' asked Tilbury, wide-eyed, 'that if you look into the *Cursed Night* you see the deepest, darkest reaches of your soul?'

'It's true,' whispered Ola.

'I'm not afraid,' said Elberry. 'I will do it. And I will unlock the *Cursed Night* from the Gilded Cage.'

Tilbury gasped. 'But no one has unlocked it. Not in two hundred years.'

'The time for change has come,' hissed Elberry.

'But what if our enemies get the *Cursed Night*?' said Tilbury, grasping his tail in his paws.

'They won't,' said Elberry, his eyes flashing dangerously, 'because I will open the cage and return the diamond to the Far Shores. I am the warrior. I am the one to save us.'

There had been whisperings amongst the rats that Elberry might be the one to open the cage. He was brave and clever too. He was a rat that knew his own mind and had saved some young ratlings from a summer flood when he was only six months old.

'Come, come,' said Pa, ushering his first-born litter along. 'The Ceremony of the Darkening will soon be starting. And we must not be late.'

Tilbury watched them go. He felt a pang of loss for the oldest brothers and sisters. He felt something else too. It washed over him. He wasn't sure what it was, but it felt like grief, or maybe a longing for something he could never have. He would never set out upon a moonlit night with a travelling coat and backpack. He would always be the one left behind. The one who always stayed and said goodbye. One day, even Nimble-Quick would leave him too.

'I'd love to watch the Darkening,' said Nimble-Quick. 'Scab-Tail in the vegetable market said the Master of the Ceremony re-enacts the Great Bartholomew's last moments with a replica of the jewel-encrusted dagger that killed him.' She lowered her voice. 'He says young rats are changed by looking into the *Cursed Night*.'

Tilbury shuddered. 'I never want to go.'

Nimble-Quick got to her feet and sniffed the air. 'Well, I'm going to watch.'

'You can't,' said Tilbury. 'Ma said not to.'

'Ma said not to talk to cats, and *you* do,' snapped Nimble-Quick.

'We're not allowed. Ma will turn us back,' said Tilbury.

'Ma won't know,' whispered Nimble-Quick. 'I'm going to go to the secret place that I found to watch. You could come too.'

'I'm not allowed outside,' said Tilbury.

The tip of Nimble-Quick's tail twitched. 'Technically, we don't

41

go outside,' she said. 'We go along an old drain from the chandlery basement.'

I'm not going,' said Tilbury, sitting down. 'And you can't make me.'

Nimble-Quick curled her tail around him. 'You said you'd love to see the Gilded Cage. This could be your chance.'

Tilbury turned his back on her and covered his ears.

But Nimble-Quick crawled closer and whispered, 'Ma and Pa won't even know we are there. We'll be back before them.'

Tilbury's mind somersaulted to the idea of the Gilded Cage. Bartholomew's invention was legendary; beautiful in design, ingenious in its making and impossible to open. And, of course, his curious mind desperately wanted to see such a creation. He turned to face her. 'And we don't need to go outside?' he asked.

'No,' said Nimble-Quick.

'Not at all?' whispered Tilbury.

Nimble-Quick pulled him closer with her tail. 'Not at all.' She smiled, because she knew that the promise of the Gilded Cage had persuaded her little brother to come.

CHAPTER NINE

The Master of the Ceremony

'This way,' whispered Nimble-Quick. 'Hold onto my tail. Let's run.'

Tilbury followed, clutching Nimble-Quick's tail in his little paw. They scurried down to the basement and entered the old sewerage system. It was pitch-black along the twists and turns of the old brickwork drain. It is well known that rats are excellent navigators in the dark, remembering routes and passages, but Nimble-Quick possessed map-making powers superior to most rats. They flew along, Nimble-Quick ahead and Tilbury behind. Sometimes Tilbury could feel a rush of cold air and it brought the worry of dangers of the outside world.

'Are there other rats here?' asked Tilbury. He'd heard Ma and Pa talk about rats from other docks that would beat you up for a lump of cheese, and if you didn't have cheese, they'd beat you up for a laugh instead.

'We'll be safe,' said Nimble-Quick. 'We're going along the mouse trails soon. Big rats can't follow where we're going. Come on. Let's go.'

Tilbury had never left the basement of the chandlery before. He could feel his little heart beating fast, but Nimble-Quick was off, and he ran to keep up. She led him almost to the very exit from the drain. He could see the bright moonlight ahead and heard the rush and gurgle of the river.

'Through here,' said Nimble-Quick.

Tilbury followed her, squeezing through an impossibly tight gap only a young rat could fit into and then along a maze of damp trails. Nimble-Quick led the way down a route that smelled saltier and felt wetter as it descended towards the river.

Tilbury sniffed the dank air. It smelled different from home. It smelled of mice too. He could hear them in the shadows, their high-pitched squeaks. He tried to be brave and remember that mice are terrified of rats.

'Here we are,' whispered Nimble-Quick. 'We must be quiet.'

Tilbury squeezed beside Nimble-Quick into a crack in the wall, concealed by a veil of slimy seaweed.

'I found this place a few days ago,' whispered Nimble-Quick. 'Look down, there's the Great Hall.'

Tilbury peered through the strands of weed and realized that they were sitting in an elevated position looking down into a vast hall. Candles burned inside broken bottles that hung from the ceiling. A breeze came in through the entrance to the hall, turning them in circles, casting dark shadows that spun around the walls.

Tilbury had heard Ma talk about the Great Hall. It was beneath the wharf of the old shipbuilders that had been sealed up and built upon by humans long, long ago. The only known way in for rats was beneath the wharf at the lowest of low tides.

'No humans can get in here,' said Nimble-Quick.

'Where is everyone?' whispered Tilbury.

'I don't think they're here yet,' said Nimble-Quick. 'I told you, we took a shortcut.'

Tilbury peered out. The floor of the hall was covered in mud that oozed and creaked, and in the centre of the hall there was a tall pillar of rock that rose up from the ground. There were steps carved into the side of the rock, and the top was flat. At the summit, a large drape covered something that could have been a table or a box, Tilbury wasn't sure. It was then that Tilbury saw a rat sitting next to it. The rat wore a long black cloak, and the hood of the cloak was pulled over its face. The rat was so still that Tilbury wasn't sure if it was real, but then he saw the tip of its long tail twitch ever so slightly. Tilbury took a sharp intake of breath and ducked behind the seaweed. The cloaked figure turned to stare in his direction and Tilbury could feel the unseen eyes boring into him. Tilbury and Nimble-Quick froze, but the strands of seaweed swished to and fro.

'Stay still,' whispered Nimble-Quick, clutching Tilbury.

The hooded figure turned away, distracted by a noise at the far end of the hall.

'Who *is* that?' said Tilbury.

'That's the Keeper of the *Cursed Night*,' whispered Nimble-Quick. 'The Guardian of the Gilded Cage.'

'Where's the Gilded Cage?' asked Tilbury. It was the reason he had come on this trip after all.

'It's under that drape,' said Nimble-Quick.

The pitter-patter of many feet began to fill the hall. The atmosphere was hushed and reverent. Lantern-bearers came first, followed by adult rats and their children, their bags packed and ready to leave their homes.

'There's Ma and Pa,' whispered Nimble-Quick excitedly.

Tilbury saw his mother and father lead their five eldest children across the hall to stand in the front row of a circle around the big rock. He could see other rats taking sideways glances at the fine clothes Ma had made for her family. They admired her jewel-embellished hat. She and Pa looked so noble and proud, but only Tilbury noticed just how tightly Ma was holding Pa's paw. He glanced once or twice at the hooded Keeper on top of the rock, but the Keeper was still again, like stone itself.

The noise of fidgeting feet and twitching tails stilled as a formidable rat swept into the hall. It was unrecognizable behind a mask of black leather studded with tiny glass mirrors. It wore a long velvet coat that gleamed with hundreds of sparkling gemstones, and it carried a staff topped with the skull of a crow.

'That must be the Master of the Ceremony,' whispered Nimble-Quick.

The Master held his staff up high and a stub of candle glowed eerily from inside the crow's skull. 'Fellow rats!' he boomed, 'Let us bow our heads to our esteemed Elders.'

The rats in the hall bowed their heads as the Elders filed in. They were flanked by large rats in leather armour and sharp metal tail spikes.

'That's the Tower Guard,' whispered Nimble-Quick. 'No rat can get past them. They guard the Elders in the Tower of London with their lives.'

The Elders climbed up wooden stairs to a gallery that ran around the upper reaches of the hall, where a feast of food and drink had been laid out before them. The Elders were white-furred, with frizzled whiskers and bent with age.

Tilbury had never seen the Elders before and was deeply curious about them. They only left the Tower of London for the Darkening Ceremonies and were heavily protected by the Tower Guard. The Elders were almost like myths themselves, for it is well known that rats are not blessed with long lives. Even those who manage to bypass disease, traps, poisons or misfortune generally only live until the grand age of three years. And there is so much living to fit in to such a short and active life. But there are some rats who live beyond their allotted years, and some of those who live to become five or six, or even seven years of age. They are revered and protected, for they are the carriers of knowledge and deep memory. They are the Elders, the ones who protect the *Cursed Night* and guard the prophecy.

Tilbury scanned the bowed heads, but he saw one rat with his head up, looking defiantly at the Elders. It was his brother Elberry. One rat from the Tower Guard looked directly at him, and Ma hastily pulled Elberry's whiskers to make him bow his head.

The Master of the Ceremony tapped his staff three times, and all the rats turned their heads towards him. He held his paws high with an air of theatrics. 'On this moonlit night we honour our children that will make haste into the wide world. We bless them with safe passage and many, many children of their own. But we ask them not to forget that they are Dockland Rats, descendants of the Great Bartholomew. We hope they are blessed with his courage, ingenuity and wisdom.' He lifted his staff even higher towards the rock. 'But we must not forget we are all connected by a curse.'

He ended the word *curse* with long hiss, like a snake.

There were audible intakes of breath in the hall.

'Tonight,' he boomed, 'as the full moon turns and begins to wane, we must honour the Darkening. We must remember Bartholomew and the prophecy. And we must seek The One to free us from this evil legacy.'

Music rose up from the dark shadows of the hall and three musicians came to join the Master. One played a pipe, one drummed tiny steel pans and another plucked at wires pulled tightly between the prongs of a fork. Then, two more rats came to stand beside the lanterns in the stone circle. They made shapes with their paws that cast huge shadow-puppets on the wall of the rock.

A expectant atmosphere rose in the crowd, for all rats love a good story and, however often it was told, the tale of the Great Bartholomew was the most thrilling story of all.

CHAPTER TEN
The Legend of the Cursed Night

Tilbury knew the story by heart.

Of course, every family had a slightly different retelling, but the diamond, the *Cursed Night*, that Bartholomew had taken for his own nearly two hundred years ago, had held every generation of Dockland Rat in fear and wonder ever since.

'Long, long ago,' boomed the Master, 'Bartholomew Belgravia, the seventh-born rat of the seventh-born litter of Bertram and Eliza Belgravia was born into this world at Tilbury Docks.'

The drummer drummed his steel pans and the two rats making shadow-puppets showed a rat mother holding her little rat baby.

'Bartholomew's intelligence was known far and wide,' boomed the Master. 'He had a thirst for knowledge and a curiosity unrivalled. His inventions were legendary at a time when man brought steamships and steam trains into the world. And upon a night like this, he set sail upon his first birthday. He was not satisfied with the barges up and down the Thames, but crossed the seven seas on a sailing ship bound for far-off lands.'

A shadow puppet ship bounced along the waves. Tilbury and Nimble-Quick found themselves drawn even closer to the actors, and both their little noses poked through the veil of seaweed to get a better view.

Even the Elders had paused in their eating and were leaning forward to listen too.

'And it was in the mythical Sky-Mountains,' said the Master, 'that Bartholomew found himself a welcome in the City in the Clouds, ruled by the Golden Rats. There, the Golden Rat King recognized Bartholomew's genius and offered him his own weight in rubies and gold in exchange for creating a flying machine. The king wanted the power of flight to command the skies, for he feared that his enemies would try to steal the black diamond from the City in the Clouds. For the legends have been told of this diamond that instils envy, greed and obsession in all those who seek it. But it is also said that its power makes the one who desires and possesses it invincible.'

Tilbury found his paws trembling at the thought that such a powerful diamond was right here in the hall. He wondered if he would feel its pull of dark magic.

The Master of the Ceremony raised his voice even louder. 'Bartholomew spent many, many months creating a flying machine that he named the Silk Wing.'

'But Bartholomew was betrayed,' whispered Tilbury.

'He was,' said Nimble-Quick. 'Shh! Listen.'

'But,' continued the Master, raising the crow-skull staff higher, 'when Bartholomew completed the Silk Wing, the Golden Rat King threw him into the dungeons, for he feared that Bartholomew would raise an army against him and steal the diamond for himself. But Bartholomew escaped from the dungeons, destroyed the original plans to the Silk Wing and, indeed, he took the diamond in revenge for the king taking his freedom. Then he escaped on the Silk Wing into a moonlit night.'

The shadow puppet of Bartholomew glided over the mountains and then showed his journey back to Tilbury Docks across the seas.

'But how *did* he escape from the dungeons?' whispered Tilbury, who had often puzzled how Bartholomew had managed it.

'Nobody knows,' said Nimble-Quick. 'Some say he had an accomplice. Others say he could pick any lock. Some even say he possessed magic.'

'He was a genius,' murmured Tilbury, wriggling further to watch the action, for he knew this part of the story where Bartholomew arrived back in London to find the Golden Rat warriors had followed him, led by the king's brother, Prince Obsidian.

'The Golden Rats and the Dockland Rats fought many a battle,' said the Master. 'Every rat wanted the diamond for themselves. Its power turned rat against fellow rat and brought violence and greed. Bartholomew named the diamond the *Cursed Night*, for it was only then that he understood that his moonlight escape with the diamond had brought mortal danger to the Docklands.'

The Master raised his voice up high. 'So Bartholomew made the Gilded Cage here, encased in this rock. And he placed the

Cursed Night inside so that none could possess it. None could possess its power. He said one day there would come a warrior of wisdom and great ingenuity, who could open the cage and return the diamond to its rightful owners. Then, and only then, could the Dockland Rats be saved from its terrible, terrible curse.'

The Keeper on the rock stood up and pulled the drape away, showing the ornate cage. Tilbury couldn't take his eyes off it. It was beautiful, made from curls and twists of wire, and cogs and wheels and strange circular bolts. And encased behind the wires sat an inner cage and, inside that, a large diamond, the size of a walnut. The formidable *Cursed Night*. It was so dark and black that it seemed to suck all the light out of the room, except for a faint sparkle that seemed to make it shine with a light of its own making.

The audience collectively leaned forward, and the Master raised his voice. 'Prince Obsidian of the Golden Rats wanted the diamond for himself. He fought Bartholomew. "Open the Gilded Cage," he roared. "The diamond belongs to me." But Bartholomew refused. He roared back, "The *Cursed Night* belongs to . . ."'

The Master let suspense and silence hang in the air. The listening rats held their breath. Despite knowing what was going to happen next, they waited, each hoping something new would be revealed.

The Master wielded the replica of the weapon. 'Before Bartholomew could finish speaking, the prince plunged his jewel-encrusted dagger into Bartholomew's chest. And Bartholomew's heart never beat again.'

Tilbury clutched Nimble-Quick's paw. 'Who does the diamond belong to?'

'We don't know,' whispered Nimble-Quick. 'Bartholomew didn't get a chance to say.'

The Master of the Ceremony turned to the Gilded Cage. 'Bartholomew was dead, but we know that he had entrusted his mother with a secret, a secret kept by every Keeper of the *Cursed Night* since. For this secret will be told to the one that unlocks the Gilded Cage, to the one who must fulfil the prophecy.' He bowed low to the Keeper, with a flourish of his paw. 'We must listen carefully to the Keeper, and hope that one day, we can be free.'

The Keeper paced slowly around the Gilded Cage, and when the Keeper spoke, Tilbury was surprised to hear it had the voice of a she-rat, soft but brittle with age.

She began to chant, and the words that spilled from her seemed to echo and chase each other like flame-thrown shadows around the walls. They were ancient words, passed from Keeper to

Keeper, words that carried the fate of every Dockland Rat within their meaning.

> 'This *Cursed Night*, holds both evil and a prophecy
> Its darkness, is ever calling to our enemies
> A rising tide, of danger and adversity
> For there will come a time, when we decide our destiny
> A time to choose between greed and our integrity
> There will come forth a rat, of Bartholomew's ingenuity
> To unlock the Gilded Cage, and release us from this legacy
> And return the *Cursed Night* far across the seven seas
> To the rightful owners of this rare piece of jewellery
> A journey fit only for a warrior of great bravery
> A warrior to find a truth we cannot see
> To this one, I will reveal the secrets of the prophecy
> Only this one, and one alone, can truly set us free.'

In the deathly silence that followed, the Master slowly looked around all the young rats, pointing at them with the end of his staff. 'And I ask each of you, who dares try to open the Gilded Cage? For this diamond will try to possess you and find the darkness in your soul.

'I ask again – who will dare to look into the *Cursed Night*?'

CHAPTER ELEVEN

In a Diamond Darkly

An excited buzz rose within the crowd, for all the young rats knew this was the moment they would be called forward to try to unlock the cage and dare to look into the cut surface of the black diamond.

The Elders clapped their paws for the Tower Guards to refill their glasses and for more food to be served. The Tower Guards scanned the crowd, and Tilbury felt the gaze of one guard turn his way. It was one of the biggest rats Tilbury had ever seen. He was battle-scarred, with ripped ears and a silver patch over one eye. His tail spikes looked long and lethal. It was as if this rat could see him though the veil of seaweed.

Tilbury felt Nimble-Quick's paw on his shoulder. 'Stay still, little brother,' she whispered. 'That's Yersinia, the General of the Tower Guard.'

Tilbury shivered and waited for Yersinia to turn his attention back to the ceremony. The Master was leading the young rats in a line up the steps cut into the rock. He invited each to take their turn. Some edged forward, too frightened to look. Others swaggered with bravado. Ola went ahead of Elberry, and Tilbury could see Ola's face turned away from the diamond. Ola hardly tried to open the locks and looked relieved to head back down the other side of the rock.

When Elberry stepped forward a deep hush descended. For Elberry was a young rat of great confidence. He was good-looking too, with sleek fur and neatly shaped ears. He bowed to the Keeper and then the Elders. Tilbury noticed the Elders had stopped eating and were leaning forward, intently looking at Elberry. Elberry then turned to the other rats, showing the best view of his handsome features. He bent down and began working with his paws at the intricate locks. There were some loud clunking and clicking of locks opening, and gasps rose up from the crowd.

But then another set of locks firmly closed up again, with another loud clunk.

Elberry tried again, turning and twisting the mechanisms. The clicks and whirr of locks opening up again echoed around the Great Hall. It seemed all the rats were holding their breath. But once again, the locks closed back up before Elberry could reach the inner cage. He snarled in frustration, hitting his clenched paws upon the cage.

'Enough,' said the Master of the Ceremony. 'You have had your turn.'

'I can do it,' cried Elberry, lashing his tail against the locks. 'Let me have another go. I know what to do –'

'Stop!' came a stern voice from the gallery.

All rats turned to the Elder who had spoken. It was Elder Elreath, the oldest rat. He was tall and so very thin, his fur silver and sparse. 'Master Elberry, you are not The One.'

Elberry bared his teeth at the Elders, spittle flying from his mouth. 'I can open it, you know I can. But you don't want me to have it, do you? You don't want anyone to have it. You say you protect the prophecy, but all you want to do is protect yourselves. You want to keep the diamond here so you can get fat and drunk in the Tower while we feed you all.'

There were sharp intakes of breath and in the silence that followed, Tilbury could hear Ma squeak, 'Hush, Elberry. Hush now.'

It was too late. Two of the guards climbed up and held Elberry by the shoulders.

'You dare question the Elders?' said Yersinia, the General of the Tower Guard.

Elberry squirmed beneath the guards' grip. 'I will return the *Cursed Night*,' he snarled. 'I'm the warrior you seek.'

Ma rushed forward. 'Forgive him, please. It's the diamond. It has cursed his mind.'

Elberry turned his head to the diamond. 'It's mine,' he screeched, reaching out his paws and biting the cage with his teeth. 'Let me open it.' But in that moment, he caught his reflection in its surface and stifled a scream. He froze, clasping his paws to his mouth. 'No, no, no . . .'

'What do you see?' asked the Keeper.

'I cannot tell,' squeaked Elberry. 'It cannot be me . . .'

'You must tell,' said the Keeper, 'for then you can understand who you are.'

'I see great weakness,' whimpered Elberry. His shoulders slumped, and he let the guards carry him away from the Gilded Cage and down the stone steps.

'Poor Elberry,' whispered Nimble-Quick gravely. 'The diamond possessed him, and he saw the truth of his soul.'

Tilbury shuddered. He was fascinated by the cage, with its intricate workings, but equally afeared of the *Cursed Night*. He did not want to feel its power and did not want to see himself at all.

The long line of young rats waiting to attempt to open the cage became shorter and shorter until all the year-old rats had tried to open the cage, but none had succeeded.

Tilbury watched the eldest Elder sit back and take a sip of wine. A small smile played at the corners of his mouth and Tilbury couldn't help thinking that he looked somewhat relieved. Doubt crept into his mind. Perhaps Elberry was right, and the Elders didn't want to find the warrior rat. By protecting the prophecy they could live life in luxury.

The Master held the crow-skull staff up high. 'Let us wish good luck and fortune to those young rats as they venture forth, and let us give praise to the moon and hope our saviour will come with its return.'

'To the moon,' all the rats murmured in unison. 'The moon.'

Tilbury and Nimble-Quick watched the year-old rats head out first into the moonlit night. Only Elberry remained, held by two guards that were talking to Ma and Pa. Then they filed out with the Elders, followed by all the adult rats, and lastly the Keeper.

Then the Great Hall was empty. The candles still swung in the breeze, the strange greenish light spinning in the darkness. The creak and swirl of the incoming tide could be heard, creeping and curling into the hall.

'We must get back too,' whispered Nimble-Quick, crawling back into the dark drain. She looked back for Tilbury, but Tilbury hadn't followed.

'Tilbury!' called Nimble-Quick. She edged forward but saw that Tilbury had jumped down onto the soft mud below.

'Tilbury!' she called again, but little Tilbury didn't hear. He seemed in a trance, walking toward the Gilded Cage on the rock. He was drawn by its intricacy and beauty.

He was drawn to it, like a moth to a flame.

CHAPTER TWELVE
The Keeper

Tilbury wanted to see the Gilded Cage for himself. This might be his only chance. He scrambled up the steps cut into the pillar of rock and stopped beside the cage, careful not to catch his reflection in the dark diamond within.

The Gilded Cage was beautiful.

Intricate.

It was the most wondrous thing Tilbury had ever seen.

The cage was cuboid, made from rods of a metal that Tilbury couldn't identify. The metal was the colour of white gold, but it was much harder and colder than gold. There was no rust or sign of age. Maybe Bartholomew had been a metalsmith too.

Tilbury ran his little paws along the tightly coiled spring locks and latches. He traced the pull direction of the interconnecting bolts. Each tiny sophisticated mechanism was connected to the next, such that Tilbury could see each lock had to be opened in order, to release the next. It was a puzzle of confounding design.

If one opened one set of locks in the wrong order, the other locks would not open at all. And Tilbury could see that Bartholomew had laid false trails; sets of locks that appeared to be the beginning of a series but, once opened, locked the central inner cage. *It was clever*, thought Tilbury. Very clever indeed. There had to be another way. Unseen. Obscured.

Tilbury tapped the metal rods as he thought, listing to the ping as his little claws rapped against them. But his claws sounded different on the corner rods. They rang a different note. Tilbury noticed that each corner post turned by forty-five degrees. And after he turned each one, a tiny pin revealed itself in the fourth rod. Tilbury pressed that pin and other latches opened above him. He could see that he was three lock mechanisms away from reaching the inner cage.

His mind was so absorbed in its task that he didn't notice a shadow fall across him.

A scrawny but powerful paw gripped his shoulder.

Tilbury shrieked and looked up. In the cut surface of the diamond, he could see the reflection of the hooded Keeper. And there, below the Keeper's reflection, he saw his own.

He recoiled in horror, twisting away from the image of himself. He closed his eyes and wailed. He wailed and wailed. He felt the darkness of the *Cursed Night* consume him. It was worse than he ever could have possibly imagined.

For he had just seen into the deepest, darkest reaches of his soul.

'Tilbury!'

'Tilbury, open your eyes.'

'I can't wake him.'

'Is he dead?'

'Tilbury. Open your eyes. It's Ma. I'm here now. You're safe.'

Tilbury heard the voices as if they were far away.

He felt the ice-cold water of the incoming tide swirling around him, and he clutched his tail and shivered. The ice seemed to wrap around his heart.

The dreadful fear of what he had seen in the diamond overwhelmed him, and he began to shake and wail again.

'Tilbury,' said another voice. It was the Keeper's voice, soft but somehow commanding authority. 'Tilbury. Open your eyes and look at me.'

Tilbury opened his eyes and found himself looking into the brightest, bluest eyes he had ever seen.

'I am Marfaire,' said the rat, pushing the hood back from her head. 'I am the Keeper.' The rat was an Elder, with fur that was so silvery white it seemed to glow in the darkness. She was tall and wiry and did not have the paunch or stoop of the other Elders. Only the white scarf around her neck seemed yellowed with age.

Tilbury still couldn't stop shaking and he took big gulping gasps that seemed to make him more lightheaded and breathless. However fast he breathed, he just couldn't catch the air.

'He's dying,' wailed Ma.

'Tilbury,' said Marfaire gently. 'You need to quieten your unquiet mind.'

'But how?' gulped Tilbury, in between gasps.

Marfaire put her paw on Tilbury's head. 'Close your eyes,

63

Tilbury. Every feeling you have, you must sink into your tail.' She ran her paw from his head, and all the way down his back. 'Your tail is your balance, for your mind as well as your body.'

Tilbury closed his eyes, and tried to shift his worries into his tail. At first it didn't feel any different. He thought of his reflection in the *Cursed Night* and he gasped for air again. He tried to concentrate on Marfaire's paw pulling his worries down his spine. After another try, he managed to separate his worries from his thoughts and carried them down into his tail. He felt his neck and shoulders relax and a heaviness sink down into his tail tip. He could breathe again, and felt a stillness take hold of him.

'See?' said Marfaire. 'You can open your eyes now. Breathe deeply, in and out.'

Slowly, Tilbury became aware of the Great Hall around him. He saw Ma and Pa, and Nimble-Quick, as well as the Master of the Ceremony. Their faces were fuzzy and coming into focus. There were two Elders watching him too, with Yersinia, the General of the Tower Guard, by their side.

Ma put her warm paws against Tilbury's cheeks. 'Oh, my sweet child.'

He looked up into her worried face 'I'm sorry, Ma.'

Nimble-Quick crouched down and took Tilbury's paw in hers. 'It was my fault, Ma.'

Pa wrapped Tilbury in a blanket and lifted him up. 'Let's get you home.'

The Master of the Ceremony was still holding the crow-skull staff, but he had taken off the mask and jewelled coat, and was wearing just his vest and trousers. The vest was stained with old gravy and his trousers were held up with a piece of string. Tilbury was somehow surprised and disappointed that the Master wasn't some worshipful Elder, but just Erik who ran the alehouse; Erik who had a penchant for theatrics and a loose tongue for gossip.

'You shouldn't have brought him,' said Erik. 'Only year-old rats can attend. Why, if everyone brought their whole family to the ceremony, there wouldn't be room in here.'

'I brought him,' whimpered Nimble-Quick.

Erik turned to Ma and wiped his drippy nose with the back of his paw. 'Really, Mrs Twitch-Whiskers, if you cannot control your youngsters, I will have to ask the Elders to ban you from the ceremony.'

'That's enough, Erik,' said Pa.

The Master looked Ma up and down and sneered. 'Maybe you should pay more attention to your children and what they get up to. Your eldest, Elberry, was a disgrace to the Elders.' He bared his teeth. 'A traitor, no less.'

Pa pushed himself between Ma and the Master. 'Get away home, Erik. I can smell ale on your breath. The drink is talking.'

The Master lifted the blanket and peered at Tilbury. A leering grin spread on his face.

'You know there's talk that your little weird child can speak Sphinx.'

'Away with you, Erik,' said Pa.

'You know what else they say about him, don't you?' goaded Erik. 'Everyone knows he's a seventh seventh-born. Everyone does.'

'Away,' snarled Pa showing his teeth. 'Before I rip your ears.'

The Master snarled back, and he and Pa stood face to face, tooth to tooth, glaring at each other with Tilbury between them, clutched in Pa's paws.

'Enough!' Marfaire's voice cut the tension between them. 'Enough,' she said again. 'The tide has turned, and we must make haste. Erik, let us not spoil this night with a quarrel, for we are all Dockland Rats, and we must not fight battles between ourselves. Let's save them for our enemies.'

The Master of the Ceremony took a step back but kept staring at Pa and Tilbury. But Tilbury was looking past Pa's shoulders towards the Gilded Cage on the top of the rock.

Marfaire gave Tilbury a curious look. 'Tell me, Tilbury. Do you think you know how to open the Gilded Cage?'

Tilbury clutched his tail and nodded. 'I th . . . think so.'

Marfaire turned to the other two Elders. 'Elder Elreath and Elder Pauncher,' she said gravely. 'It appears that young Tilbury here may be the one we have been waiting for. The one to save us and fulfil the prophecy.'

Elder Pauncher was a rotund rat, with greasy yellowed skin and a scabby tail. He scraped at a piece of cheese that was stuck between his rotten teeth and belched loudly. 'The prophecy says we must await a warrior. He does not look like a warrior to me.'

'Warriors come in all shapes and sizes,' said Marfaire. 'We must be ready when that warrior comes.'

Elreath leaned forward. Being the eldest Elder, he was the most revered, having reached the grand age of seven years and three months old. He had barely any fur at all and his papery skin was so thin that Tilbury could see the veins beneath. 'Tell me, young rat,' he said, looking at Tilbury with his cloudy eyes, 'what did you see in the *Cursed Night?*'

Tilbury closed his eyes tightly. 'I cannot tell you.' His whole body started to shake again.

'What did you see?' he asked, pulling Tilbury's nose up to face him.

'I saw . . .' began Tilbury. 'I saw . . . fear . . . I saw nothing else.' His teeth chattered together. 'I am nothing. I saw no head, no heart, no soul. Just fear. Eternal fear.'

Elreath nodded and turned to Ma and Pa. 'If your child is truly a seventh seventh-born, then I ask you not to bring him here again. You must never show him the Gilded Cage.'

'But I insist,' interrupted Marfaire. 'I am the Keeper, and I say Tilbury is the one we seek. Only a rat of Bartholomew's ingenuity can open the cage. If we delay, our enemies may rise and gain strength from the *Cursed Night*. There is unrest among some Dockland Rats. I hear rumours that some have forged links with Underground Rats to overthrow you.'

'Ridiculous,' said Elder Pauncher. 'The Tower Guards protect us with their lives. No one can get past them.'

'Elder Pauncher,' said Marfaire, the exasperation evident in her voice. 'The curse could destroy us all. We must let Tilbury try to open the Gilded Cage.'

'He cannot be the one,' said Elder Elreath. 'We must never

speak of this again. He turned to them all. 'What we have seen tonight must not leave this hall. Our silence will protect us.'

'Quite so,' said Elder Pauncher. 'Tilbury must never come near the Gilded Cage again.'

'Why not?' squeaked Ma, quickly covering her mouth with her paw, as if the words had spilled out too soon.

Elreath lowered his voice. 'Because one day, there will be a young rat to open the cage, and when they do, they must be a warrior, fit for a journey and fit for a battle. Our future depends upon it.' He looked at little Tilbury shaking in Pa's paws. 'Your little son has an inventive mind. But I fear that a small rat with a weak heart and in want of adventure will not last long enough in the world to save us.'

'But, Elreath,' said Marfaire. 'We cannot violate the prophecy.'

Elreath glared at Marfaire, his yellow teeth visible underneath his curled lip. 'And you would risk all the Dockland Rats' lives entrusting a ratling with a diamond of this power?'

'But . . .' said Marfaire, her eyes flitting between Elreath and Tilbury.

'I am the eldest,' said Elreath, 'and therefore blessed with wisdom even beyond your years, Marfaire. And I can clearly see that what matters most is to keep the *Cursed Night* safe inside the Gilded Cage.'

'Exactly,' said Elder Pauncher taking a hip flask from his belt and swigging the contents down.

Elder Elreath turned to them all, pointing at each of them with his gnarled paw. 'And the only way to protect the prophecy is never to speak of this night again.'

CHAPTER THIRTEEN
Shadow Rat

'Hurry up, hurry up,' said Pa. 'It's market day and we'll miss the riverboat if we don't get a move on.'

Market days for the Dockland Rats always fell on the day after the Darkening Ceremony. It was known as a day of truce, when all the Dockland Rats from up and down the docks on the Thames, put aside their quarrels. Goods were traded at low tide on the riverbank at Waterloo. It was a time for the year-old rats who had just left the family homes to meet other rat families and find safe passage into the big wide world. It was time to meet up with old friends and to eat and drink and make merry.

Ma had packed her bags with all the finest clothes and jewellery to trade; silk gowns, tweed waistcoats, fancy hats with pigeon feathers, pearl-bead necklaces, blue cotton dungarees with periwinkle buttons. She fretted with the bag she was holding. 'I don't think we should go,' she whispered to Pa. 'Not after last night.'

'It will look suspicious if we don't go,' said Pa. 'Other rats will talk.' He tied up his cheese packs with string and looped them over his neck.

All the other uncles and aunts and cousins in the attic rooms were getting ready with their wares too.

Ma buttoned her coat. 'I really think someone should stay back with Tilbury.'

'We usually leave him on his own,' said Pa.

'I'll be fine, Ma,' said Tilbury.

'But what about last night?' whispered Ma. 'Perhaps we should take you with us this time.'

'He's safest here,' said Pa. 'Nobody knows about last night.'

'Are you so sure?' asked Ma. 'I'm sure Aunt Swinney was giving him a funny look this morning.'

'No one knows,' assured Pa. 'We all promised to keep it secret.'

'I'll stay with Tilbury,' whispered Nimble-Quick.

Ma wagged her paw at her. 'Definitely not. Who knows where you might take him.' She sighed. 'Oh, it's been such a worrying time. We haven't seen Elberry since last night. He spoke out so rudely against the Elders. Maybe they will punish him.'

'He's here,' said Nimble-Quick, pointing to the door to the attic room, where Elberry had just appeared.

Ma rushed over to him, smoothing down his fur. 'Oh, Elberry, what happened? Have they punished you?'

Elberry brushed her off. 'I've been forgiven.'

'Forgiven?' said Pa.

Elberry nodded. 'Yersinia has shown mercy. He said I was

70

cursed by the diamond. He said he will show me the ways of the Elders, to help me understand all they do for us.'

Ma wrapped her paws around Elberry. 'Thank goodness. At least one thing has worked out well. Maybe you could stay with Tilbury today.'

Elberry scowled and pushed her away. 'I can't. Yersinia has ordered me to meet with the Tower Guards to learn my respect for the Elders.'

'I'll be fine on my own, Ma,' said Tilbury. 'I've always been fine before.' Secretly he loved the peace and quiet when the others went to market. The events of last night were so entangled in his thoughts that he wanted time to make sense of them.

Ma sighed. 'Well now, make sure you stay away from the windows and promise me not to go down to the basement.'

'I promise,' said Tilbury.

'Come on, everyone,' hurried Pa. 'We can't miss our boat.' He picked up Ma's bags with his cheese boxes.

'Don't put your stinkiest cheeses next to my fine woollens,' Ma scolded, 'or the Canary Wharf rats will complain.'

Pa chuckled. 'They have no taste for good food. Their idea of fine dining is a half-eaten hot dog.'

Ma fussed, getting Pa's collar straight, then she called upon her children to come and take a bag each to carry.

Nimble-Quick stopped beside Tilbury. 'Are you sure you're all right?'

Tilbury was silent for a moment. 'Did you hear what they said last night? Is it true?'

'Is what true?' said Nimble-Quick.

Tilbury clasped his paws together. 'Am I a seventh seventh-born?'

Nimble-Quick curled her tail around him. 'It doesn't matter what you are to me.'

'Nimble-Quick!' called Ma. 'Hurry, we'll miss the boat.'

Nimble-Quick gave Tilbury a hug. 'I've got to go,' she said.

She scurried after her family, and little Tilbury, once more, found himself alone.

Tilbury watched them all leave.

He heard the patter of feet as his family and all the other aunts and uncles and cousins scurried out of the attic rooms. He crept to the window and hid beneath his box, and he looked down to the docks and the river.

Was he really a seventh seventh-born? Could it be true? The very possibility of it felt like a crushing weight upon his chest. Ma was right, he thought. He was safest here. He vowed never to leave the chandlery again.

It was a bright, clear morning, with mist rising up from the river, and the sun a low ball of light in the sky. There were a few humans about, heaving boxes and containers on the ships that set sail for far shores. Tilbury could see his family running in the shadows, unseen by the humans. He often wondered how humans never seemed to see rats, even though they knew they were there. But as long as a rat stayed unseen and learned to stay away from traps and poisons, then the world of humans offered rich pickings

in food, materials for fine clothes, precious metals and gems to trade. The city offered a whole network of rivers, rail tracks and sewers to travel through.

Tilbury sighed. He only saw these places through the maps Nimble-Quick drew for him on the dusty floor. He could only experience them through Nimble-Quick's re-tellings. Sometimes he could almost smell the roasting chestnuts at the markets. He could imagine the hustle and bustle of so many rats weaving their way through the stalls. Nimble-Quick described the mountains of cheese, the crystallized fruits, the soft fabrics and the rainbow colours of the beads. Tilbury could almost hear the suck and squeak of the incoming tide as it slid across the mud, hurrying the rats to sell their wares at the end of the market.

But if he couldn't go to the market, at least he had the attic rooms all to himself. He enjoyed the peace and the silence. He loved to explore his aunts' and uncles' homes in the attic when they were away. Lily-Mae's suitcase home was lined with shredded wool. It always smelled musty and Ma disapproved of Lily-Mae letting her children eat biscuits in the bedding. *She'll be infested with mice if she leaves food in her house*, Ma would say.

Uncle Eddy and his family slept in the pockets of fur coats in the wardrobe. Tilbury poked his nose inside, but the pungent scent of mothballs made his chest feel tight and so he went on to explore Cousin Jak's house. Cousin Jak lived alone in a large trunk full of books and rarely allowed visitors. Tilbury tiptoed inside. Everything was so neat and ordered, not like his own home. A page of a book was open, showing the most wonderful picture of a landscape Tilbury had never imagined before. There were high snow-capped mountains and lush green forests. Tilbury turned the pages of the book to see all sort of different animals. Birds of so many vibrant colours. He was so engrossed looking at the book that he was only half aware of a scuttling sound.

It sounded again.

Tilbury froze.

If Cousin Jak found him in his house looking at his books, he'd bite his tail for sure.

He quietly left the book as he'd found it and peeked out.

There was no one there. Tilbury listened and waited. But there were no more sounds. Maybe it was mice searching for crumbs while the rats were away.

Tilbury tiptoed to Uncle Tubs and Aunt Swinney's house. They had the finest house in the attic rooms. The old Victorian doll's house. Tubs and Swinney slept in a vast bed in the master bedroom and their children slept beneath embroidered blankets in the other bedrooms. They even had lightbulbs that were attached to batteries and so could have electric lighting anytime, though Uncle Tubs only switched them on for special occasions as he said batteries were hard to come by. Tilbury sat on the rocking horse in the hall and imagined himself galloping along the muddy shores of the Thames. He walked into the kitchen and settled himself at the table. He marvelled at the plastic loaves and apples and bananas that Aunt Swinney kept on display. Uncle Tubs often unkindly said that the plastic food was better than Aunt Swinney's cooking. He ran his paw along the embroidered swirls on the tablecloth. Ma had made it with the matching curtains. He stood up and looked out of the window, imagining what it must be like to live in this house and see this view every day.

He looked out past the trunk full of books and the wardrobe to his own saggy sofa home. It might not be as posh as Aunt Swinney's, but at least it was home, and the food was edible. He yawned and decided that the saggy sofa was the best place to be.

But then the fur on the back of his neck prickled.

There was a shadow moving near the sofa.

A big shadow.

Not a mouse shadow.

A rat-shaped shadow.

It seemed bigger than an average rat. Maybe it was Uncle Tubs, whose rather large belly could make him look big. But this was a different shape of big. Besides, this rat was moving silently and there was nothing silent about Uncle Tubs. The rat was rummaging in the cushions, pulling out feathers and throwing them in the air. It was searching for something.

Maybe it was after their hoarding, even though Pa had hidden their jewels on the rafters.

Tilbury felt his heart pitter-patter even faster. His little paws felt clammy.

He was on his own.

With a big rat he didn't know.

Totally alone.

He hid behind the curtain and watched.

Eventually the rat came out from the sofa.

Tilbury watched it cross the attic to the wardrobe. It wore dungarees and carried a sack. Its dungarees were black, its fur was black, its sack was black, and it even left little black sooty paw prints across the wooden floor.

Tilbury trembled. This wasn't a Dockland Rat. This was an Underground Rat. It lived in the underground railways in the soot and the Everdark. Underground Rats were to be feared, Ma said. They took Dockland Rat children into the darkness and made them their slaves. There was talk about them wanting the *Cursed Night* for themselves and waging war on the Dockland Rats. Tilbury had never seen one before, but he guessed this was one.

The rat came out from the wardrobe and sniffed. It passed Cousin Jak's house and headed straight for the doll's house, straight for Tilbury.

Tilbury pressed himself against the wall. He heard the front door creak open. He could smell the rat, the soot and underground dirt. If the rat came into the kitchen it would all be over. But Tilbury heard the rat tread upstairs and the creak of the floorboards above. Soon it would come down the stairs and into the kitchen. Tilbury felt frozen to the spot, his mind spinning and his little heart racing inside his chest. Oh, he wished Nimble-Quick were here now. What would she do? And in his mind he could almost hear her voice. *Come on Tilbury, hold onto my tail and run.*

And run he did.

He knew this was his only chance.

He dashed out of the kitchen and ran.

He ran and ran as fast as his little paws could carry him.

But when he turned, he could see the huge rat bounding after him across the attic room floor, swiftly narrowing the distance between them, its black teeth bared and its long claws slicing the air.

CHAPTER FOURTEEN
Soot and Grime

Tilbury headed for the only place he could escape. He'd promised Ma not to go to the basement, but surely even Ma would let him go this time.

He skittered across the wooden floor, feeling the hot breath of the large rat just behind him. He reached the narrow crack in the wainscot and dived through, hearing the heavy thump of the rat against the wood. The rat was stuck in the gap, but it was wriggling and pushing its way through, its claws scraping on the wood. Tilbury ran to the chimney breast and scrambled down, his paws remembering all the little cracks and crevices. Behind him came the rat, jumping and falling in the darkness after him.

Tilbury shot through into the basement, blinded by the sunlight that sliced through the dusty air. He bounded away but felt something tight around his leg and he was pulled back.

The large rat had thrown a lasso of fine wire, which had caught him by the leg, and Tilbury found himself on his back being dragged toward the large rat.

Closer . . .

And closer . . .

And closer.

Little Tilbury clutched his own tail and squeaked. But it was such a small squeak that no one could have heard.

The rat drew a short dagger from a sheath at its chest and knelt down, pressing the sharp point against Tilbury's neck.

'Are you the young rat that opened the Gilded Cage?' said the rat. Its voice was deep and gravelly, and somehow commanded authority.

'I didn't open it,' squeaked Tilbury. His mind spun, wondering how this rat could possibly have known about last night.

The rat pressed its face closer to Tilbury's. 'But you know how to open it?'

Tilbury looked into the rat's dark eyes and felt the point of the dagger press harder against his skin. 'I . . . I . . . I think so,' he stammered.

The rat stared hard at Tilbury; its eyes narrowed. 'Then you must come with me.'

Neither the rat nor Tilbury heard the velvet paws on the dusty floor behind them. For although Marmalade Paws was more of a sun-catcher cat, he still had the deep instinct to hunt. He knew how to stalk, how to hold still and crouch down and then wiggle his bottom and jump.

And jump he did, his outstretched claws closing on the large rat. When the rat turned to slice the dagger at Marmalade, the cat clamped his jaws around the rat's throat, and held it tight.

Tilbury scrambled backwards, pulling off the lasso of wire. He saw the dagger the rat had dropped and picked it up. It was heavier than he'd imagined. Now that he held it in his paw, he could see the handle was made from gold and was encrusted with diamonds and emeralds.

The large rat was twisting and wriggling in Marmalade's mouth. Its paws were scratching at the cat's skin, but its sharp teeth could only gnash the air. Its tail whipped wildly to and fro, but Marmalade would not let it go. Tilbury crept closer, drawn by a morbid curiosity. The rat grew weaker, as Marmalade's grip closed on its airway.

It fell limp in his mouth, gasping for breath.

The rat's eyes locked onto Tilbury's as it hung dying in Marmalade's jaws.

And somehow, Tilbury felt responsible for this rat's life. He knew he could let it live or die. It would be his choice.

'Don't kill it,' squeaked Tilbury in Sphinx.

Marmalade turned to look at him. He couldn't speak with a mouthful of rat.

'Please,' implored Tilbury.

Marmalade took a long look at Tilbury and then unceremoniously dumped the rat in a full bowl of water. He gagged and retched. 'Ugh! I forgot how much I hate catching live prey.'

They watched the large rat splash about in the water bowl, spluttering and clawing his way out. Then it stood watching them and eyeing the gold dagger in Tilbury's paws.

Tilbury clung on to Marmalade's fur. A question burned in his mind and he had to know the answer. 'How did you know?' he said, his voice trembling. 'How did you know I can open the cage?'

A sneer played on the rat's mouth. 'Erik at the alehouse has a loose tongue after a few drinks. He told everyone last night. You were the talk of town. I followed your aunt and uncle back here.'

Tilbury couldn't speak. The secret was out and the Dockland Rats were in mortal danger.

The rat took a step towards Tilbury and Marmalade.

'Go,' squeaked Tilbury, pointing the dagger at the rat.

The rat took another step, shaking the water from its fur, and it was only then that Tilbury noticed something different about it. Its fur wasn't brown, like the Dockland Rats. Beneath the soot and grime, it had a sheen that caught the sun and glinted in the light. This rat's fur burned gold and bright.

Tilbury's little paw shook, and he clung to Marmalade. 'Go, or I will set my cat upon you.' He turned to Marmalade. 'Do something . . . please,' he said in Sphinx.

Marmalade puffed up his fur up to look twice his size, then he opened his mouth wide and hissed, cat-spit flying in the air.

And the large Golden Rat turned tail and ran. It scuttled up on to the workbench and scrambled up a pole, through a wire grille and escaped out onto the street.

The next thing Tilbury knew, Nimble-Quick was flying across the floor to hold him. Ma and Pa eyed the big cat and called to him.

'Get away from that cat,' cried Pa.

'Marmalade saved me from the giant rat,' said Tilbury.

'What rat?' squeaked Ma.

'A rat came when you were out,' said Tilbury. 'It searched through all our houses.'

'We saw,' said Pa. 'We thought something terrible had happened to you.'

'It almost did,' squeaked Tilbury. 'But Marmalade saved me.'

'Marmalade?' said Ma.

Tilbury smiled up at the big ginger tomcat. 'He's my friend.'

Nimble-Quick wrapped her tail around Tilbury. 'I'm glad you're safe.'

Ma and Pa cautiously walked past Marmalade, and Ma gave an awkward little curtsey and a 'thank you' before hurrying on.

'What was this rat searching for?' asked Pa.

Tilbury trembled. 'It was searching for me.'

Ma gasped out loud. 'But how did it *know*?'

'It was Erik,' whispered Tilbury. 'Everyone knows.'

Ma gnashed her teeth. 'Wait till I get my paws on him.'

'What did it look like?' said Pa. He reached down and ran his paw in the soot and grime. 'Was it an Underground Rat?'

'I thought it was,' said Tilbury. 'But under the soot, its fur shone bright gold.'

Pa's head jerked up. 'Don't tell lies, Tilbury.'

Tilbury opened his eyes wide. 'I'm not, Pa. Really I'm not.'

Ma laid a paw on Tilbury. 'Tell the truth, Tilbury,' she said.

Tilbury backed away from them. 'I'm telling the truth. It left this,' he said, lifting up the jewel-encrusted gold dagger.

Ma and Pa both stared at it.

'It can't be,' said Ma. She clutched her paws to her mouth. 'The Golden Rats were gone years ago. The Dockland Rats fought them and won. The last of them were killed in the Battle of Bakerloo.'

Pa frowned. He walked in tight circles, tapping his paw against his head. 'Maybe the rumours that Elberry heard about the Golden Rats being seen are indeed true.'

'Do you mean the ancient warrior rats?' whispered Tilbury.

Nimble-Quick took Tilbury's paw in hers. 'The very same ones,' she said. 'The legends say they show no mercy. They're known for their brutality too.'

CHAPTER FIFTEEN
The Offering

'A Golden Rat? Are you sure?' said Elder Elreath, peering closely at Tilbury.

Tilbury nodded, and Pa held out the jewel-encrusted dagger to show the Elders.

All the Elders had been summoned and now they stood in the attic rooms of the chandlery with the Tower Guards and Tilbury's aunts and uncles all crowding round him. Tilbury counted about twenty Elders; their pearly white fur seeming ghostly in the dying afternoon light.

Ma shook her head. 'But, Elder Elreath. Surely there are no Golden Rats left?'

Elder Elreath stroked his whiskers and looked slowly around his audience. 'We have known they walk among us for some time,' he said gravely.

There were gasps from Tilbury's aunts and uncles.

'But why didn't you warn us?' squeaked Lily-Mae.

Elder Elreath turned to her. 'In our wisdom, we chose to protect you all from this news. The Tower Guards kill any Golden Rats they find.'

'But where do they live?' said Uncle Tubs. 'Surely we'd have seen them.'

Elder Pauncher pulled a short knife from his belt and held it high. 'They're a cowardly lot. When we defeated them at the battle of Bakerloo, some of them ran to the Underground, which was being built by humans at the time. They have lived in the Everdark since then, biding their time. The Underground Rats welcomed them, for they saw a day they might join together and defeat us. The soot and darkness cover their golden fur and they have been walking among us along the riverside. It is certain one was at the alehouse. There were sooty pawprints on the drinking glasses.'

'Well, it's made a right mess of my house,' sniffed Aunt Swinney. 'It left soot all over my clean floor.'

'But why have they shown themselves now?' asked Pa.

'Like us, the Golden Rats have been waiting for the chosen one to open the Gilded Cage,' said Elreath. 'They want the diamond for their own.' He walked in a circle around Tilbury. 'But the dark is rising. The power of the *Cursed Night* is getting stronger. The Golden Rats are getting bolder. And if it falls into their paws, we will lose it forever. Once they possess the *Cursed Night*, they will kill us all.'

Uncle Tubs swivelled his gaze on Tilbury. 'It was looking for Tilbury, wasn't it,' he said. 'Everyone knows Tilbury can open the Gilded Cage. It wants Tilbury to get the *Cursed Night* for them.'

Tilbury shrank back against Ma.

Aunt Swinney nodded. 'Your Tilbury has put us all in great danger.'

Ma whipped her tail across Aunt Swinney's face. 'Idle talk has put us all in danger. Who was in the alehouse telling tales? Who blabbered where he lives? You tell me that?'

Aunt Swinney stepped back. 'I said no good would come of you letting him play in the basement. Look where it's got us.'

Marfaire stepped forward. 'Enough,' she said. 'We must not waste time talking about what cannot be undone, but what we need to do. Tilbury knows how to open the Gilded Cage. He is the one to fulfil the prophecy.'

Elder Elreath shook his head. 'With respect, Marfaire, all the other Elders agree that Tilbury is too young for such a journey.'

There was a murmur of agreement across the Elders.

Tilbury felt eyes upon him, and all he wanted to do was to shrink away.

'Too small,' said Elder Pauncher, helping himself to a piece of ripe Camembert that was sitting on a pile of Pa's cheese hoarding.

Another Elder stepped forward. 'The journey would be too difficult for such a weak rat.'

'We must trust the prophecy,' said Marfaire. 'The chosen one will find a way.'

Aunt Swinney stifled a laugh. 'Tilbury couldn't find his way out of a paper bag.'

Ma held Tilbury close. 'But he's not safe. The Golden Rats will come for him again.'

Elder Elreath nodded. 'We must take the *Cursed Night* to the sanctuary of the Tower of London where we will keep it safe with our hoardings of gemstones. Tilbury must open the cage on the next low tide and give it to us.'

'I agree,' said Elder Pauncher, pulling a string of cheese from a whisker and eating it. 'We must protect the *Cursed Night* from our enemies.' He began rummaging deeper into the pile of Pa's cheeses. 'You don't happen to have any Gouda?' he asked, guzzling a large piece of Emmental. 'And a drop of sherry wouldn't go amiss.'

Marfaire turned to the other Elders. 'We have been chosen as guardians of the *Cursed Night*. But it is not ours to keep. The prophecy tells us this will be the time we must choose between greed and our integrity.'

Elder Elreath turned on Marfaire. 'What are you suggesting?'

Marfaire looked back defiantly, her whiskers bristling. 'The *Cursed Night* has the power to possess even the greatest of minds. Have we mistaken our wisdom with our greed?'

Tilbury could feel the tension in the room. He clutched onto Ma's velvet skirt, burying his nose in the soft fabric, and entwined his tail with hers.

Elder Elreath pointed a bony paw at Marfaire. 'Can you guarantee this young rat can keep the diamond safe from our enemies? The truth is that we must protect it for the good of all.'

Marfaire looked at Tilbury trembling behind his mother's skirt. 'But Elreath . . . the prophecy . . . it says the chosen one will find a truth we cannot see . . .'

Elreath put up a paw. 'It is decided. You said yourself, Marfaire, that there will come a time we must choose our destiny. The *Cursed Night* will be safest in the Tower with the Elders. Tonight, at low tide on the waning moon, Tilbury will open the cage and will entrust the *Cursed Night* into the eternal safekeeping of the Elders.'

'And we shall have a feast,' roared Elder Pauncher. 'A moon-feast, to celebrate its offering to the Elders.'

Marfaire spun around. 'Elder Pauncher, I wonder if you do not want to lose the diamond for fear of losing your fine dining too?'

Elder Pauncher spluttered, little bits of cheese and spittle flying through the air. 'Preposterous,' he roared. 'Apologize at once. We must keep the *Cursed Night* safe. It is for us to use our wisdom to protect it.'

Elreath smiled, his eyes glittering in the candlelight. 'And in doing so, we shall become invincible.'

CHAPTER SIXTEEN
Moonfeast

Tilbury hid in his favourite spot by the window and watched as the moon lumbered its way into the sky over the city. It shone brightly in the dusky light of early evening, pulling the tide away from the shore. There was a small crack in the window glass that let in the breeze and Tilbury shivered. A deep feeling of unease had settled inside him and would not shift.

Nimble-Quick came to sit next to him then and glanced back at the rats gathering in the attic rooms. There were rats arriving from all the docks up and down the Thames to witness the opening of the Gilded Cage. Food and drink were being brought for the moonfeast and an atmosphere of anticipation and festival was in the air, for rats love nothing better than a spontaneous party. Ma and Pa and all the aunts and uncles were laying out a long dining table for the Elders, and Aunt Swinney put out her best silver. The attic rooms filled with the scent of ripe cheeses and fragrant spices. Erik brought flasks of beer and wine and filled cups and glasses.

Nimble-Quick held Tilbury's paw. 'Are you nervous?'

Tilbury nodded his head. 'Oh, Nimble-Quick, we should never have gone to the Darkening Ceremony, for the diamond would still be safe if we hadn't, and ready for the chosen one – a warrior – to come.' He clutched her hand tightly. 'What have we done?'

TING, TING, TING!

Nimble-Quick's answer was interrupted by Elder Elreath ringing a bell.

'Welcome, fellow Dockland Rats,' said Elder Elreath. 'Tonight, we honour the *Cursed Night* being given into the safe keeping of the Elders. We live in a dangerous time. We are in mortal danger from our enemies who seek the *Cursed Night*. Young Tilbury can open the Gilded Cage, but it would be foolish of us to let a young ratling bear responsibility for the diamond, for it would put us all at risk. The prophecy tells us that *there will come a time when we decide our destiny*. And we know this time is now. We will use our wisdom and the fortress of the Tower to protect the *Cursed Night*.'

There were cheers and the sound of glasses being clinked together.

'But first,' said Elder Elreath, 'while we wait for the tide to fall to reveal the Gilded Cage, let us drink and eat and be merry.'

Elder Pauncher raised his glass. 'Let the moonfeast begin.'

Nimble-Quick got to her feet. 'Come on, Tilbury, let's not miss this fine food.'

Tilbury shook his head. He felt sick in the pit of his stomach.

'I'll get us some chocolate peanuts,' she said.

He watched her walk away as Marfaire came to join him.

'Good evening, Master Tilbury,' said Marfaire.

Tilbury glanced up at her. 'Is it?' he said. 'I'm not sure what is good about it.'

Marfaire smiled. 'I share your unease.'

The noise in the attic rooms buzzed with chatter and food being eaten. The Elders all sat around the long table being waited upon by rats of the Tower Guard, while the rest of the Dockland Rats stood talking and eating, or sitting in small groups on the floor. The noise filled Tilbury's head such that he could not think.

'I'm sorry,' said Tilbury.

'What are you sorry about, Tilbury?' said Marfaire.

I shouldn't have tried to open the cage,' he sniffed. 'Bartholomew wanted a warrior.'

Marfaire sat next to Tilbury. 'Bartholomew wanted a rat of his equal, and one who would undo what he had done.'

'There has never been a rat as clever as Bartholomew,' said Tilbury. 'Maybe there never will be.'

Marfaire unwrapped her silk scarf from around her neck. 'I wonder if you might like to look at this,' she said. 'It has been passed from Keeper to Keeper to give to the one who can unlock the cage. Why, I believe it belonged to Bartholomew himself.'

'A scarf?' said Tilbury.

Marfaire looked over her shoulder to make sure no one was watching them, and then unfurled it. It was a long rectangular piece of yellowed silk, hemmed on three sides. The fourth side was torn as if someone had violently ripped a square of silk in half. It was patterned in faded brown ink. But as Tilbury looked, he realized that it wasn't a pattern, it was a strange drawing in the shape of an arrowhead. The arrowhead had curious lines drawn from it to the ripped edge of silk, as if it were only half of a drawing, and the rest of it was on the missing half. But then Tilbury noticed that the arrowhead itself was marked with pleats and folds.

Tilbury's paws began to tremble with excitement. 'It can't be,' he whispered.

Marfaire nodded, watching him intently. 'It belonged to Bartholomew himself.'

Tilbury traced his paws over the drawing. 'Ingenious,' he whispered. 'Bartholomew designed a new type of wing in the shape of an arrowhead. This must be half of Bartholomew's original plan for the Silk Wing. It's the design of the wing itself.' He looked up at Marfaire. 'But where is the other half of the plan?'

Marfaire pulled the scarf away, as Elder Pauncher waddled over. He breathed hot cheesy breath over them. 'And what are you two doing hiding over here?'

Marfaire wrapped the silk scarf around Tilbury's neck, tying it in a knot under his chin. 'I was just telling Tilbury here that if he doesn't wear a scarf, he could catch his death of cold.'

'We wouldn't want that,' chortled Elder Pauncher. 'Certainly not before he's opened the cage. Come, Tilbury, you are our guest of honour.' He pushed Marfaire and Tilbury towards the long table. 'Sit with us and eat.'

Yersinia pulled out chairs for Marfaire and Tilbury to sit down with the other Elders. Marfaire's glass was filled, though Tilbury noticed she didn't touch it.

She took a napkin and dabbed it at her mouth, and as she did so Tilbury heard her whispering urgently to him.

'Tilbury,' she said. 'Do not react. Do not appear as if I am talking to you, but I want you to settle your mind. Look beyond what you can see, hear between the sounds, and tell me what you feel.'

Tilbury reached for a piece of cheese and nibbled the corner, trying not to react to Marfaire. His thoughts wouldn't settle, as Marfaire's words had unsettled him, but he forced himself to try. He pushed those worries into the base of his tail and tried to still his unquiet mind.

The talk and clink of bowls and cutlery faded into the distance. The moving jaws and paws reaching for food became background to Tilbury's vision and the room took on a different feel. The Elders were engrossed in food and drink and idle chatter. But Tilbury noticed a shift in the energy in the room. Two rats of the Tower Guard were standing by the long table with trays of food. They stood stiffly, the tips of their tails twitching ever so slightly. They gripped the edges of the trays they carried a little too tightly. He noticed they were in sightline with Yersinia on the other side of the table. Then Tilbury saw it, an almost imperceptible glance from Yersinia with the two guards. It was not one of expected attention, it was one of collusion.

'Something is not right,' whispered Tilbury. 'It feels as if something is planned, as if something is going to happen.'

Marfaire nodded. 'Then I did not imagine it.'

'What?' whispered Tilbury. 'What is going to happen?'

Elder Pauncher plunged his head between Marfaire and Tilbury. 'What are you whispering about?'

Marfaire forced a smile. 'I was just telling Master Tilbury about the time my great aunt outwitted the banded bandits of Belgravia.'

'There are better stories to tell him,' said Pauncher swigging another glass of wine and pushing himself between them. 'Why, my great, great, great, great, great, great, great, great, great grandfather was the general who led the charge at Bakerloo. Now there's a fine tale to tell.'

And so, Tilbury spent the rest of the moonfeast having to listen to Elder Pauncher's drunken tales of chivalry and derring-do. He managed to filter out Pauncher's droning voice and settled his mind to see beyond the superficial layers of Elder etiquette and notice what was really happening in the room.

TING! TING! TING!

Elder Elreath tapped his glass of wine with a spoon. 'Good evening, my fine fellow Elders and rats of the Docklands. As we come to the end of this moonfeast, let us raise a glass to young Tilbury here. For soon, the ebbing tide will reveal the *Cursed Night* and Tilbury will bestow it into our safekeeping.'

The other Elders and the Dockland Rats raised their glasses.

'Hear! Hear!' said Elder Pauncher.

Yersinia clapped his paws together, and two rats came forward carrying trays. One rat carried a large pot of coffee, its rich aroma rising with its steam into the air. Then Tilbury saw the rat behind him was his own brother, Elberry. Elberry carried a huge tray piled high with chocolates wrapped in bright metallic foil.

Yersinia bowed his head to Elder Elreath. 'For a special night, we have sourced your very favourite chocolate liqueurs from the food hall at Harrods. The best quality chocolate filled with Jamaican rum, Portuguese port and Speyside whisky.'

There were little whoops of delight from the Elders and a buzz of excitement, for the Elders were well known for their fondness for fancy food from their favourite food hall.

Elberry carried the tray of chocolates high above his head.

'Not for you,' hissed Elberry, his eyes sliding over Tilbury. 'These are for the Elders. You're too young for liqueurs.'

'All the more for us,' chortled Pauncher.

Rich dark coffee was poured too, in tiny silver thimbles.

Tilbury's mind seemed to see everything in slow motion. He saw the flicker of a glance between Yersinia and Elberry. He saw greedy Elder paws reaching out for the chocolates. Elder Pauncher beside him, snuck two more liqueurs beneath his napkin and then guzzled them down. Tilbury saw the tweak of a smile on Yersinia's mouth; not a smile of contentment but one of embittered hatred. He wanted to warn Marfaire not to eat the chocolates and felt relief to see she had left hers untouched. She sipped her coffee instead and Tilbury could see her eyes lock briefly with Yersinia.

It was a moment of change. A sudden squall of wind gusted through the window and blew out the candles on the table, the smoke rising up from the burned wicks like grey ghosts in the dim light.

Groans and moaning gasps came from the Elders.

Elder Pauncher was the first to fall. One paw outreached for another chocolate, his eyes rolled back into his head and he toppled forwards, his mouth slack and a dribble of rum leaking from his mouth.

'Pauncher?' said another Elder, getting to her feet, but she too swayed sideways, and fell to the floor, her head hitting the wood with a thud.

Elder Elreath stared at the chocolate in his paw. He turned to Yersinia, and seeing Yersinia's leering grin, Elreath's face changed from one of confusion, to understanding and then to terror. Elreath too, stumbled back and collapsed. His tail twitched twice and then he was still. One by one, all the Elders were falling.

Tilbury turned to Marfaire who was crouched by Pauncher.

She felt his neck. 'He's dead.' She turned to Tilbury. 'Oh, Master Tilbury, I thought we would have more time. You must be brave; do you understand me?'

'But I'm not brave,' squeaked Tilbury, clutching his tail.

'My dearest Tilbury,' whispered Marfaire urgently. 'You are braver than you think. You must believe it so.' Her eyelids dropped and she stumbled forward.

'You didn't eat the chocolate, did you?' said Tilbury.

'No,' said Marfaire, but she clutched at her throat and started to sway. She tried to stand again but slumped on the floor. She stared at Yersinia who was walking over, kicking at Pauncher's dead body on the way.

'Marfaire,' squeaked Tilbury. 'Don't die.'

98

But Marfaire's tongue lolled sideways and she gasped to breathe. Her legs twitched but she couldn't stand up.

Yersinia stood over her. 'You are not so clever as you think, Marfaire,' he laughed. 'I didn't just poison the chocolates. I poisoned the coffee too.'

CHAPTER SEVENTEEN
Open the Cage

Yersinia pulled his sword from its sheath and raised it high. 'Dockland Rats,' he announced. 'The Elders have fallen. They were too weak and foolish to lead us and protect the *Cursed Night*. Only I can do that and keep you safe. I will make us invincible.'

In the shocked silence that followed, the rats of the Tower Guard closed around Tilbury and Yersinia. They raised their swords in unison too.

'We have waited a long time for this moment,' said Yersinia. 'For we come into a new dawn, a new era. You will all live and prosper under me.' He turned to Elberry. 'Come, bring your brother with us to open the Gilded Cage.'

Tilbury had been holding his breath and began to feel light-headed. But Elberry grabbed Tilbury by his collar and steered him out of the attic rooms and down the fire escape to the dock below.

'What are you doing?' whispered Tilbury.

'Yersinia has chosen me,' said Elberry. 'He knew I despised the Elders. The Elders were fools. The *Cursed Night* could never be safe with them. It belongs to the Tower Guard now.'

Tilbury twisted under Elberry's firm grip to look at him. 'But Elberry, you said yourself that if you unlocked the cage you would fulfil the prophecy and return it across the seven seas.'

Elberry gripped Tilbury's collar even tighter. 'But I wasn't given the chance to try again, was I? My pathetic little brother did it instead.'

'I didn't mean to,' stuttered Tilbury.

'But you did,' snarled Elberry. 'You took what was mine. You stole my glory.'

'Come with me,' said Tilbury. 'Let's return it together.'

Elberry stopped to look deep into Tilbury's eyes. 'Why would I do anything for you? You are nothing, Tilbury. Nothing. The *Cursed Night* is safe with the Tower Guard.'

'But you're not a Tower Guard!' squeaked Tilbury.

Elberry nodded. 'I am now. Yersinia saw something in me none of you ever did.'

'But, Elberry,' said Tilbury. 'The chocolates were poisoned. You handed them to the Elders!' He paused, his eyes becoming wider and wider. 'Did you *know*?'

Elberry didn't answer but shoved Tilbury forward, until they descended down to the muddy riverbank. The tide had slipped further out and the entrance to the Great Hall could be seen by moonlight.

Tilbury was half pulled, half carried to the top of the stone pillar, while one rat from the Tower Guard lit the candles. Behind the Tower Guard, Tilbury could see Dockland Rats following them into the hall, scared but curious to know what was going to happen.

Yersinia turned to face the shocked faces staring up at him. He laughed. 'The Elders thought they were well guarded. They believed the rumours of rebellion were from the Underground Rats. They were too arrogant to believe it would come from their own people instead.'

Tilbury caught a fleeting glimpse of Ma, her hand held to her mouth as she watched Elberry raise his sword with the rats from the Tower Guard too.

Yersinia turned to Tilbury. 'Open the cage and give me the *Cursed Night*,' he thundered.

Tilbury swallowed hard. Already his mind was twisting and turning the bolts and screws. Already he knew that the intricate openings could be found.

'Don't open it,' cried a voice.

Tilbury looked down to see Erik from the alehouse had pushed his way through.

'Don't open it, Tilbury,' he cried. 'If it gets into the wrong paws, no Dockland Rat will be safe again. We will stay cursed forever.'

Yersinia gave Tilbury a shove forward. 'Open the cage.'

But Erik climbed the stairs to the top of the pillar. He put his paws together and knelt in front of Yersinia. 'Please, Yersinia. We must honour Bartholomew's words. We must honour the Elders.'

Yersinia laughed. 'Ha, you who told everyone about Tilbury! The Elders may have tolerated your fawning loyalty, Erik, but I do not.'

Tilbury wasn't quite sure what happened next, but Yersinia lunged forward, and when he stood back, Erik was clutching his chest, blood spreading like a red flower across his smock. Then, with a flick of his spiked tail, Yersinia knocked Erik into the air and he fell backwards, in a slow arc. Whether or not he died before he hit the ground, it was impossible to say. But he lay dead for all to see.

The Dockland Rats gasped in shock and horror, pushing back against each other.

Yersinia turned around and smiled. 'The old order is gone. There is no Keeper to pass on Bartholomew's secrets of the prophecy. They are lost. Gone forever. The power of the *Cursed Night* is now mine.'

Tilbury felt his whole body tremble in fear. He tried to still his mind, but he couldn't find the quiet place where his thoughts could settle.

'Open the cage,' roared Yersinia.

Tilbury closed his eyes tightly. If the *Cursed Night* fell into the wrong paws, the Dockland Rats would be cursed for eternity. He shook his head. 'I won't.'

There was an audible intake of breath from the Dockland Rats.

Elberry pushed Tilbury forward. 'Didn't you hear him? Open the cage.'

Tilbury turned to face Elberry. 'Oh, brother, don't you see? Look what the *Cursed Night* is doing. It is bringing death and evil into our world. It is even turning us against each other.'

'Do it,' ordered Elberry. 'Now!'

Tilbury shook his head. 'No.'

Yersinia pushed his face next to Tilbury's. 'What did you say?' he snarled.

'I won't open the cage,' said Tilbury. His teeth were chattering with fear, and his little heart was beating so fast that he felt it might break.

'Do it,' screeched Yersinia.

Tilbury took a deep breath. He forced the tightness in his chest down, down, down through the base of his tail. And as he did, he felt all his tension disappear. He felt strangely detached as if someone else, not he, was doing the talking. 'No,' he said calmly. 'I won't.'

Yersinia drew his sword and held it against Tilbury's chest. 'Open it, or I will kill you too.'

A deep calm filled Tilbury. By protecting the *Cursed Night*, he was protecting his family. He would give his life for them. 'No,' he said again. He would die for them, willingly.

But a panicked voice called out from the Great Hall. 'Open it, Tilbury. Open it now.'

He turned to see Ma pushing her way through the crowd until she stood at the bottom of the rock. 'Open it, Tilbury,' she called. 'Do it for me, your ma.'

A smile curled on Yersinia's mouth, showing his sharp orange teeth. He turned to one of the guards. 'Scat, bring her up here,' he called.

Tilbury's chest began to tighten again. 'No,' he whispered. 'Leave her alone.'

Scat, a short, bulky guard hauled Ma up the steps, his claws digging into her fur, and this time, Yersinia turned on her. He held the point of the blade at her chest.

'It would be a shame to mess up these fine clothes,' Yersinia hissed.

Tilbury's little paws shook. 'Let her go.'

Yersinia pushed Ma to the edge of the rock. 'If you want to see your ma alive, then open the cage.'

'Ma!' squeaked Elberry, but his voice was so soft it was barely heard.

Tilbury glanced at Ma, but her eyes were wide in fear.

'Open the cage,' ordered Yersinia, his blade cutting the thin fabric of Ma's shirt. 'Open it, now.'

CHAPTER EIGHTEEN
Golden Arrows

Tilbury stepped towards the cage, but his mind went blank. Panic rushed through him. He wanted to save Ma. *Think*, he told himself. *Think*. But his thoughts scattered like windblown sand. His paws trembled as they touched the cold metal, but he couldn't focus on the sequence of locks.

'Come on,' ordered Yersinia.

Tilbury's teeth chattered in fear. 'I c . . . c . . . c . . . can't.'

Scat pulled out his dagger and pushed the blade against Tilbury's neck. 'You'd better hurry,' he snarled.

Tilbury was aware of something that whooshed past his ear and landed with a dull *thwack*. Scat's hand uncurled, releasing the dagger, and Tilbury turned to see the rat staring at the end of a golden arrow sticking out of his chest. It had pierced the leather armour, like a blade through butter. An expression of confusion and surprise spread across Scat's face before his eyes rolled into his head and he toppled backwards from the stone pillar.

Yersinia spun around, as another golden arrow whizzed through the air and struck him in the shoulder.

'Attaaaaaack!' came a cry from the back of the hall.

Tilbury could see more rats swarming into the hall. They were big Golden Rats in shining armour, and they were fighting the Tower Guards and moving closer to the Gilded Cage. In the chaos, Dockland Rats were pressing themselves against the walls of the Great Hall, trying to avoid the flying arrows.

Yersinia held his good paw high. 'Kill the enemies! Kill the Golden Rats.'

But golden arrows flew through the air, picking off the rats of the Tower Guard at the bottom of the stone pillar with exact precision. Yersinia flattened himself on the pillar to avoid another arrow and Ma slipped past him and wrapped her paws around Tilbury.

'Ma!' squeaked Tilbury.

'Tilbury!' said Ma, pulling him inside her coat. She looked down at the fighting rats and couldn't see any safe passage between them to get out of the hall.

The fighting raged in a clash of daggers and the flash and whistle of arrows overhead. The rats of the Tower Guard were no match for the Golden Rats. They had been taken by surprise and were not armed with weapons to counter the speed and ferocity of the Golden Rats' bow-and-arrow attack. Rats from the Tower Guard lay dead and dying at the bottom of the stone pillar.

Then one Golden Rat rushed forward, leaping over the bodies and scrambling up the stone stairs. Tilbury recognized it as the Golden Rat that had crept into the attic rooms looking for him before. The Golden Rat and Yersinia faced each other, each with a short dagger that they thrust towards each other. Yersinia was a bigger stronger rat, but the Golden Rat was fast and nimble. It forced Yersinia closer and closer to the edge, and when Yersinia could see there was no way he could win this battle he snarled and scuttled down the steps, calling the remaining guards with him.

'Elberry!' cried Ma.

Elberry gave one backward glance, his eyes locking briefly with Ma's, but he turned away and followed close behind Yersinia.

'Elberry!' wailed Ma, a deep guttural call of grief from her heart.

Tilbury clutched Ma's tail. He felt the intense power of the diamond swirl around them, pulling his brother away from them, drowning him in its darkness. He understood, then, the weight of its darkness, for the *Cursed Night* had the power to tear even love apart.

Yersinia turned at the entrance to the hall. 'This is not the end,' he screeched. 'The *Cursed Night* will be mine.'

Then he, Elberry and the remaining Tower Guard disappeared into the night.

There was a brief hush, and all that could be heard was the tide sucking and swirling into the entrance to the Great Hall.

The Golden Rat turned to Tilbury sheltered by Ma's coat. 'Open this cage,' he snarled, holding his dagger out in front of him.

But Ma was faster. She whipped the long hat pin from her hat and held it out, its needle-sharp tip pressed against the Golden Rat's chest. 'No one gets near my boy again,' she snarled. 'No one.'

'I am Obsidian,' roared the Golden Rat, 'the direct descendant of Prince Obsidian of the Golden Rats. The diamond belongs to me.'

'This diamond belongs right here,' said Ma. 'Until the Chosen One releases it and fulfils the prophecy.'

'Fool,' snapped Obsidian. 'There is now no Keeper alive to pass on the words of Bartholomew.'

'I carry the words of Bartholomew,' came a voice.

Tilbury turned at the sound of the voice – one he recognized even though its owner was still hidden in the darkness at the entrance to the hall.

'I am the only surviving Keeper,' said the voice.

'Marfaire?' said Tilbury. 'Is that you?'

Marfaire stepped out from the shadows. She pulled the hood back from her face and her blue eyes met Tilbury's.

Several Dockland Rats stepped forward to get a better view.

'But how?' said Tilbury. 'I thought you were dead.'

'I didn't drink the coffee. Yersinia wanted me dead, so I had to pretend to die,' she said. 'And as you have seen, he spares no one in his greed for the *Cursed Night*.'

'So, Bartholomew's secret is safe?' asked Tilbury.

Marfaire nodded. 'I am the last Keeper of the Gilded Cage. I am the only living rat to know the secret Bartholomew told to his mother. And I can only reveal it to the warrior who opens the Gilded Cage.'

Tilbury clutched his paws together. 'Then I must leave now,

Marfaire. And you must await the true warrior to open the cage and save us all.'

Obsidian lashed his tail but was kept back by Ma's hatpin. 'The *Cursed Night* was stolen by Bartholomew. I am Obsidian, descendant of the prince. This diamond belongs to the Golden Rats.'

The Golden Rats around him called out in agreement, raising their bows into the air.

'No,' said Pa, 'the *Cursed Night* belongs to the Dockland Rats until the true warrior comes. Hurry now, Tilbury, we will leave with you while we can. We must never return.'

Marfaire lit her own candle and held it high. 'The prophecy says that the one who opens the Gilded Cage must be the one to return the *Cursed Night* to the rightful owners.'

'The rightful owners are the Golden Rats,' hissed Obsidian.

Marfaire turned her eyes on Obsidian. 'We don't know that. Only the chosen one can reveal the true owner. The *Cursed Night* must be returned across the seven seas, for I have been entrusted with an ancient secret map, held in my mind. And I must take the chosen one on a long journey, for they must be the one to return the diamond.'

'Where is this place?' snapped Obsidian.

'To the Sky-Mountains,' said Marfaire, 'and a place known as the City in the Clouds.'

Obsidian paused, and there was a collective gasp from the rest of the Golden Rats. He fixed his stare on Marfaire. 'The City in the Clouds is our ancestral home, a place of legend, lost in time. Do not treat us like fools.'

Marfaire stared back at him, piercing him with her blue eyes. 'I believe it still exists.'

Obsidian's whiskers twitched. 'And you actually know how to get there?'

She nodded. 'And I must take Tilbury there. For he is the one chosen to return the *Cursed Night*.'

'Then tell me how to get there, and I will take it,' snarled Obsidian. 'It belongs to the Golden Rats.'

Marfaire shook her head. 'The map has been held secret by every Keeper. The *Cursed Night* must be returned by the one who opens the Gilded Cage.' She chanted lines from the prophecy, '*A warrior to find a truth we cannot see. To this one, I will reveal the secrets of the prophecy. Only this one, and one alone, can truly set us free.*'

'But I'm not a warrior,' squeaked Tilbury.

Marfaire turned to face him. 'Master Tilbury,' she said softly. 'You were prepared to die for your family and for all the Dockland Rats. You have the makings of a great warrior.'

'He's not a warrior,' said Ma, tears streaming down her face. 'He's my little boy. He belongs to me.'

Marfaire nodded. 'You should be proud of your boy for he has great strength.'

Ma sniffed loudly. 'He has weak bones and a weak chest and . . .' the words stuck in her throat, words she had never said out loud before. 'He is my seventh seventh-born. What if he doesn't survive this journey?'

Marfaire smiled gently. 'And what if he does? He is stronger than you think.'

'He stays with me,' wept Ma.

Tilbury stared at his paws, tears welling in his eyes. 'Oh, Ma, I do not think I am a warrior. But Bartholomew warned the dark is rising. The evil has turned the Dockland Rats against each other. It has turned my own brother against me.' He took Ma's paws in his own. 'I can open the cage. I have no choice, Ma. I must return the *Cursed Night* across the seven seas, to the City in the Clouds, or at least die trying.'

'Then you will need protection,' interrupted Obsidian. 'A skinny ratling like you and an old maid will not get far. I and my warrior rats will come with you. For we too will find our destiny in the legendary city that was once our own. We will return with the diamond.'

Marfaire looked at him. 'The journey will be dangerous, and we cannot risk being seen. The bigger the group, the bigger the danger. But I admit, it could be useful to have some protection, especially from one who is seeking the same city as we are. I will take one Golden Rat with me, but no more.'

'Then it will be me,' said Obsidian locking his eyes with Marfaire. 'This diamond is part of my story too.'

Marfaire nodded. 'So be it. Make haste, Tilbury. Open the Gilded Cage before the tide covers it and be ready soon. We must leave on the dawn tide, before Yersinia and the Tower Guard raise more troops and come and take their revenge.'

CHAPTER NINETEEN
Perseverance

Water was swirling around the base of the stone pillar, bringing urgency with the tang of salt and whiff of raw sewage. Tilbury told himself not to look into the surface of the *Cursed Night*. He tried to settle his mind, and it was only when he touched the cold metal with his paws, that he knew what to do. He turned the outside bars unlocking the mechanisms of the outside cage, and then had one more lock to undo to open up the inner cage. He could see it was a reverse lock. When the first cage opened there was a gasp from the watching rats. But Tilbury didn't hear it. He had to concentrate. He had to focus. The inner cage had a series of sliding rods that had to be pushed in a precise order. He needed to think two steps ahead all the time.

Each time a rod moved forward, another rod was blocked. It seemed impossible. He sat still, trying to force his rising panic down into his tail. *What would Bartholomew have done?* he thought.

In the corner of his eye he could see the diamond glinting darkly. It had a flat cut surface and eight cut facets around that. He saw it then, what Bartholomew must have thought, the intricate sequence of locks falling into place like the pattern of cuts on the diamond. One last turn, and the inner cage door swung open, and the *Cursed Night* was freed.

Marfaire had guessed Tilbury wouldn't want to touch it, because she reached in, slipped a black silk bag over the diamond and lifted it out. Tilbury turned back to the cage one last time to marvel at its intricacy, but he stopped and frowned. There was a short silvery metal tube in a crack of rock that had been concealed by the *Cursed Night*. He leaned forward and picked it up, turning it over in his paws. There seemed no way to open it, and when he tapped it, it sounded hollow.

'We must go now,' insisted Marfaire, 'or we will be trapped by the water.'

Tilbury slipped the metal tube into his pocket and followed Marfaire and the other rats out of the Great Hall, wading out through the incoming tide.

Up in the attic rooms of the chandlery, all Tilbury's brothers and sisters and aunts and uncles and cousins gathered around him and an urgent excited buzz rose up. Nimble-Quick flung her arms around him and would not let go.

'Oh, Nimble-Quick,' he whispered. He ran his paws along the scarf with the plans to the Silk Wing. 'I must tell you about the Silk Wing!'

Nimble-Quick's eyes opened wide. 'What about it?'

'Make haste,' said Marfaire. 'We must pack for our travels and head to the dock for the ship that will take us to the Far Shores.'

Nimble-Quick tried to hold on to Tilbury, but he was ushered away. 'What about the Silk Wing?' she called after him.

'He'll need cargo,' said Uncle Tubs. 'The ship rats will only give you safe passage in exchange for rum and wine.'

'Ship rats?' exclaimed Ma.

'Evil rats,' nodded Aunt Swinney. 'Watch your back. They'll steal the socks off your feet and throw you in the sea.'

'Pay them well,' said Cousin Jak. 'Offer them promises of more to come.'

'No!' wailed Ma. 'I won't let him go.'

Tilbury clutched Ma's paws. 'Ma, I can't stay, you know this. I have to take the *Cursed Night* back to the City in the Clouds, or our enemies will rise, and the curse will destroy us all. I have no choice.'

Pa held his son against him. 'Be safe my little child. I will pack you the finest fare to see your way across the high seas. The ship rats' bellies will be so full of my fine cheese that you will come to no harm.'

Ma sniffed. 'And I will pack you all travelling cloaks.' She pointed her hat pin at Obsidian pressing the end into his chest. 'You too, for now I must trust you with my son's life.'

Obsidian curled up his lip and turned to Pa. 'Control your wife.'

Pa laughed. 'I do not own her. She is her own rat.'

Obsidian sneered. 'She is just a seamstress. My ancestors

revered their wives. They did not send them out to work. They decorated them with a thousand jewels. But look at your wife's cheap gemstones. Is that all you can afford? Glass beads?'

Pa's face fell a little, for he had not sold enough cheese to buy the emerald she had so desired.

Ma pressed her hatpin a little harder against Obsidian. 'I am a tailor and designer. I can buy my own hoardings if I wish. If Mr Twitch-Whiskers chooses to buy me a jewel, it is a sign of his love, not of his wealth.'

Pa nodded. 'And you will be glad of her travelling cape. For no rat makes them like she does. It will hide you in the shadows and may well save your life. But I want to know how we can trust you with our son's life?'

'You have my word, a golden oath, that I will see your son has safe passage to the City in the Clouds,' said Obsidian. 'But how do I trust your son and Marfaire to take me there?'

Pa reached into his bag and pulled out the jewelled dagger that Obsidian had dropped in the basement. 'Here's your dagger returned in exchange that my son will return safely too.'

Obsidian took the golden dagger and travelling cape and nodded. 'So be it.'

Nimble-Quick curled her tail around Tilbury. 'I'm coming with you.'

Ma shook her head. 'I cannot lose two of my children today.'

'But, Ma!' protested Nimble-Quick.

But it was Marfaire who spoke next. 'I will not take charge of two young ratlings. One is quite enough.'

Ma nodded. 'There now. It is decided.'

Nimble-Quick wrapped her paws around Tilbury. 'But he needs me,' she cried. 'Who will read maps, who will keep him safe? Who will tell him wild stories?'

'Marfaire says you can't come,' said Tilbury.

Marfaire arrived at Tilbury's side. 'We are ready. Say your goodbyes. We must make haste. The sun is almost up, and time is not on our side.'

'Come down to the docks and say goodbye,' said Tilbury to Nimble-Quick.

She shook her head. 'I can't. I'll say my goodbyes here.'

Tilbury hugged his sister, feeling her tense and angry beneath his paws.

'What did you want to say about the Silk Wing?' she said as furious tears fell.

'Oh, Nimble-Quick. I have been given half of the plans to the Silk Wing on this scarf . . .'

'Hurry,' said Marfaire, pulling him along. 'We must go now!'

'Tilbury!' called Nimble-Quick.

Tilbury cast one last glance before he left to see her glaring at him, but then she turned away, her tail whipping angrily to and fro.

Ma gave them all travelling capes, and Tilbury put the metal tube he had found beneath the *Cursed Night* into its deep inside pocket.

'Come,' said Marfaire. 'Let's go.' She looked at the trunk that Pa was filling with biscuits and cheeses. 'We cannot carry this all the way with us.'

Pa nodded. 'But the boat journey may be long, and you may not find food so easily.' He started searching in his stores. 'I have some rum and brandy somewhere for the captain. Go ahead. I'll bring the trunk down soon.'

'How will we know which boat to travel in?' asked Tilbury.

Marfaire nodded. 'This has been passed from Keeper to Keeper. There were once sail boats that travelled to the Far Shores. We have a connection with the ship rats that come ashore. The boats now are huge things burning black smoke from their funnels. And I know there is a boat on this high tide. I hear it's named the *Perseverance*. We must go before the Tower Guard come back.'

Marfaire put the silk bag containing the *Cursed Night* inside a rucksack. 'Here, Tilbury. It is for you to carry the *Cursed Night*. Put the rucksack beneath your travelling cape.'

'Must I?' whispered Tilbury.

Marfaire nodded gravely.

Tilbury pulled it over his shoulders and put his travelling cape over the top. He felt the diamond like a heavy weight, its ice cold presence burning into his back. Then Tilbury, Obsidian, Ma and the aunts and uncles, brothers and sisters and cousins followed Marfaire down to the docks.

The ship's horn blasted a long note.

'Come on,' called Marfaire, hurrying aboard along a gangplank.

'Wait!' called Pa. He and Uncle Tubs and Aunt Swinney were carrying the trunk down to the dockside. It swung between them as they struggled with its weight, until Aunt Swinney dropped it down with a thump. 'How many cheeses have you put in here?' she complained, rubbing her back. 'It weighs more than a dead cat.'

Ma came to help carry it up the gangplank.

Tilbury noticed the ship rats watching them as they boarded. There were tall rats, short rats, stocky rats and skinny rats, and all were wearing white shirts, blue shorts and little peaked caps.

The ship's horn blew a second time and Tilbury's ma and pa and all his siblings and cousins scuttled off the ship back to the harbour wall.

'Feed Marmalade Paws for me,' called Tilbury.

'We will,' said Pa.

Tilbury watched as the ship pulled away from the harbour wall, leaving a gulf of foaming froth between him and the land. He searched the crowd for Nimble-Quick, hoping she had changed her mind and come to wave goodbye. He couldn't see her and looked up to the glass window of the attic rooms. He had often looked out of that window on the world, watching Nimble-Quick leave to go foraging or to market. Now he was the one leaving. He waved, hoping she would see him. Maybe she was waving back, but the rising sun reflected in the windows and he couldn't see her at all.

Tilbury tried not to cry, holding back gulping sobs that wanted to come.

He waved and waved until he could no longer see Ma and Pa. Then he stood with the sea wind blowing in his face and tears streaming down his cheeks.

'Chin up,' said Marfaire with a smile. She inhaled deeply. 'Do you smell that?'

Tilbury took a deep breath and sniffed. 'I can't smell anything, only the salt of the sea.'

'Then breathe in more deeply,' said Marfaire. 'Fill your lungs with it.'

'What can *you* smell?' asked Tilbury.

Marfaire took another deep sniff and smiled. 'That, Master Tilbury, is the smell of adventure.'

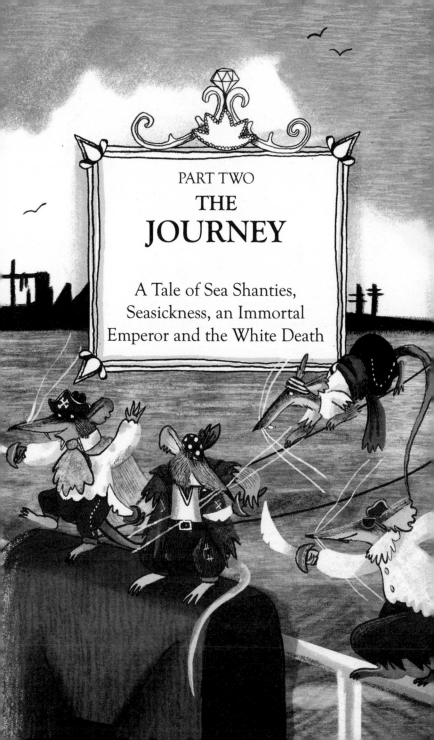

PART TWO
THE
JOURNEY

A Tale of Sea Shanties,
Seasickness, an Immortal
Emperor and the White Death

CHAPTER TWENTY
Ship Rats

Tilbury watched the land slip away. Further and further and further. Until all around them was only sea. Thoughts buzzed inside his head. *How big is the sea?* and *How deep?* and *How do we know where we're going?* and *How do we find our way back?* and *Will we ever come back at all?*

He glanced at Marfaire and Obsidian. They were both lost deep in their own thoughts, staring at the wide blue horizon that lay ahead of them. This was not the moment for questions.

But an answering call came from somewhere above Tilbury's head.

It was a voice, singing:

Say farewell to the land-ho.
One last kiss to your family.
You'll not be back for a long time yet,
If you ever come back at all.

Tilbury looked up and there on the deck above him, stood a ship rat. Soon, other ship rats lined up, joining in with the singing.

Hey ho and off we go
On the rolling waves
O'er the fathomless sea,
Hey ho and off we go
It's a ship rat's life for me.

Give me wine, and give me cheese
Give me a hammock, I can call my own
A kick of spray and a following wind
And I call this ship my home.

Hey ho and off we go . . .

Fate throws me to the wind and waves
To the wild storm's frightful rumpus.
A guiding star in the black night sky
And my heart becomes my compass.

Hey ho and off we go . . .

Fare-thee-well, to my old life
Come wind, fill these sails and blow.
Oh ship, ride these tempests
Or to the bottom of the sea, we go.

When the ship rats had finished singing their sea shanty, Tilbury felt even further from home than ever before.

Obsidian turned to look at the ship rats and scowled. 'Would you just shut up!' he snarled. 'Or at least get someone to teach you to sing.'

'Sea shanties are some of the oldest songs,' said Marfaire. 'They connect stories from all around the world.'

Obsidian snorted. 'They are the tales of spies, thieves and lay-abouts. No self-respecting rat would join a ship.' He turned to look out at the horizon again. A cool wind ruffled his fur and he looked even more golden in the light of early morning.

Marfaire turned her face to the sun. 'You must have many stories of the City in the Clouds?'

'We have many, many stories,' said Obsidian. 'We have kept them alive in the Everdark in the London Underground. They have given us light and hope when there was no light or hope to be found.' Obsidian paused, his focus still on the far horizon, as if he was trying to look beyond the ocean. 'I thought the City in the Clouds had been lost to myth and legend. But maybe it does still exist. The tales tell of a city so beautiful that it hangs within the clouds. To reach it, you must walk beneath the Rainbow Falls and climb the ladder to the sky.' He turned to Marfaire. 'You may think it's a silly story!'

Marfaire shook her head. 'It is the story that has been passed to me too.'

Tilbury looked at Marfaire, wide-eyed. 'Do you think such a place really exists?'

Marfaire smiled. 'I believe it to be so.'

Obsidian nodded. 'Then we will find it. And we will find the most beautiful place imaginable, a place where Golden Rats are revered, a place of order and magnificence. It will be the most perfect city in the world. The Great Palace will shine with gemstones where the eastern towers are encrusted with sapphires to catch the morning sun and the western towers are covered in rubies, citrine and topaz. The stories tell of a place where the Golden Rats ruled wisely over the mountains and valleys.' Obsidian frowned, a dark shadow crossing his face. 'But Bartholomew stole that from us the day he stole the *Cursed Night*. Of course, the Golden Rats had a different name for the diamond.'

Marfaire nodded. '*Aurun's Eye*. The eye of the great warrior rat who built the City in the Clouds.'

Obsidian turned to her. 'Then you must know the diamond belongs to the Golden Rats,' he said sharply. 'We are the rightful owners.'

Marfaire smiled but said nothing.

Tilbury scratched his ear. 'But Marfaire, if Bartholomew had wanted the *Cursed Night* to go back to the City in the Clouds, why don't we just give it to Obsidian and tell him how to get there?'

'Exactly,' said Obsidian. 'For when I find the city, I will send for the Golden Rats hiding in the Everdark, and we shall return triumphantly to our ancestral home.'

Marfaire smiled. 'I have been instructed to take the chosen one to the city with the diamond. And I have more questions than answers. And so, we often need to go on an adventure in search of answers.'

Tilbury's head felt full of questions. *Was Bartholomew a thief or a hero? Who did the diamond belong to?* Thoughts tangled inside his brain in knots. Tiredness washed over him, and he couldn't help a huge yawn.

'Come,' Marfaire said. 'These ship rats will take us to our quarters. Our journey across the sea will take forty days, and we must try to make ourselves at home.'

Two ship rats arrived beside them. One was plump and wore a greasy cook's hat and apron. The other was thin and wore stained dungarees and a belt of kitchen knives around his waist. Both had ripped ears, scarred tails and smelled of tobacco and rum.

'I'm Retch,' said the plump rat. 'And this is Spew,' he said, nodding to the skinny rat. 'We're the ship's cooks. We've orders from the captain to look after you.'

'How kind of you,' said Marfaire. 'Perhaps you could help carry our sea chest.'

Retch and Spew took an end each and Retch grunted as he lifted it up. 'What you got in 'ere? A sea monster?'

Marfaire smiled. 'Rum and wine in payment for a comfortable passage,' she said.

Spew mumbled in what sounded like appreciation. 'Captain'll be pleased. Come on. This way.'

But before Retch and Spew could carry the chest, the chest began to rattle and shake of its own accord. Strange growling and huffing sounds were coming from within.

Something was inside, scrabbling to get out.

''Tis a monster!' exclaimed Retch.

'Stand back,' said Marfaire. She held out her dagger and undid the latch, flipping up the lid. The clothes and bags began to shift, and something was emerging from the chest.

Tilbury gripped Marfaire's travelling cape and watched as clothes and biscuit crumbs spilled out on the floor.

And as the figure revealed itself, it gave an incredibly long and very loud . . .

BURP!

CHAPTER TWENTY-ONE
Retch and Spew

'Nimble-Quick?' gasped Tilbury.

Nimble-Quick stood up, pushing away the jumble of clothes. 'Thank goodness. I wondered when you'd let me out. I couldn't breathe in there.'

'What are you doing?' said Tilbury.

'Coming with you, of course,' said Nimble-Quick.

'Does Ma know?' asked Tilbury. 'Does Pa?'

'They do now,' said Nimble-Quick. 'I folded my nightshirt on Ma's pillow and I took my travelling cape. I had to take out some of the cheese Pa put in the trunk so that I could fit inside instead. So, I'm sure they've guessed.'

'You took out the cheese?' said Tilbury, his stomach rumbling loudly. 'How could you?'

Nimble-Quick folded her paws and frowned. 'Not all of it. Besides, which would you prefer, Pa's cheese or me?'

Tilbury wrapped his tail and paws around Nimble-Quick. 'You, of course. I want it to be you. But oh, Nimble-Quick, we do not know what will happen on this adventure.'

Nimble-Quick laughed. 'It wouldn't be an adventure if we knew what was going to happen.'

Marfaire had been watching them all this time, her face unreadable.

But it was Obsidian who spoke. 'Another ratling, and a she-rat too. I made no promises to look after another.'

Retch narrowed his eyes. 'No one said nothin' 'bout a fourth rat.'

Spew picked up a fallen piece of cheese and chewed it slowly. 'Stowaways walk the plank. Captain's orders.'

Marfaire shut the lid of the sea chest and turned to Spew, fixing him with an icy stare. 'Then I should like a word with your captain.'

Retch and Spew lifted the sea chest again and led them down, down, down to the stores near the hold of the ship. The room was stacked high with boxes and tins and fresh fruit and veg.

In one corner of the room was an open cigar box, lined with red velvet, and inside the cigar box, amongst empty crisp packets and rotten fruit, reclined a rat. He was a huge middle-aged rat, with a large belly and wearing an old, faded blue jacket trimmed with gold tasselled epaulettes to show his rank. His black trousers were decorated with gold piping too. He looked battle-worn with a long scar across his face and a white clouded eye. One tooth stuck out like a tusk and had been filed to a sharp point. His ears were ripped and torn, but one bright diamond glinted from an earring in his left ear.

Retch stood to attention. 'Captain Spurious, we have travellers.'

Captain Spurious rose to his feet and walked a circle around them. His eyes lingered on Obsidian, taking in his golden fur. He stroked his whiskers. 'A Golden Rat!' he said. 'No Golden Rat has passed through these shipping lanes since . . .' He paused, casting his eyes over the trunk and all their belongings. '. . . well . . . since Bartholomew came this way with a cursed diamond two hundred years ago. It is a strange tribe; a Golden Rat, an old maid and two ratlings barely out of the nest.'

'That one's a stowaway,' said Spew pointing at Nimble-Quick.

Marfaire smiled. 'This ratling is with us,' she said. 'She is no stowaway.'

The captain nodded. 'If you say so.'

'I do,' said Marfaire.

Tilbury looked between Marfaire and the captain, and somehow Marfaire's authority radiated into the room.

The captain looked curiously at Marfaire. 'So, pray tell me, where you are headed on this journey?'

'We are hoping to disembark at the Port of Wonders,' she said.

'Port of Wonders?' said the captain, his whiskers twitching in surprise. 'I haven't heard that name for it, in many a year. That's the old name, passed down through legend. It's the name from the time of tall ships and sailcloth.'

'What is it called now?' asked Tilbury.

'It's been called many things since then,' said the captain. 'The

Port of Thieves, the City of Lost Dreams, the Capital of Angels and Demons.' He paused, enjoying his audience. 'It still holds its magic, for it is a place of wealth and poverty, a place of polished marble and filth, a place of plenty and hunger and a place of hope and despair . . .'

'Get on with it,' muttered Obsidian.

The captain ignored Obsidian and leaned towards Tilbury, embellishing his description of the fabled port. 'It is a melting pot of stories,' he said. 'You will find the lost and the abandoned. You will meet your assassin and saviour in the same alley, and you will not know who you can trust.'

'But what is the Port of Wonders called now?' said Marfaire in such a voice that only Tilbury could detect a note of impatience.

The captain regarded her for a moment. 'It's called Felinport,' he said abruptly. He watched them all for a reaction and where there was none, he smiled. Retch and Spew sneered too, and Tilbury felt that a shared secret passed between them, as if the very word *Felinport* should provoke some reaction.

'What brings you to Felinport?' asked Captain Spurious.

'We need to find guides,' said Marfaire. 'Where do we look?'

The captain reclined back in his cigar box. 'Go to the Traveller's Rest at the far end of Snake Street. It's beneath the rice store. It's a travellers' tavern and many a guide passes through there.' He chewed a mouldy grape and looked at Marfaire. 'You'll be safe, old maid that you are, but I doubt the Golden Rat and the ratlings will even get out of Felinport.'

Obsidian glowered at him. 'Why not?'

A smile flickered at the captain's lips. 'Do you know why it's called Felinport?'

Obsidian scowled. 'No?'

The captain leaned forward. 'The port and saltpans between the sea and the Sky-Mountains are ruled by the felinrats.'

Obsidian's head jerked upwards. 'But felinrats are monsters of myth and legend. They have two heads – one of a rat and one of a cat – and the body and claws of a cat. Surely they are not real?'

The captain sneered. 'It is said they are ruled by the Immortal Emperor who sends his enemies to face the White Death. And the Golden Rats are their greatest enemies of all.' He turned to Tilbury and Nimble-Quick, a nasty smile playing at the corner of his mouth. 'As for you two,' he said. 'You'll have no chance.'

'Why not?' squeaked Tilbury. 'We're just ratlings.'

'Exactly,' said Spurious. 'And it is well known that any ratlings out on the streets are snatched by felinrats and never seen again.'

Tilbury's eyes widened. 'What happens to them?'

Captain Spurious sat back, a knowing grin spreading across his face. 'I don't think you want to know.' He pulled a toothpick from his pocket and removed a grapeseed from between his teeth. 'I suggest you turn back when you can. Unless of course, your journey is of such great importance you would put all your lives in danger. For the old sea shanties sing that the fabled diamond, the *Cursed Night*, will pass this way again in the possession of a Golden Rat.'

Tilbury could feel the captain's eyes burning into them and wondered if he could sense the presence of the *Cursed Night* hidden in Tilbury's rucksack. He felt it sap all the energy from him and tried to stifle a loud yawn.

'The ratlings are tired,' announced Marfaire. She opened the trunk and pulled out a small flask and a lump of cheese wrapped in brown paper. 'We have brought fine cheese and wine in exchange for a comfortable passage. Where do we sleep?'

'Over there,' said the captain, taking the flask and cheese and inhaling its pungent smell. 'Retch and Spew will carry your things.'

Tilbury was relieved to see they were to sleep on the other side of the stores, away from the captain and other ship rats. Three hammocks had been strung between the shelving and there was even a porthole that looked out across the sea.

'This will be just fine,' said Marfaire to Retch and Spew. 'You can put our chest here.'

When they had gone, Marfaire turned to Tilbury, Nimble-Quick and Obsidian. 'We will need to keep our wits about us on this voyage. The captain suspects we may have the *Cursed Night*. If the ship rats find out we have the diamond they will surely kill us for it.'

'Then it is all the more reason that I should carry it,' said Obsidian. 'I will keep it safe.'

Marfaire shook her head. 'They would expect you to carry it. They would not believe it would be entrusted to a ratling. The *Cursed Night* is safest where they will never look.'

'No ship rat could come near me,' snarled Obsidian.

But that night, as darkness fell and Tilbury curled up with Nimble-Quick in a hammock, he heard the soft scuttling of ship rats' feet from across the stores towards them. He heard thieving paws searching through the sea chest and rummaging in Obsidian's pockets and Marfaire's bags as they slept. Sharp little claws reached beneath his own pillow and patted down his blanket.

Tilbury curled his tail even more tightly with Nimble-Quick, entwining it with hers, their travelling capes wrapped around them. The *Cursed Night* lay safe between them, out of reach of searching paws and prying eyes.

But for how long could they keep it safe? thought Tilbury. They were alone on a wide ocean, so very far from home. He did not think he would ever sleep. But the gentle rolling and swaying of the ship, and Nimble-Quick's soft snores soon lulled little Tilbury, pulling him down into a deep and dreamless oblivion.

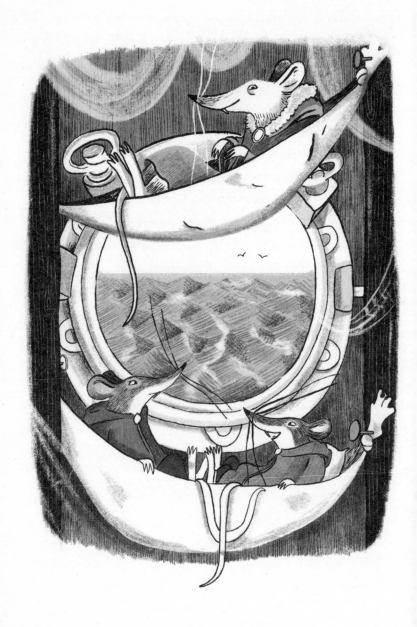

CHAPTER TWENTY-TWO
Ratiffi

When Tilbury woke, the whole ship seemed to be rolling around him. His rucksack was safe, but Nimble-Quick was already up and out of the hammock sitting next to Marfaire on the ground, and they seemed to be swinging up and down too. Tilbury's head spun. His eyes couldn't make sense of what was up or down.

'We've hit some rough weather,' explained Marfaire.

Tilbury clambered down from his hammock trying to hold on to the floor as the ship pitched and rolled.

'Cheese?' said Nimble-Quick.

Tilbury pulled a face. 'I don't feel well.'

'You'll get your sea legs soon enough,' said Marfaire, tucking into a dry cracker.

'Where's Obsidian?' asked Tilbury.

'He's still in his hammock,' said Marfaire. 'He's not feeling well either.'

Tilbury looked across and could see the shape of Obsidian and hear him groaning and retching loudly. The ship rats in the stores must have heard too, for they started up a new song. Their singing voices drifted across the space between them. There were too many words in some lines and sometimes their verses didn't rhyme but it didn't seem to stop them singing:

Oh, landlubber, 'tis best not eat
When the sea's so rough and restless.
'Tis a waste of good fine food
To say hello again to your breakfast.
T'will take three days of pitch and toss
Three days of retch and spew
Then when you find your sea legs
You'll become a ship rat too.

Obsidian pulled his cape over his head. 'Stop your hollering, or I'll throw you to the bottom of the ocean.'

The ship rats burst into peals of laughter and set about singing another sea shanty about having a picnic with an octopus on the seabed.

Tilbury covered his ears and crawled into a corner, feeling more ill than he ever had in his life. He stayed curled tightly in a ball and didn't even move when Retch and Spew came across carrying three bowls of porridge gruel.

Retch left the porridge on the floor. 'Captain says he's not seen a storm so bad as this. Says one of you might be cursed.'

Tilbury felt the dark pull of the diamond. Could it have the power to curse even the winds and the waves? He groaned loudly and pressed himself against the ground that rolled around beneath him.

Spew fixed his eyes on Tilbury. ''Tis best to throw a cursed passenger to the sea to save us all.'

Marfaire stood up and put herself between Spew and Tilbury. 'This is no more than a storm in a teacup,' she said. 'Is your captain scared of a little breeze?'

Retch narrowed his eyes at her. 'Captain says he smells a bad omen on his ship.'

A smile twitched at Marfaire's lips. 'Maybe the captain has indigestion from the ripe cheese we gave him. I recommend peppermints for trapped wind.'

Retch muttered and turned tail and left with Spew.

Tilbury watched them go. He glanced at the greasy porridge and his stomach churned. He crawled back into his hammock, feeling like he would never, ever feel well again.

The storm raged for the next ten days. Tilbury didn't eat for the first few days, but hunger got the better of him and he soon found his appetite and found his balance too. He had wanted to show Nimble-Quick the design for the Silk Wing on the scarf, but somehow the ship rats' eyes followed him wherever he went, and he didn't get the chance. Instead, he spent the days looking out of the small porthole at the wild storm. Sometimes the waves washed right over the porthole, and when the ship rolled, sometimes Tilbury found himself looking up at the sky.

But the storm did end, quite suddenly, and Tilbury woke on the eleventh morning to look out at clear blue sky and a sparkling flat sea.

Obsidian peered out of the porthole and announced he was going out on deck.

'Can we go too?' asked Nimble-Quick.

Marfaire paused for a moment. 'Yes, I think we all need some fresh air.'

Tilbury pulled on the rucksack with the *Cursed Night*, concealing it beneath his travelling cape. The diamond seemed even heavier than before, the rucksack straps digging into his shoulders. He could feel the curse's dark power weighing him down and filling him with a sense of impending dread.

Outside, the sun was so bright in the blue, blue sky that Tilbury had to squint to see. It was much hotter than Tilbury had expected. The metal deck was too hot for their paws, and so Tilbury, Nimble-Quick and Marfaire kept to the shadows. The ship was huge. It was a large container ship with brightly coloured shipping containers stacked on top of each other. It was like a whole city at sea. The funnel belched out thick black smoke as the ship cut its way through the water, leaving a frothy white wake spreading out behind it like the lace Ma used to unfurl for her dressmaking.

Tilbury noticed the ship rats seemed to be everywhere. Wherever he, Nimble-Quick and Marfaire sat down to rest, a ship rat would pop up, or spy on them.

'We can't get away from them,' said Tilbury.

'In here,' said Nimble-Quick, scrambling up a rope and

dropping down into the deep hull of one of the lifeboats. 'It'll be cooler in here too.'

But it wasn't cooler in the lifeboat. The sun shone in with all its ferocity, but at least it was away from prying eyes.

Tilbury tried to find some shade under one of the oars. He glanced around, checking that no ship rat had followed, then unfurled the scarf, showing Nimble-Quick the design in faded ink.

She marvelled at the arrowhead design and the pleats and tucks, but her eye was drawn to the ripped edge.

'Where is the other half with the rest of the design?' she said. 'We only have the wing.'

'We don't know,' said Marfaire. 'I looked all over the Elders' hoarding in the Tower and never found it.'

Tilbury reached into his pocket and pulled out a silver tube. 'Why didn't I think of this before,' he said. 'I found this beneath the *Cursed Night*. It must be important.' He shook it, but couldn't hear anything inside. 'It could be silk folded up in there.'

Nimble-Quick took it from him. 'It's a tube inside a tube,' she said. 'How do we open it?'

Tilbury nodded. 'The inner tube looks like it's made from a different metal from the outer tube. But there doesn't seem to be a way of getting one tube out from the other. It's like they're sealed together.'

'Maybe they're rusted,' said Nimble-Quick.

But there was no rust to be seen. The metal of the inner tube was silvery while the outer tube looked a pale golden colour. 'We could try to cut it open.'

'With what?' asked Tilbury. He took it back and worked his little paws, trying to find some hidden mechanism to open it, but there was none. There were no marks or scratches to suggest any force had been used to slide one tube inside the other.

Marfaire peered closer to look. 'How curious,' she said. 'Bartholomew was known for his engineering, yet here he has invented something without any mechanism at all.'

Tilbury took it back and tried to twist and bend the metal, but it would not budge. He threw it down in frustration, where it rolled in hull of the lifeboat, glinting in the hot sunlight. He wrapped the silk scarf around his neck again and shuffled back into the shade, feeling hot, tired and hungry.

Nimble-Quick pulled out a piece of dry biscuit she had been saving and offered some to Tilbury and Marfaire. 'No one in our family has been on such an adventure before,' she said. 'Imagine the tales we will have to tell when we get home.'

'If we do get home,' snapped Tilbury. He pulled his travelling hood over his head and closed his eyes, because surrounded by the ocean, he felt very, very far away from all he'd ever known.

Nimble-Quick curled her tail around him. 'I'm glad I stowed away with you.'

Tilbury put his head on her shoulder. 'And I'm glad you did too.'

'Come on,' said Marfaire, 'Retch will be serving food soon. Not that it's much to look forward to.'

Tilbury reached forward to pick up the tube. It was almost too hot to touch where it had soaked up the direct sunlight. But as he picked it up, he felt the metal tubes rattle against each other.

He peered at them closely, turning them over in his paws, and as he did so the inner tube slid out. 'That's so clever,' he said. 'And so simple too. Bartholomew made the tubes out of different metals. When they heat up, the outer metal tube expands more in the heat and so the inner tube can be pulled out.'

A piece of parchment was fluttering out from the separated tubes into the breeze, and Tilbury snatched it in his paw.

'What is it?' asked Nimble-Quick.

Tilbury gently unfurled the fragile parchment. On its yellowed surface were strange faded black markings and symbols. Some were the same, but they were arranged differently on the page. 'What *are* these?' he said.

Marfaire looked over his shoulder, then spoke quietly. 'Oh my!' she said. 'If I'm not mistaken, this is ratiffi.'

'Ratiffi?' said Tilbury.

Marfaire nodded. 'Bartholomew said the Golden Rats used ink to put their thoughts on paper. They used repeating symbols that can be arranged in infinite ways, and they called it ratiffi. This ratiffi must have been inked by Bartholomew himself.'

Tilbury looked at the strange markings. 'That's impossible,' he said. He stared hard at the piece of parchment in front of him. 'For if I could understand this, I would know exactly what Bartholomew thought two hundred years ago, as if he were here with us now.'

'Exactly,' said Marfaire. She lowered her voice even more. 'The Elders thought ratiffi was some form of dark magic. It frightened them that thoughts and images could be conjured in another's mind by black marks on paper, even when the teller is dead. They believed our history must be passed by word of mouth and guarded by the Elders.'

Tilbury frowned. 'But stories change with the teller,' he whispered. 'This is the truest word, if told by the thinker.'

Marfaire nodded. 'You are wise beyond your years, Master Tilbury.'

Nimble-Quick slowly traced her paws across the black squiggles, as if she was trying to absorb their message. 'I wonder what Bartholomew is saying.'

'Yes, I wonder that too,' said Marfaire. 'There is no way of knowing, because the Elders destroyed all parchments with ratiffi that they found.'

'We must keep this secret,' whispered Tilbury.

But above them, two voices began singing. Two ship rats were peering into the lifeboat.

Tilbury shoved the parchment back into the metal tubes and slipped it in his pocket. But it was too late. They had been seen.

And as he, Marfaire and Nimble-Quick walked back to the stores, the ship rats followed, keeping up their song:

The young rat found an ancient code
Black ink marks on a parchment olde.
He'll tell you he ain't got it
But it's hiding in his pocket.

Obsidian's ears pricked at the ship rats' song and he swung out of his hammock, grabbed Tilbury by his cape and had thrust his paw deep in the pockets before Tilbury could stop him.

'What are you hiding?' he said, holding the tube up high.

'Give it back,' snapped Nimble-Quick, jumping to try to reach it.

'It belongs to Tilbury,' said Marfaire.

Obsidian shook it. 'What's inside?' he hissed. 'Is it really parchment with ratiffi?' He tried to prise the ends apart but could not, and Tilbury was relieved to see the metals had cooled enough to seal together again.

'Then I will keep it,' said Obsidian.

Marfaire's whiskers bristled. 'It belongs to Tilbury. If you do not give it back, I will not take you on this journey with us.'

Obsidian stood staring at Marfaire. 'I can understand ratiffi,' he said. 'It is passed from one generation to another in the Everdark. It could be a message of great importance.'

'All in good time,' said Marfaire. 'Now, give the tube back or we will have to part ways when we reach port.'

'I don't need you,' he snarled.

Marfaire narrowed her eyes. 'Oh, but you do. For I hold the map in my memory.'

Obsidian scowled. He thrust the tube at Tilbury and stalked away.

'Maybe we should let Obsidian read it,' said Tilbury.

'No,' whispered Marfaire. 'Not now. We do not know his motives well enough yet.'

'He doesn't like us,' said Tilbury.

Nimble-Quick narrowed her eyes. 'Well, I don't like him.'

'Bartholomew betrayed his people,' said Tilbury. 'Maybe we need to show him that he can trust us.'

Marfaire shook her head. 'We do not know the truth of all things.'

149

Tilbury frowned. Marfaire often spoke in riddles he did not understand. And there was so much he did not understand.

Nimble-Quick went to lie in her hammock and when Tilbury was alone with Marfaire, he turned to her.

'Marfaire,' he said, 'What was the secret that Bartholomew told his mother? You haven't told me yet.'

Marfaire sighed. She looked around to check no one else was listening. 'I wasn't sure of the right time to tell you. Maybe that time is now. Indeed, I do not understand the message myself.' She closed her eyes, reaching back into her memory. 'These are the words he told to her: *Upon my death, I, Bartholomew Belgravia, wish to make amends, for I am nothing more than a common thief. But in my thievery, I have committed a crime of such wickedness that I have too much shame to tell this story in my lifetime. There will come a warrior rat greater than me, to atone for my sins and return the diamond to the City in the Clouds. For only there, in the deepest darkness, can a light shine on the truth and set my soul free.*'

'So, Bartholomew *was* a thief?' said Tilbury.

Marfaire opened her eyes and looked at him. 'Yes,' she said.

Tilbury frowned. 'But what was his wicked crime?'

Marfaire shook her head. 'I do not know. It seems Bartholomew had secrets he didn't want others to know.'

Tilbury held the metal tube in his paws. The ink on the scroll inside remained a mystery, its message out of reach.

It was a scroll holding secrets of the past, but those secrets could be the keys to unlock the future too.

CHAPTER TWENTY-THREE
Felinrats

The ship cut through the wide, flat sea, peeling a long wake that broke up into braids of white foam behind them.

Days slipped by, each one becoming a little hotter, each one taking them further and further from home.

Tilbury and Nimble-Quick often sat in the shade and shelter of a lifeboat and watched the unchanging ocean. Once, Tilbury spotted dolphins rising up from the depths, and he wondered what worlds lay below the waves that could hold such astounding creatures of speed and beauty. But most of the time, the ocean concealed its secrets and lay flat and featureless, reflecting a cloudless sky. Tilbury lost count of the days. The relentless heat made everyone sleepy, even the ship rats. They were often to be found curled up under ropes or snoozing in their hammocks.

Then, one evening, just as Tilbury began to feel that this would

be their life forever, a sweet earth scent drifted on a fresh breeze. The horizon seemed a little hazy and covered in cloud.

'Land!' squeaked Nimble-Quick. 'Oh, Tilbury. I can see land.'

As the ship drew nearer, they could see palm-lined beaches and jumbles of small towns at the shoreline. Humans in small fishing boats cast nets out to the water. There were other ships too, blasting their horns as they passed. Birds from the land flew overhead. Some bright scarlet with huge bills, others iridescent green. Tilbury and Nimble-Quick watched as the ship passed along the coastline all night. As dawn approached, they neared a city, its neon lights bright across the water. Tilbury could hear the hum of traffic and the mechanical sounds of a city waking up. It was like a living beast, Tilbury thought, pulsing with life; mysterious, unpredictable, while at the same time hypnotic and enthralling. They were entering a place of thieves and assassins, where two-headed monsters roamed the streets. Somehow, life on the ship with the sea-shanty-singing rats seemed remarkably tame. The ship turned and edged into the port, where huge cranes were unpacking containers from other ships.

'Come on,' said Tilbury. 'Let's tell Marfaire.'

But Marfaire was already out of her hammock and packing her bag. 'We cannot take your pa's sea chest. We must put what we

need in our travelling packs.'

Nimble-Quick grumbled as Marfaire made her take thick winter clothes for the mountains, and she carefully folded and included her sky-blue bird-suit too.

Tilbury packed his clothes, his short knife and a few ship's biscuits and the remains of the cheese, carefully arranging them around the *Cursed Night*.

Marfaire instructed them all to wear a cool cotton smock beneath their travelling capes, as she said the port would be hot, but they would need their travelling capes to remain out of sight. Tilbury pulled on his rucksack, then his cape, and tucked the metal tube safely in the inside pocket.

Nimble-Quick looked into the chest. Only Ma's finest clothes remained.

'Ma would want us to look respectable if we were asked to dinner,' said Tilbury, running his paws along the lace and ribbons.

'Well, Ma's not here and the chances of us being asked to dinner are zero,' said Nimble-Quick. 'We're most likely to end up as dinner inside one of the felinrats.'

Tilbury buried his nose in one of the frilly shirts. He hadn't allowed himself to think too much of Ma and Pa, but suddenly it was as if Ma was beside him, fussing with the frills and telling

Tilbury to sit still. His little heart ached, because it dawned on him just how far he was from home, and he wondered if he would ever return.

'Come,' said Obsidian, when their bags were packed. 'Let's go.'

They scrambled up the decks to where they could see the gang-plank had been lowered. Tilbury looked up to see the captain and the ship rats in a line watching them go. A shanty rose up into the thick, humid air, and one verse filled Tilbury with a deep fore-boding that weighed on the diamond in his bag.

> *Ye cannae trust a ship rat*
> *We'll trick ye in the end.*
> *Assassins, cheats and fibbers*
> *No ship rat is your friend.*

'Hoods up,' said Marfaire. 'Let's go.'

Marfaire led the way down the gangplank, and when they could, they slipped into the shadows and hurried along an alley-way deep in shade.

This port smelled different from London. The warm humid air held the scent of nutmeg and pepper. The buildings were different too. They were ornate and painted in reds and ochres. But the port was strangely quiet and, unusually for a port, there were no rats to be seen. The only signs Tilbury could see were scuttling feet and flicks of tails beneath doorways and in the cracks between broken fences.

When they came to the shelter of some rubbish bins, Marfaire stopped. 'We need to find our way to Snake Street and the Traveller's Rest,' she said.

But before any of them could move, a small, skinny rat dashed past them, its feet skittering on the cobblestones. When it saw them, it spun on its tail and dived into the shadow of the bins next to them. Its chest heaved up and down and a gash in its ear oozed thick red blood. It stared at Tilbury, its eyes wide in fear. 'Felinrat,' it mouthed.

Tilbury clutched Nimble-Quick's tail.

He couldn't move. He couldn't breathe.

The monster of nightmares was here, right now.

And they had nowhere to run to, and nowhere to hide.

On the opposite wall, a huge shadow reared up. It was the shadow of a beast with two heads and a cat's body. One head was that of a rat and one was of a cat.

The cat's head opened its massive jaws and hissed.

CHAPTER TWENTY-FOUR
Snake Street

The creature that emerged from the shadows was not a giant monster, but a rat riding on the back of a large spotted cat. The cat wasn't fat and furry like Marmalade, this one was sleek, rippling with pure muscle. Its green eyes glittered. It wore a leather bridle with tassels of gold, and a gleaming saddle. And astride the saddle rode the rat, in leather armour and a helmet with a plume of feathers.

'Felinrats are just rats, like us,' whispered Nimble-Quick.

The cat's ears swivelled towards them and Nimble-Quick covered her mouth with her paw.

The cat was sniffing the air and prowling down the alleyway.

'Show yourself,' said the rat riding the cat. 'There is no hiding place.'

'They know we're here,' squeaked Tilbury.

Obsidian drew his sword and Marfaire stood in front of Tilbury and Nimble-Quick, protecting them.

The skinny rat stared at them briefly, then flicked its tail and was gone, sprinting down the street.

The cat bounded after it, its feet making no noise at all. The felinrat drove the cat on, digging sharp spurs into its sides, screeching strange yowling sounds to the cat.

But only Tilbury could understand the Sphinx it was saying, the language of cats. And the words the felinrat called chilled him to the bone.

'Kill, kill, kill.'

The cat pounced, picked up the skinny rat, and in one swift movement bit down on its head, and it hung dead and limp in its mouth.

Tilbury covered his eyes to hide from the brutal moment.

The felinrat pulled on the reins and swung the cat around. 'Hear me, hear me,' it shouted. 'Death to the enemies of the Immortal Emperor. Death to the Rebel Mothers.'

Tilbury became aware of rats in gutters and roof spaces, all watching, all silent, all drawing back in revulsion at the skinny rat's death.

Marfaire, Tilbury, Nimble-Quick and Obsidian edged back into the deep shadows as the felinrat rode his cat past. Tilbury couldn't help looking at the emerald eyes of the cat. They held no warmth, only the cold-blooded gaze of a killer.

'We need to hide,' whispered Obsidian.

'We have already been seen,' whispered Marfaire, nodding in the direction of a broken door. A large she-rat was watching them. Her eyes darted left and right and then she scuttled over, her tail twitching. Five others followed and stood behind her, looking up and down the alleyway.

'State your business,' said the rat.

'We're looking for the Traveller's Rest,' said Marfaire.

The rat pulled back Tilbury's hood and clicked her tongue. Then she glared at Marfaire and Obsidian. 'I'm guessing these two ratlings are no kin of yours? No one would set their own ratlings on the streets of Felinport.'

'We are visitors,' said Marfaire. 'Passing through. We need safe passage to the City in the Clouds. These young ratlings are my wards. I have been entrusted by their mother for safe passage.'

The rat glanced back at the other she-rats and they whispered among each other. She turned back to Marfaire. 'I'll take you as far as Snake Street,' she said. 'Go to the Traveller's Rest and wait there. We'll send Jinkwene to find you. She will hear your story and may help you.'

The other rats melted into the cracks and crevices of the buildings and the she-rat set off at a fast trot.

'Follow me. Keep to the shadows. Watch out for the sentinels.'

And so Marfaire, Tilbury, Nimble-Quick and Obsidian hurried after her. Tilbury barely had any time to take in the world waking up around him. Humans were on the move, on foot, by bicycle and in cars and small trucks. Stalls of vegetables were being set up and delicious sweet scents filled the air. The alleyways and back roads were crisscrossed high above with wires and bright washing hanging on lines between the houses. Tilbury noticed cats on street corners. Some were lying in the sun, some sat on walls, their paws tucked under their chests. Did they belong to the felinrats? Were they the sentinels? Were they spying on everyone's movements? Soon, he began to feel quite lost; he couldn't imagine where the port was any more, but Nimble-Quick was switching her head this way and that as they crossed roads, building a mind-map of the city.

The she-rat came to a sudden stop at the beginning of a narrow street. The sides of the street were filling up with humans carrying cages and placing them down. Tilbury could see animals inside the cages: chickens, monkeys, cat-like animals with spotted coats and lots of brightly coloured birds.

'This is Snake Street,' the she-rat said with a shudder.

'Where is the Traveller's Rest?' asked Marfaire.

The she-rat pointed. 'At the far end beneath the rice store.'

'Thank you,' said Marfaire. 'Take care travelling home.'

The rat placed her paws tenderly on Tilbury and Nimble-Quick. 'Keep them safe,' she whispered. 'We have lost too many of our own.' She looked up the street of cages and chained animals. 'Keep away from the cage bars too.'

Obsidian led the way this time, past the cages. Tilbury shrank back, feeling the eyes of the caged animals watching him. Some of these creatures had the smell of the wild on them. Some were terrified, slinking to the back of their cages. Others launched themselves at the bars, snarling and clawing. A skinny monkey reached through and grabbed Obsidian by the tail. He made a quick stab to its paw, and it let go, screeching at him and rattling the bars. At the far end of the row, the cages were filled with serpents of all

160

colours and sizes. They coiled and writhed and filled each rat with a deep primal fear.

Not many London Dockland Rats have ever seen a snake, but olde ratlore told of vicious, limbless creatures with poisoned fangs that could swallow a rat whole. There were stories of rats being hypnotized by them. Serpent stories were told by mothers to keep their curious children safe and by their side. Seeing serpents here in Snake Street was even more terrifying than the stories. They hissed and struck the bars, trying to reach the rats as they passed. Flecks of venom landed on Tilbury's cape and he recoiled at the dark stains of poison. Obsidian was strangely engrossed, drawn to a huge mottled snake that flickered its tongue at him. One snake lay asleep, a large rat-shaped bulge in the middle of its belly.

Even Marfaire's whiskers trembled. She tugged Obsidian's coat. 'Cover your eyes, don't look at them. They can spit poison too.'

They all hurried on, and Tilbury could feel his little legs shaking by the time they came to the end of Snake Street. Before them, on the corner of the road, rose a huge warehouse on wooden stilts. Two sides of the warehouse were open to the road. Beneath the stilts were many rats sitting around tables, eating and drinking. Metallic music tinkled out from an old wind-up radio. There was an air of insouciance yet underlying disquiet too. The tavern was a meeting point of strangers at crossroads on their journeys.

'This must be the Traveller's Rest,' said Marfaire.

Heads turned to look at them. Obsidian kept his hood up, and Marfaire tried to keep Tilbury and Nimble-Quick close, hoping the other rats would not take much notice.

The floor was covered in rice husks and the space was deep in shade. Marfaire led them to a table at the far edge of the area from where they could easily escape should they need to.

An old rat, with a fat belly and wearing a bright yellow tunic stained with brown grease spots walked over to them. He had the bored air of one who has heard too many travellers' epic tales. He held a tray of cups and a flagon of water that he set down at the table. 'Lunch is boiled rice balls and fried banana.'

Marfaire nodded. 'Thank you.'

Tilbury slumped into his chair, and looked around the room. There were all sorts of rats here, some with long travelling capes of silk and gold. One rat sat at a table with a cockroach chained to his paw, which he was feeding small pieces of bread, and at another table there was a rat with pale, almost lilac, fur.

But then, Tilbury saw three other rats troop inside. Rats that Tilbury recognized: Retch and Spew and Captain Spurious. They sat down on the far side of the room and the waiter served them drinks. The captain dealt out cards to Retch and Spew, and as he did so, his eyes met Tilbury's across the crowded room. He raised his glass to Tilbury and smiled.

But Tilbury didn't smile back. Beyond the background hum of chatter and clinking glasses, he could feel the air was thick and heavy. The energy in the room fizzled with tension, like a thunderstorm about to break.

CHAPTER TWENTY-FIVE
Jinkwene

Tilbury noticed an urgency about Marfaire too. Although she was still, her eyes scoured the other rats in the tavern. Even when the waiter laid down a plate of rice balls and fried banana on their table, she still kept up her watch.

Her eyes darted from side to side, then they fixed on a rat walking purposefully through the throng. 'She's coming,' whispered Marfaire. A tall she-rat wearing a dark blue travelling cape swept towards them. There was nothing that made her stand out from the other rats, but the moment she sat down, Tilbury could feel her presence. She seemed to take up more space than everyone else at the table, and even Obsidian moved aside. Beneath her travelling cape she wore a bright red dress. A string of small bones hung around her neck like a necklace and she wore silver rings on the end of her very long tail.

'Jinkwene?' asked Marfaire.

'I am she,' said the rat. 'Do you have a story to trade? A truth for a truth?'

Marfaire nodded, and Tilbury noticed that Marfaire's whiskers trembled ever so slightly.

'I trade knowledge for stories,' said Jinkwene. She took the bones from the string and rolled them on the table. 'The story must be true.' She paused. 'And it must be one you have never told. A deep and dark secret of your soul.' She looked directly at Marfaire. 'Do you have such a story? For I will know if it is not true. It must be pertinent to your journey.'

'I do have such a story,' said Marfaire in a hushed whisper.

'Then tell it,' said Jinkwene, 'for the bones are telling me that time is not on your side.'

'Where I come from, I was a Keeper,' said Marfaire. 'A keeper of knowledge and entrusted with the secret words of Bartholomew to unlock a curse to fulfil a prophecy.' Marfaire clutched her paws together. 'I knew my Elders did not want the cursed diamond to be returned. They knew a young rat had come with the power to open the Gilded Cage. They knew he was the one.'

Tilbury's eyes opened wide. 'Me? They knew it was me?'

'Why didn't they say?' said Nimble-Quick.

Marfaire frowned. 'There was a time when the Elders gathered knowledge for good, but they became greedy. They lost connection with the ordinary rat. They feared they would lose their position and power if they lost the *Cursed Night*. They intended to keep the *Cursed Night* for themselves.'

Tilbury gasped.

But Jinkwene leaned forward. 'So, what did you do?' she asked, as if she already knew the answer.

'I betrayed the Elders,' said Marfaire closing her eyes. 'I knew there was an uprising. I knew a rat named Yersinia was at the heart of it, but I did nothing to stop it. I suspected the rebels had poisoned the Elders' food and drink, and I let it happen. The Elders died because of me.' She sank her head onto her chest. 'It is a great weight I carry. Not just because I sealed the fate of the Elders, but because I have put Master Tilbury in great danger too.'

'Let me see the *Cursed Night*,' said Jinkwene.

Marfaire looked at Tilbury and nodded. Tilbury reached into his rucksack and brought out the silk slip holding the diamond.

Marfaire pulled back an edge of silk to show the diamond's glittering surface.

Jinkwene looked into the diamond, and Tilbury noticed she gazed in deep sorrow at her reflection.

Jinkwene threw the bones again and stared at the pattern they made. 'You tell the truth,' she said. 'Only history can bear witness to your actions. And what truth do you desire from me?' she asked, gathering her bones and stringing them on her necklace again.

'I must know the safe passage to the City in the Clouds. We need a guide to take us there to fulfil the prophecy.'

Jinkwene took a deep breath and glanced around, aware other rats were watching, but they were out of earshot. 'There are no trusted guides in Felinport any more. You must catch the next train bound north across the Dustlands. The train stops at the end of the line at a human town called Hilzen. Beyond Hilzen, the Badlands are battlegrounds of felinrats, and beyond those are the Sky-Mountains, where you will find the City in the Clouds.'

Obsidian leaned forward. 'It really exists?' he said in hushed wonder.

Jinkwene looked at him for the first time. 'No one has been there for two hundred years. The felinrats gained power over Hilzen and the Badlands when the Golden Rats lost the diamond. The Golden Rats have not been seen since. But,' she paused, 'sometimes, when the air is clear, you can look up at the Sky-Mountains and see the gemstones of the Great Palace gleaming in the sun.'

'My home,' whispered Obsidian.

'It will be a dangerous journey,' said Jinkwene. 'The Palace of the Immortal Emperor lies in the Badlands. The Badlands is a place ruled by beasts, bandits and felinrats. No one knows a safe route through the Badlands any more.'

'I do,' said Marfaire. 'The map has been entrusted to me, but we will need supplies and escorts for our journey.'

'At Hilzen, you will find the help you require,' said Jinkwene. She took a ring from her tail. 'Look for Kadma. Give her this and tell her Jinkwene sent you. Tell her the Rebel Mothers of Felinport send their strength and love.'

'Thank you,' said Marfaire, curling her paw around the ring.

Jinkwene stood up. 'You must go. Now!' she said urgently. 'The bones tell me your time has run out.'

There was a ripple of unrest from the other side of the room. Tilbury glanced around, his little heart hammering at the arrival of six felinrats riding cats. They stood at the exits to the Traveller's

166

Rest, the cats' tails swishing in impatience. One was the large spotted cat they had seen earlier that day. It moved with precision and power. The felinrat riding it raised his sword up high. 'My name is General Malice. And I tell you there are enemies among us,' he snarled. 'We have heard rumours that a Golden Rat is in our port. This rat may be carrying a fabled black diamond.'

Gasps rose up from the rats sitting at tables.

General Malice guided his cat into the Traveller's Rest to walk among the tables. 'This Golden Rat is travelling with an old maid and two ratlings.'

Tilbury pulled his hood up further and pressed into Nimble-Quick. Obsidian sank lower in his seat, and Marfaire sat perfectly still, but the tip of her tail twitched to and fro.

'Has anyone seen these rats?' roared the general. 'There is a bounty on their heads. Whoever finds them will be generously rewarded.'

Silence rippled like a wave across the rats, but then Captain Spurious stood up. 'There,' he said, pointing directly where Tilbury sat. 'There they are.'

Marfaire leaped up, snatching the silk bag with the diamond in her paw. She pulled Tilbury and Nimble-Quick with her. 'Run,' she ordered. 'Now. You must run for your life.'

CHAPTER TWENTY-SIX

Dustlands

Tilbury took hold of Nimble-Quick's paw and ran.

Their escape route was blocked by a large cat and so Tilbury and Nimble-Quick leaped up on the tables, jumping from one to the next, drinks and food flying in the air. Paws grasped at them as they tried to reach the back wall of the Traveller's Rest, hoping to find an exit there.

Marfaire and Obsidian were following, their paws skidding on the dry rice husks. Tilbury glanced around to see the cats leaping over tables, hissing and spitting. He heard the felinrats screaming at them, urging them on. Part of him wondered if he could speak Sphinx with the cats and persuade them to stop, but these cats had none of the softness of Marmalade. These cats were killers.

Tilbury could see a small gap in the brickwork on the back wall. It was big enough to fit a ratling. Would it be big enough for Marfaire? Could Obsidian fit through too?

Nimble-Quick dived through the gap, and Tilbury turned. 'Come on, Marfaire,' he yelled. But the two cats were almost upon them, their lips curled back in snarls, their claws outstretched. One swiped at Marfaire, but she leaped and twisted, the silk bag with the *Cursed Night* flying from her paw. Another knocked Obsidian off his feet, and he spun on the dry rice husks until a cat closed its jaws on him and picked him up. Marfaire tried to grab the *Cursed Night*, but a paw from the spotted cat pinned her down, its claws piercing her travelling cape. General Malice reached down, and swept up the bag holding the jewel. He pulled out the *Cursed Night*, his eyes glittering in triumph. 'The fabled black diamond,' he screeched. 'The Immortal Emperor will become invincible.'

Marfaire struggled, but couldn't get free. 'Run, Tilbury,' Marfaire screamed. She threw the ring that Jinkwene had given her, and it flew in an arc through the air and then rolled straight through the gap in the wall.

Tilbury dived after it, narrowly missing a paw that swiped the space where he had just been standing. He squeezed and wriggled through the gap and he and Nimble-Quick found themselves in an alleyway next to Snake Street.

Tilbury bent down and grasped the ring.

'Come on, run,' yelled Nimble-Quick.

'What about Marfaire?' said Tilbury.

'No time,' said Nimble-Quick. She pointed over Tilbury's shoulder.

Tilbury spun around to see two felinrats riding their cats towards them, the cats' bounding strides quickly covering the ground between them. Then Tilbury heard the harsh words from the felinrat.

'Kill, kill. Kill them both.'

'This way,' screamed Nimble-Quick, pulling Tilbury towards Snake Street.

Snakes struck at the bars as they fled past. The cats chased them down the street. They were agile, quick to turn, with a powerful leap. Tilbury felt white panic rise inside him, but he forced it down as Marfaire had made him do so many times. He forced his fear into his tail, and as he did the world slowed, but his mind sped up. He used his tail to launch into the air, and as he did so he pulled a wooden peg from one of the snake cages, then with his foot, he flicked it open.

The angry snake shot out, straight at the cats, rising up and swaying in front of them. The cats came to a halt, their fur on end and their tails like bottle-brushes, for all animals fear snakes. The snake flickered its tongue, scenting the air. But Tilbury and Nimble-Quick didn't wait around, they scuttled between cages of geese that honked at them, past a cage with two monkeys that screeched and tried to grab them, and then on to a large straw-filled crate with a potbellied pig. The sow was suckling her ten piglets, which grunted and snuffled beside her.

'Under here,' said Nimble-Quick, pulling Tilbury beneath the pile of warm piglets. The piglets grunted but settled again beside the sow.

Through the straw, Tilbury could see one of the cats pacing between the rows of cages.

The cat was sniffing the air to catch the scent of Tilbury and Nimble-Quick.

'Can you smell them?' said the rat riding the cat.

'They have been this way,' replied the cat.

'They could be miles away now,' said the second rat.

'We've orders to kill them,' said the first rat.

'They are unimportant. Let's say we disposed of them ourselves,' said the second rat. 'General Malice has the diamond and will take it with the prisoners to the palace. The train leaves at sundown.'

A nasty smile crept across the first rat's mouth. 'Come, let us get on that train. The Immortal Emperor will feed the Golden Rat and the old she-rat to the White Death. That will be a spectacle we won't want to miss.'

Tilbury watched them turn their cats around and leave. He breathed out, aware he had been holding his breath for a long time.

'We need to be on that train too,' said Nimble-Quick. 'It's the only way we can save Marfaire and Obsidian. It's the only way we can get the diamond back.'

Tilbury shuddered. At sundown they would catch a train and be bound across the Dustlands towards a palace, an Immortal Emperor and the White Death.

Tilbury and Nimble-Quick stayed hidden beneath the piglets as the afternoon wore on. As the sun lowered in the sky, the humans began packing up their crates and cages, and Nimble-Quick led the way back to the port, keeping to the shadows. Between the gaps in the alleyways, Tilbury could see the *Perseverance* still in dock. A big part of him wanted to scramble back aboard and head back to London and Ma and Pa and forget all about the *Cursed Night*. But the felinrats now possessed the diamond, and he knew his destiny was bound up with it. Even the Elders had known that.

'Look,' said Nimble-Quick, pointing. 'There's the station.'

They scurried inside towards a huge scarlet engine puffing thick steam into the air. Further up the platform several felinrats patrolled on their cats, watching everyone that climbed aboard.

'Up here,' said Tilbury.

Together, they scrambled up the last carriage, up and up until they were on the very roof of the train. It was flat, with a small air vent that they could curl up inside. The carriage suddenly jolted forward and Nimble-Quick and Tilbury had to hold on tightly. Then the carriages jolted again and they were off, the train like a huge red snake, uncurling and sliding out of the station. They watched the big iron girders of the railway station pass overhead. Then they were travelling through the sprawl and messiness of the city, and then finally out across green fields and through rolling valleys. The sun was setting in the sky and the last sliver of ocean disappeared around a corner.

Tilbury pulled his travelling cape around himself and Nimble-Quick. Part of him never wanted the train journey to end, because the thought of what lay ahead terrified him. They were on their own, without Marfaire or Obsidian. 'Are you scared?' he whispered to Nimble-Quick.

Nimble-Quick curled her tail around him. 'Not when I'm with you.'

Tilbury held onto Nimble-Quick's paw, but he didn't feel brave at all.

The train veered ever northwards, and they became accustomed to the sway of the train and to the shrill whistle before it disappeared into a tunnel.

As stars pricked out above them, across the dark blanket of sky, they were soon falling into a deep, and much-needed, sleep.

Nimble-Quick was the first to wake.

She rubbed her eyes and stared out at the landscape. They had left behind the green lushness of the south, and for miles and miles all she could see was an endless dust plain. In the early dawn light, the land and sky seemed to merge in hues of blue and purple.

'The Dustlands,' she said.

Tilbury woke up. 'I'm hungry.'

'Me too,' said Nimble-Quick.

'I'm thirsty,' said Tilbury.

'Me too,' said Nimble-Quick.

Tilbury rummaged in his bag hoping for some crumbs he had missed before, but there were none.

The sun rose higher and higher, turning the landscape to shades of fiery red and yellow. The heat rose quickly too and the vent gave little shade. Not even the rush of air over the train seemed to cool them down.

Tilbury felt his mouth become dry, and his head thumped with the need for water. As the day wore on, a shimmering lake formed either side of the train across the dust plains. 'Oh, Nimble-Quick, shall we jump off here? How I'd love to dip my toes in that water.'

'It's not what it seems, little brother,' she said. 'Look how it ripples in the heat and disappears. It's not real.'

Tilbury peered through bleary eyes. 'And is that city not real?'

Nimble-Quick looked around. There, above the shimmering mirage, rose a city of pale stone. 'That must be Hilzen.'

'Look at those clouds too,' said Tilbury, craning his neck to look high in the sky.

'Those aren't clouds,' said Nimble-Quick, her eyes opening wide. 'Those are mountains.'

Tilbury gripped Nimble-Quick's paw, because although he had heard the legends of the City in the Clouds, he had never imagined the scale of the Sky-Mountains. They shone pink and white in the midday sun, their sharp peaks stark against the blue sky. They seemed to reach up and up and up, forever.

'We have to rescue Marfaire and Obsidian, and get the diamond first,' said Nimble-Quick.

Tilbury shivered. He watched the city approach. From a distance it looked almost picturesque, but the nearer they came, they could see it was a busy city. Dust rose in plumes from the traffic on the streets. The stench of sewers and human rubbish filled the air.

'Remember, Jinkwene told us the felinrats patrol this city,' said Nimble-Quick. 'They'll probably be at the station. Maybe we should jump off before we get there.'

Tilbury nodded. 'I think you're right.' He looked down at the ground passing quickly below.

'See over there,' said Nimble-Quick, pointing into the distance ahead of the train. 'There's some bushes. There'll be shade and maybe water. We'll be safe there.'

So as the train began to slow at the outskirts to the city Nimble-Quick and Tilbury climbed down the carriage as far as they could.

'Jump, now,' insisted Nimble-Quick.

'I can't,' said Tilbury clinging on to her.

'We'll be fine,' she said.

Tilbury shook his head.

But Nimble-Quick held onto Tilbury tightly and jumped for them.

They hit the ground and rolled and rolled in the dust, coming to a stop against a thorny bush.

Tilbury rubbed his head and sat up.

'See!' grinned Nimble-Quick. 'I told you we'd be fine.'

But Tilbury watched in horror as a sack came down over Nimble-Quick's head.

He was about to call out, but something swept over his head too. Everything went dark. And he couldn't see anything at all.

Rope was bound around his paws, pinning them to his sides.

He squeaked loudly, but it was no use.

He and Nimble-Quick had only just arrived, but already they had let themselves be caught.

CHAPTER TWENTY-SEVEN
The Rebel Mothers

Tilbury felt himself pushed and shoved.

'Don't make a sound,' said a harsh voice behind him. 'Or you die.'

Tilbury tried to guess how many captors there were. Maybe two or three? They moved with such silence it was hard to tell.

They walked for a long time, and Tilbury's feet felt sore where he stubbed his toes on the rough, uneven ground. Occasionally their captors stopped and loosened the sacking over Tilbury's and Nimble-Quick's heads to push a gourd of water against their lips. Tilbury drank and drank, trying to fill his body with much-needed water. They were climbing higher and higher and Tilbury was relieved to feel a cool breeze through his fur. The throb inside his head began to ease and he could focus on his surroundings. The noise of the city seemed far, far away, down below them. *Were they in the Badlands already?* he wondered. *Were they being taken to the Palace of the Immortal Emperor?*

From somewhere above came the shrill cry of a bird and Tilbury crouched down.

'Almost there,' said the voice. 'Keep moving.'

Then they were out of direct sunlight and being led in deep cool shade, and then, quite suddenly, the breeze was replaced by still air and the ground became soft and sandy underfoot.

'Sit,' came the voice. The voice echoed around them and Tilbury guessed they were in a big, empty space.

Tilbury and Nimble-Quick sat down and the sacking was removed from their heads, although they were still trussed up. Tilbury blinked in the dim light. They were in a cave, with rough-hewn walls. Beyond the cave opening he could see the dust plains below them and the city spread out, glistening in the rising sun.

Three rats stood opposite them, but Tilbury could hear murmurings further inside the cave and didn't know how many more there were.

One of the rats crouched down to look at them. She was wiry, with intense black eyes. The tip of her tail twitched back and forth.

'What brings ratlings on their own to such a place?' she said.

Neither Tilbury nor Nimble-Quick answered.

'I said they were spies,' said one of the other rats. She was older than the first, with a greying muzzle. She flicked sand at them. 'Who sent you?'

The wiry rat leaned closer. 'Hilzen is not the place for a young rat. What is the purpose of your journey?'

178

'We're passing through,' whispered Nimble-Quick.

The wiry rat gave a curious smile and turned to the other rats. 'Passing through! We have tourists.'

The other rats laughed.

'Well now,' said the wiry rat. 'Where would you be going? Beyond the city are the Badlands and the Palace of the Immortal Emperor, beyond them lie the Sky-Mountains and the City in the Clouds. If you're not killed in the Badlands, then you will not be permitted to enter the City in the Clouds.'

'Why not?' asked Tilbury. He still found it hard to believe this place of myth and legend was real, yet these rats talked so easily about it.

The third rat stepped forward. Her face was softer than the others' and she reminded Tilbury of Ma. 'Well now, the border has been closed for two hundred years. The Rainbow Falls are heavily guarded.'

The wiry rat narrowed her eyes. 'Surely everyone knows that. So why don't you? So we ask again, what brings ratlings to Hilzen?'

Neither Tilbury nor Nimble-Quick answered.

'Search them,' said the older rat.

The wiry rat untied them. 'Take off your travelling capes and leave them with your bags on the ground.'

Tilbury stood up. He felt his legs shaking and pulled off his cape and left it for the rats to search. He watched as they rummaged through their belongings.

One rat held up the silver tube. 'What's this?'

But before Tilbury had time to answer, the wiry rat held up the ring Jinkwene had given them. She thrust it in front of Tilbury and her eyes blazed. 'Where did you get this?'

'I was given it,' said Tilbury.

'Liar!' said the rat. 'Did you kill for it?'

'No,' said Tilbury. His legs buckled beneath him, but the rat grasped him and held him up, her face pressed close to his.

'Where did you get it,' snarled the rat.

'Jinkwene,' spluttered Tilbury. 'She gave it to us.'

'Jinkwene?' The rat released her grip a little. 'Jinkwene is still alive? What did she say?'

Tilbury didn't want to answer, and the rat drew a knife and held it against Tilbury's neck.

'What did she say?' growled the rat.

'She said to look for Kadma,' blurted out Nimble-Quick. 'She said Kadma would help us.'

The rat let go of Tilbury and he fell in a crumpled heap. 'And why would I help you?' she said.

'You're Kadma?' asked Nimble-Quick.

Kadma stared hard at her. 'This can't be. Why would Jinkwene send you? She said she would send warriors to start the revolution.'

'We were travelling with a warrior,' said Nimble-Quick. 'A Golden Rat. But he was captured.' She sighed. 'It's just us.'

The words started to tumble from their mouths.

'We have to save him,' said Tilbury, 'and Marfaire too. They've been taken into the Palace of the Immortal Emperor.'

'To be sent to the White Death,' said Nimble-Quick.

180

'And we have to get the *Cursed Night*,' said Tilbury, 'and return it to the City in the Clouds.'

Kadma put a paw up. 'Wait! Are you telling me that there is a Golden Rat with you?'

'Yes,' said Tilbury catching his breath.

'Then we need to hear this story and see how we can help you,' said Kadma. 'For if Jinkwene has sent you to us, then she believes you are the ones to set us free.'

Tilbury and Nimble-Quick found themselves the centre of attention of a group of rats. Tilbury noticed they were all she-rats of varying ages. More and more were arriving in the cave. Plates of dried apricots and bread were placed in front of him and Nimble-Quick.

'Eat,' said Kadma. 'Then we will hear your story and you will hear ours.'

And through mouthfuls of delicious food, Tilbury and Nimble-Quick told their tale.

'We have to save Obsidian and Marfaire,' said Tilbury. 'We have to get the *Cursed Night* too.'

'But it's impossible,' whispered one rat.

'Why?' asked Tilbury.

She shook her head sadly. A single tear fell and ran down a whisker, dropping to the floor. 'Because no ratling that enters the palace ever comes out.'

'We are the Rebel Mothers,' explained Kadma. 'The felinrats steal our ratlings.'

'And you never see them again?' asked Tilbury.

181

There was a silence across the rats that felt heavy with their grief.

'A few young rats have escaped,' whispered one rat. 'But they are broken from what they have seen and heard.'

Kadma looked Tilbury in the eye. 'The felinrats feed our children to their cats. And those that defy the felinrats and the Immortal Emperor face the White Death.'

Tilbury clutched his tail. 'What can we do?' he asked.

'There is nothing any of us can do,' said Kadma. 'Jinkwene has read the bones wrong.'

'We have to go into the palace,' said Nimble-Quick. 'Tilbury and me. We won't be suspected; we will blend in with the other ratlings.'

'No' said Kadma. 'Because we would be sending you to your deaths, and you will have a mother wanting you home.'

Tilbury's eyes burned hot with tears, for he thought of Ma and wanted her paws around him.

'We have to go in,' said Nimble-Quick. 'We have no choice. If Tilbury does not return the *Cursed Night*, then our people will never be free. It is said in the prophecy. We have to do it for our families.'

'How do we get in?' asked Tilbury.

Kadma glanced around the other Rebel Mothers. 'Sadly, that will be only too easy. You must let yourself be caught on the streets of Helzin.'

'We can't let them,' said another rat. 'They are ratlings, and we would not let our own go on such a foolish mission.'

182

Kadma paced circles in the sandy floor. She came to a stop and stared out of the entrance of the cave down at the city. 'We cannot hold out forever here. We have nowhere else to run before the winter. We cannot promise their safety with us.'

The other rat nodded. 'Then we must trust the reading of the bones.'

Kadma's face darkened. 'And we must let these ratlings go to the palace.'

'Leave your bags and capes with us,' said Kadma. 'You must be dressed in the brown frock of the Helzin rats.' She rummaged in her own bag and pulled out a smock. 'This belonged to Padme, my eldest daughter.' She lifted up the hem to show a small embroidery flower. It had four blue petals and a bright yellow centre. 'This was her favourite flower.' She buried her head in the fabric, breathing in the scent of the dress. 'If you find her, bring her home to me.'

Another rat came forward. 'My son is named Barille.'

Soon the names of lost ratlings were swirling in the cave, their names rising and echoing in the still air.

And Tilbury and Nimble-Quick found themselves in the embrace of mothers who had lost their own children.

Kadma put her paws on Tilbury's cheeks and looked deep into his eyes. 'Bring them home,' she wept. 'Bring our children home.'

CHAPTER TWENTY-EIGHT

The Palace of the Immortal Emperor

Even though Tilbury was expecting them, the speed and ferocity of the felinrats came as a surprise.

Tilbury and Nimble-Quick were playing in the dust in the streets of Helzin, waiting for the felinrats. Tilbury thought they would have to pretend to try to run, but the cats were so fast, so agile, that Tilbury had no time even to move. He felt the jaws of a cat around him and hoped that the cat was not hungry enough to swallow him whole. He looked across to Nimble-Quick who was in the mouth of another cat, her eyes wide with fear. Then the felinrats urged their cats on and they bounded away.

They travelled fast out of the city, along back alleys and storm drains, and then out onto the scrubland of the Badlands. Tilbury could see behind them and looked high up into the hills where the Rebel Mothers were waiting for their children.

The cats turned off from a human road, along a dusty path

that wound between scrubby thorn bushes. Tilbury could see Nimble-Quick in the cat's mouth beside him. He wanted to talk to her, but felt the sharp points of the cat's teeth dig into his skin. He looked ahead to see an old, derelict house. Fire had destroyed part of it, but what remained hinted at a grandeur of times past. Creepers had grown up all around it and in through the broken windows. He could see faded wallpaper on the walls and ragged velvet drapes hanging from broken curtain poles. It wasn't the palace he had been expecting. It held an air of decay, and a stench drifted across on the breeze. Felinrats patrolled the perimeter, pacing a well-worn path around the building. It seemed like a fortress, and Tilbury began to understand why it was so hard to escape.

Tilbury and Nimble-Quick were carried across an open dusty courtyard into the house. It had been a grand place once, but broken china and glass were strewn across the floor. Everything was covered in a fine layer of dust and grime. Food was left rotting on the ground and dirty water leaked from old, rusted pipes.

Tilbury and Nimble-Quick were dropped in front of a rat riding a spotted cat.

It was General Malice.

'Ah,' said the general, 'two more helpers. We're a bit short of helpers. Keeping so many cats fed is not easy.' A nasty smile curled on his lips. 'Did you not heed your mother's words when she told you not to go out to play?'

Tilbury kept his head down, hoping the general would not recognize him from the Traveller's Rest.

'Take them away,' said General Malice, dismissing them with a wave of his paw. 'Make use of them.'

Another felinrat pushed and shoved them through a doorway. 'These are the servants' quarters for the ratlings,' it said.

The hallway was long and thin and opened out onto another courtyard at the back of the building. Tilbury wrinkled his nose. A bad stench came from the courtyard, a smell of filth and stale cat urine. He hurried on, following the rat into a big room that was used as a food store and kitchen.

'Your job is to serve the felinrats,' said the rat. 'Obey orders. Do your job diligently. Do not talk to any other rat. Do as you are told, obey the chef-rat, or you will be fed to the cats.' He gave two blasts on a whistle and immediately ratlings formed rows and lines in front of him. He indicated to Tilbury and Nimble-Quick to join a line, although separated them, so they were too far apart to talk.

Tilbury and the ratling next to him were paired and handed silver platters of ripe figs and cheese and cups of rosewater.

'Dining hall!' ordered a rat in a white jacket and checked trousers, and a tall white pleated hat. The chef-rat, Tilbury assumed.

Tilbury scurried after the ratling. When they were out of earshot of the felinrats, he hurried alongside. 'Excuse me,' he whispered.

The ratling hurried faster, ignoring him.

'Excuse me,' Tilbury whispered again.

The ratling spun around. 'Didn't you hear,' she hissed. 'If we talk to each other we are dead. We are cat food.' She strode away, leaving Tilbury in her wake.

Tilbury followed her into the dining hall. The felinrats were reclining in soft cushions, drinking and eating. Tilbury served them cups of rosewater, bending down to pick up the used plates and cups. When he stood back up, he noticed the ratling staring at him for a moment too long.

When the platters of food had been eaten, he followed the other ratling back out of the dining hall. As they walked alone down the hallway, the ratling spoke in harsh hurried whispers.

'Where did you get your smock?' she said.

'I was given it,' said Tilbury.

'Liar!' snapped the ratling, daring to glare at him. 'I know that embroidery on the hem. That is my sister's smock.'

Tilbury gripped his tray a little more tightly. 'Then you must be Padme's sister. Your Ma gave this to me.'

'Ma?' said the ratling. 'You've spoken to Ma?' Her eyes flitted about, checking they went unheard.

'I'm here to take you home,' said Tilbury, although the words sounded grander than he felt. Indeed, he had no plan at all.

A felinrat turned the corner and Tilbury and the ratling kept silent and walked with their heads down.

'I'm Zorris,' said the ratling when they were alone again. 'My sister Padme tried to escape, and persuaded others to join her. She was caught and sent to the death-yard. I haven't seen her for two weeks now. She may already have been . . .' Unable to say her worst fears, the words stuck in her throat.

'I'm looking for a Golden Rat and an old she-rat. Have you heard anything about them?' asked Tilbury.

188

Zorris nodded. 'They are here. They have been sent to the death-yard too. They will face the White Death. The Immortal Emperor has ordered it.'

'Where's the death-yard?' whispered Tilbury. He could see they were almost back at the kitchens again and would not be able to talk there.

'The courtyard at the back,' whispered Zorris.

'And how do I get there?' asked Tilbury.

'Get on slop duty,' hissed Zorris.

'And how do I do that?'

'Be clumsy, drop things,' said Zorris. 'Make the felinrats want to punish you.'

And Tilbury felt some relief that getting to be on slop duty wouldn't be all that hard to do.

The sleeping quarters where the ratlings slept were controlled too. As Tilbury curled up on the thin blanket of his sleeping space, he looked over to the far side of the room to see Nimble-Quick. He desperately wanted to speak with her. She looked at him too, but there was no way they could talk. It was impossible, and the short distance between them seemed an ocean wide.

Tilbury woke to the sound of a gong and a short stick being brought down on his back.

'Get up, get up,' said the felinrat. 'Move it. Line up.'

Tilbury rubbed his eyes and joined the other ratlings in their lines and rows, ready to take orders. The sky was not yet light, but the chef had the ratlings cutting vegetables and fruits and carrying vast pails of milk from the nanny goat across the yard.

General Malice rode in, eyeing a silver platter with fruits and sweet pastries piled high. The chef nodded to him. 'The Immortal Emperor's breakfast is ready.'

Malice looked at the silver tray. 'Where is the coffee? The emperor does not want to be disappointed.'

The chef scurried away and brought back a steaming pot.

'Good,' said Malice. 'For today I am the one to bravely test each food for poison before I deliver it to His Excellency.'

Tilbury noticed the spotted cat watching him, and the fur on the back of his neck prickled. It licked its lips and curled one paw showing the needle-sharp claws. Tilbury wanted to get as far away from General Malice as he could and it only took him a few purposeful trip-ups and broken bowls to be sent to slop duty in the death-yard. Nimble-Quick had already been placed on slop duty for sullen behaviour. Tilbury glanced at Nimble-Quick as they grabbed two pails each. He dared not speak, but followed Nimble-Quick out into the yard.

He squinted in the bright sunlight, trying not to breathe in the stench. There were small cages set all the way around the walls and a huge cage in the centre of the yard. The felinrat guard screeched at them to hurry up, then sat himself down in the shade and watched from half closed eyes. A snore caught in his throat as he snoozed in the heat.

Tilbury looked at the rows upon rows of cages. In each cage was a cat. It struck him that the cats did not share the same space with the felinrats, but were caged here when not being ridden, willing prisoners of the rats. He wondered how the cats had given up their freedom so easily. Maybe it was the promise of ready meals of fresh ratlings that the cats did not have to hunt for.

He could see the other ratlings on slop duty slipping in between the bars to clear out the litter trays and fill bowls of milk. Tilbury slipped into one cage and began clearing up the litter tray and filling up the slop bucket with the mess. All the while, he kept a wary eye on the cats. The ratlings worked along the long line of cages until they came to another set of cages on the adjoining wall. Only this time the cages weren't filled with cats, but with ratlings.

Some of the ratlings were at the point of adulthood, maybe too big to control, thought Tilbury. Was this the last holding place before they became the cats' dinners? Did they see other rats being fed to the cats? He took their full slop buckets and gave them empty ones, but they did not look him in the eye and seemed broken in spirit. Maybe they had seen their end coming and knew no way out. When Tilbury reached the end cages, he could see two adult rats sitting in the gloom, with their backs to him. He recognized one white furry head above the cape.

'Marfaire?' whispered Tilbury. 'Obsidian?'

Marfaire turned around. 'Oh, Master Tilbury, you have been caught.'

Obsidian turned too, but then spat his disapproval and turned his back on them again.

Nimble-Quick came to join Tilbury, keeping a watchful eye on the felinrat guard who was still snoozing.

'We have come to rescue you,' whispered Tilbury excitedly.

Obsidian gave a hollow laugh but Marfaire touched Tilbury's face with her paw. 'Oh, dearest Tilbury, I have thought and thought and can see no escape. Tomorrow, Obsidian and I will face the White Death.'

'Maybe we can fight the White Death together,' said Tilbury.

Obsidian spun around, his manic laughter ringing out in the cage. 'Fight it? Fight it? Have you actually *seen* it?'

'No,' whispered Tilbury, 'Have you?'

Marfaire nodded. 'We have already seen it, and there is no escape.'

She was looking beyond Tilbury and he turned. She pointed at the huge cage in the centre of the courtyard. It seemed empty, but then Tilbury noticed what was lying in the centre of the cage, camouflaged by the striped shadows of the iron bars.

Nimble-Quick recoiled in fear.

The creature inside the cage was bigger than Tilbury could have ever imagined. It lifted its head from between its paws and sniffed the air, scenting him. A low growl rose inside its throat.

Nimble-Quick backed away and turned her head from its gaze.

But Tilbury's eyes opened wider and wider and his little heart quickened with excitement.

And he stepped towards the beast in total awe and wonder.

CHAPTER TWENTY-NINE
The White Death

The beast that lay before Tilbury's eyes was the most beautiful animal he had ever seen. It was a creature of myth and legend, a creature he had never thought he would ever see, and it reminded him a little of his very dear friend Marmalade and the stories he had told him of the great cat kings.

A huge, white tiger lay before him.

The cage was too small for such a magnificent beast, and the floor was caked in its filth. Scum floated on the dirty water in its bowl, and bones littered the floor. Tilbury didn't want to think too hard about who those bones might have belonged to.

The tiger's stripes were a dark chocolate brown against the white fur. But it was the tiger's eyes that fascinated him; they were bright blue, the colour of the clear mountain sky. They held mountains and whole landscapes within them, and for a moment it felt as if Tilbury was on the tip of a mountain feeling the freezing air.

Tilbury bowed low, remembering his manners. 'Greetings, great king,' he said in Olde Sphinx. 'I offer you my life as your humble servant. For you are the king of all kings. The king of all kingdoms.'

The tiger blinked and sniffed. It rose to its feet and padded over, its nose almost touching Tilbury through the bars. Long whiskers, rigid as wire, poked through.

When the tiger spoke, his voice was a low, deep growl. 'What kind of rat thinks he is worthy of speaking to a king?'

Before Tilbury could answer, he was knocked off his feet. The felinrat shoved him. 'What fool-ratling have we here?' he shrieked with laughter. 'Have you no brains? Are you so dull-witted you have no fear?' He laughed again. 'Maybe we should let you in to play with the beast?' He grabbed Tilbury and pressed him against the bars such that the tiger could have pulled Tilbury through with a single claw. 'Would you like that?'

But the tiger didn't pull Tilbury through. It took a deep breath, opened its mouth and roared. The blast of air from its lungs sent Tilbury and the felinrat rolling backwards. Four other felinrats rushed in. They came with long sticks tipped with sharp iron nails. They poked at the tiger, stabbing at him through the bars, and the tiger spun around in anger swiping at the sticks and lashing its tail.

General Malice rode through on his spotted cat and stopped in front of the tiger. 'I see the White Death is getting hungry. Maybe he is getting impatient. For tomorrow he will feed on our prisoners in front of the Immortal Emperor.'

'Move it,' said the felinrat, shoving Tilbury. 'Get back to work.'

Tilbury picked up the pails and scuttled back with Nimble-Quick. He turned around to see General Malice tormenting the tiger, jabbing it with a spiked pole and laughing. 'Get back, pussy cat.'

The tiger lashed at the cage again and it shook as if the bars might break. Tilbury noticed the cage was crude in design but strong. The iron bars were thick enough to prevent the tiger's escape, and an iron bolt was drawn across the cage door. Unlike the Gilded Cage this had only one bolt, but that was no use at all to the tiger, thought Tilbury, if it still couldn't undo the door.

'You were a fool,' snapped Nimble-Quick later, when they were emptying slop buckets out of earshot of felinrats. 'What did you think you were doing? You could have got killed.'

But Tilbury's thoughts were racing, and he wasn't listening to Nimble-Quick.

Nimble-Quick punched him hard. 'Tilbury, what's the matter with you?'

Tilbury turned and gripped Nimble-Quick's paw. 'I think I know how to get us out of here. But I'm going to need your help.'

CHAPTER THIRTY

The Immortal Emperor

Tilbury hardly slept all night. The ground was cold and hard, and his mind kept going back over conversations and lessons with his dear friend Marmalade in the chandlery basement.

Nimble-Quick was watching him from her patch of floor, her whiskers twitching in nervous anticipation, but the felinrat guard was on watch and they hadn't been able speak to each other at all since making their plans yesterday.

The morning gong rang and the ratlings all gathered in their rows and lines.

The guard stood in front of them. 'Today is a great day. It is an auspicious day, for the Immortal Emperor himself will be in attendance. It has been ten years since he has given us the great honour of his presence.' He looked around the ratlings. 'It is forbidden to look directly at him. Any ratling that casts a glance his way will be killed. Is that understood?'

The ratlings nodded silently.

'Good,' said the guard. 'Your masters will want to be well nourished before the ceremony. Make sure you attend to their needs.'

In the courtyard, the felinrats were gathering around the tiger's cage, but the tiger remained hidden in the shade. They jostled and chattered and helped themselves to the fine food from the trays the ratlings carried. There was an air of excitement and anticipation amongst them. A loud gong sounded, and all the felinrats fell silent.

General Malice rode in on his spotted cat and addressed them all. 'Fellow felinrats,' he called out. 'Today is a great day. We have the honour of the *Cursed Night* in our possession. Such is the patience of the Immortal Emperor, that time has brought it to us. He has waited for two hundred years for this moment. He was the one to defeat the Golden Rats and banish them back to the City in the Clouds. With the diamond in our keeping, they will never rule over us again. Let us show our respect for our great leader. Please kneel and avert your gaze, for the Immortal Emperor does not wish to be stared at.'

All the rats knelt down, and Tilbury did the same. From the far side of the death-yard rolled a high platform on wheels, pushed by four felinrats. All the rats kept their heads bowed as General Malice carried the *Cursed Night* up to the platform. Tilbury couldn't help stealing a glance. There was a throne on the top of the platform, and sitting there, perfectly still, was an old rat dressed in furs. It was hard to see him well, and his face looked wizened with age.

General Malice lifted the diamond high, blocking Tilbury's view. 'It is by your wisdom that we receive the *Cursed Night* into our safe keeping. Now, we have become truly invincible.' He placed the diamond on the emperor's lap, and Tilbury craned his neck to see.

Someone coughed and Tilbury stared at the floor again, hoping he hadn't been seen staring at the Immortal Emperor.

'It is time to avenge our enemies,' said the general. 'Let the White Death begin. Bring forth the prisoners.'

Tilbury watched as Marfaire, Obsidian, and a young she-ratling were escorted to the cage.

The felinrats' eyes glittered with excitement. They clambered over each other to see the prisoners walking in a line. Some placed bets to see which rat would be eaten first.

Then there was hushed silence as the prisoners were forced to climb to the top of the cage and then lowered slowly on a piece of wood. The tiger emerged from his resting place, watching the piece of wood as it came towards him.

Tilbury noticed Obsidian had been given back his sword. He stood with his sword drawn. Marfaire had her paws around the young she-rat, shielding her from the tiger. But even before they had reached the ground, the tiger swished his tail and leaped, knocking them to the floor. Obsidian and the she-ratling scurried away to hide, but the tiger had pinned down Marfaire by a claw. The claw was longer than Marfaire, and it shone like polished steel.

The felinrats roared and hooted with laughter.

'Marfaire!' squeaked Tilbury. He took a deep breath and squeezed through the gap in the cage, running towards the tiger.

The rats in the crowd leaned forward and gasped with excitement. Another rat would be killed today, and they were bloodthirsty for the entertainment.

But Tilbury stood before the tiger and bowed. 'Greetings, great king. I offer you my life as your humble servant. For you are the king of all kings. The king of all kingdoms.'

The tiger stopped and stared at Tilbury, his eyes blue and sharp as the ice-rivers on the high mountains. 'And I ask again, what rat thinks he is worthy of speaking to a king?'

Tilbury kept his eyes on the floor. 'A rat who can return a king to his kingdom.'

The tiger lowered its face and Tilbury could feel tiger breath ruffle his fur. 'And how are you going to do that?'

'We are going to open the cage,' said Tilbury. 'You can then return to the mountains.'

'And why would a rat do that for a tiger?'

Tilbury could feel his little legs shaking so badly. He became aware of the drumming of rat paws from the crowd, baying for blood. But no one else could understand the words that passed between Tilbury and the tiger.

'I am here with a Golden Rat, an Elder and my sister. We need to return a diamond to the City in the Clouds.'

'Why?' said the tiger. His voice was soft and curious but rolled like distant thunder in his throat.

'We want freedom too,' said Tilbury. 'We need to be free of a terrible curse.'

The tiger thought for a moment and then smiled. 'It *must* be a terrible curse if you'd dare to face a tiger.'

'Will you take us?' asked Tilbury. 'If you can't promise, I would rather die now. And if you do eat me, please make it quick.'

The tiger turned to look at his mountain kingdom, at the snow dust swirling from the summits. The mountains reflected in his eyes as if he and the mountain were one. He turned back to Tilbury. 'You have my word,' he said.

Tilbury turned to Nimble-Quick and raised a paw. The felinrats were hooting and screeching for the tiger to attack, and they didn't notice Nimble-Quick climb and pull on the bolt. It was heavy and however hard she pulled it would not budge.

'Hey,' came a felinrat's voice, seeing her trying to pull back the bolt. 'Stop that ratling!'

But then Zorris jumped up beside Nimble-Quick and hauled on the bolt too. 'I'm with you,' cried Zorris. 'The she-ratling in the cage is Padme, my sister.'

Together they pushed and pulled it, scraping off old rust, and the bolt flew back, letting the cage door swing wide.

The tiger burst from the cage, swiping his paws, biting mouthfuls of fleeing rats.

In the panic, felinrats swarmed from the palace, charging from the yard, and through the house, knocking over candles on the way. Fire caught on the faded curtains and rose like a wall of flames. The dry timbers of the house blazed and black smoke rose into the sky.

Tilbury scrambled out, following Obsidian to the platform where General Malice was hunched over the Immortal Emperor. The general was putting the *Cursed Night* into his own bag. Obsidian charged at him, his dagger out in front of him. But the general was faster, pulling his own sword and knocking Obsidian's dagger from him. General Malice lifted his sword to strike, but before he could plunge it into Obsidian, the tiger's teeth closed around General Malice and, dropping his sword and bag, he was swallowed whole in one large tigerish gulp.

Obsidian spun around and grabbed the *Cursed Night*. But Tilbury turned to the Immortal Emperor. The emperor still hadn't moved. He sat impassive, wrapped in furs. Then Tilbury noticed the emperor had no eyes. His face was sunken, and his paws were shrivelled. He was hardly a rat at all. The emperor was just a dried husk of a rat, desiccated by the sun and the wind.

The emperor was long, long dead.

CHAPTER THIRTY-ONE
The City in the Clouds

Padme poked the emperor with her foot. 'The felinrats were ruled by a dead king?'

Marfaire looked at the twisted mouth of the emperor. 'The felinrats were ruled by fear. And fear spills out as hatred and cruelty. There can be no greater evil than sending innocents to their deaths.'

Tilbury looked back to see ratlings spilling out of the palace. Flames licked high and Tilbury could feel the searing heat on his fur. 'We need to lead them to their mothers,' he said.

'There are ratlings in the death-yard in cages,' said Padme. 'They'll die in there.'

Tilbury turned to the white tiger. 'Oh, king of kings, please can I beg of you to help release the ratlings, and return them to their mothers who are waiting for them?'

The tiger turned to Tilbury. 'I will do as you ask, and take them to their mothers, then I shall look for mine, for I too was tricked by the felinrats as a small cub. They lured me in here many moons ago.'

The tiger jumped down to the cages in the death-yard where the ratlings were coughing in the smoke. He ripped the doors from the cages. 'Climb on my back,' he ordered.

Tilbury scrambled up too and called others up. 'Come on, you're going home.'

On the other side of the yard, cats yowled in fear as smoke billowed through their cages.

The tiger spun around and spoke in Olde Sphinx, but he chose words he knew they would understand. 'You disgrace the great kings of cats, selling your freedom to the felinrats. Cats answer to no one but themselves.' He tore their doors from the cages. 'Run now and may you live in the shadows, eating beetles and worms, for you are not worthy of living as noble cats.'

The cats scattered, fleeing after the felinrats through the burning house and out onto the road to Hilzen.

The tiger turned to look at the burning remains of the palace where he had been kept prisoner. Then he turned to face the mountains, threw back his head and roared. Tilbury had never heard such a sound. The vibrations of the roar swept through his body and he could feel the immense power of the tiger. The roar echoed in the mountains and far, far away, the mountains answered with the distant rumble and roar of an avalanche, tumbling in a puff of powder-white snow.

Then, with ratlings riding on his back, and others trotting alongside him, the tiger padded out of the burning remains of the palace and headed to the hills where the Rebel Mothers were waiting for their children.

Obsidian walked behind, and Tilbury kept glancing back at him.

'He's got the *Cursed Night*,' whispered Nimble-Quick. 'He might run off with it.'

Marfaire shook her head. 'He needs the tiger to take us across the Badlands to reach the City in the Clouds.'

Tilbury frowned. 'He still doesn't trust us.'

Nimble-Quick glared at Tilbury. 'And I don't trust him. He'd be dead if it wasn't for us. He hasn't even thanked us.'

'He's a warrior,' said Tilbury. 'Maybe it's shameful for him to accept help.'

'Pah!' spat Nimble-Quick, the fur at the nape of her neck bristling in anger.

As they neared the caves where the Rebel Mothers had hidden, the mothers lined up, watching the great tiger padding towards them, and when they saw their own ratlings riding on his back, they came running down the mountain to meet them.

'Padme, Zorris,' cried Kadma. She wrapped her paws around her daughters, and soon all the lost ratlings were finding their mothers. Tilbury felt a deep ache of homesickness for his own ma, but Kadma pulled him in her embrace. 'Thank you,' she said. 'Come and stay with us by our fire and have some supper.'

The tiger sniffed the cold mountain air and his eyes searched the mountains. 'We must go soon,' he said to Tilbury. 'The journey will be long, and I do not know the way.'

'Marfaire does,' said Tilbury. He turned to her. 'Marfaire, can you find our way to the Rainbow Falls?'

Marfaire nodded. 'The mountain pass lies between twin peaks. We must follow the meltwater of the glaciers.'

Tilbury looked across at her. 'How do you remember the map?'

Marfaire smiled. 'I have walked it every day in my mind since I was chosen to be the next Keeper.'

Tilbury and Nimble-Quick picked up the bags they had left. Tilbury was glad to wrap the silk scarf with the Silk Wing plan around his neck again.

They climbed on the tiger's back with Marfaire and Obsidian, and the tiger bounded away.

It was hard to talk, clutching on as the world unfurled below the tiger's paws, but Marfaire gave Tilbury instructions that he told to the tiger. Higher and higher they went, through scrubby Badlands where trees were short and gnarled and on, above the treeline where Tilbury could hear the roar of the river. Ahead of them lay three valleys, each with a glacier that met to form a raging meltwater that flowed down a central valley.

Marfaire squinted her eyes into the sun. 'There should be a glacier across this valley, but there is only this river,' she said. She sighed. 'The map told to me is two hundred years old. There is no ice where it had once been plentiful.'

The tiger dipped his paw into the water. 'Then we shall cross the river. You must all hold on tightly,' he said to Tilbury. And with that he plunged into the water.

The current took them, swirling the great tiger around and around, but he pulled his way forward, his head and neck above the surface. Tilbury wrapped his tail around Nimble-Quick and clung on. Freezing spray soaked Tilbury's travelling cape and sometimes it felt as if the river would swallow them whole, but the tiger found his grip on the far side of the river and hauled himself out. He shook himself, scattering diamond drops of water and Tilbury had to cling on even more tightly. Then they were off again, the tiger following the instructions Marfaire gave, across rocky scree and high mountain goat trails, until they reached a sheer cliff face. Ahead of them, a rainbow arched over a waterfall. It was the most beautiful sight that Tilbury had seen. The cliff formed an arc around a clear blue pool where the waterfall plunged from high, high above.

'The Rainbow Falls,' said the tiger to Tilbury. 'You have kept your word, and now I have kept mine. I must leave you. Farewell, brave ratling. This king has been humbled to know that true heroes can come in any size.'

Tilbury watched the tiger bound away, the pattern of his stripes camouflaging him against the pale rock and deep shadows. He seemed to dissolve into the landscape of his kingdom. And he was gone.

Nimble-Quick flung her arms around Tilbury. 'We did it.'

'Marmalade helped us,' said Tilbury. 'He taught me Olde Sphinx.'

Marfaire put her paws around them both. 'Never have I seen warriors of such bravery. What do you say, Obsidian?'

But Obsidian had eyes only upwards. Tilbury followed his gaze up the sheer cliff-face, and there at the very top were puffy white clouds, and poking through were jewel-encrusted towers, shining in the evening sun.

'The City in the Clouds,' murmured Obsidian. 'A place so long lost in time it seems like myth itself. This is my home,' he said. 'My destiny. My journey's end.'

'Journey's end,' Tilbury repeated. 'Oh, Marfaire. Are we almost there?'

'Maybe,' said Marfaire looking up where the sheer cliff disappeared into cloud. She frowned and sighed deeply. 'You have learned to be brave, my dearest Tilbury. But I fear the hardest part is yet to come. Now you must learn to be wise.'

PART THREE
MOONFLIGHT

The Return of the
Cursed Night

CHAPTER THIRTY-TWO
Ladder to the Sky

A howl rose up from behind them.

Night was drawing in, and the shadows of the Badlands stretched towards them, reaching out like long claws. Tilbury crept a little closer to Nimble-Quick. He wondered what creatures might steal forwards with the shadows too. It was colder up here in the mountains than the searing heat of the valley floor. A wild screeching cry split the air and Marfaire pulled her dagger from the sheath, holding it at her side.

Obsidian knelt down and dipped his paw in the clear blue pool. 'Ice cold,' he said, blowing warm breath on to his paws.

'How do we get across?' asked Nimble-Quick. 'Is it too cold? Is it deep?'

Tilbury shuddered. 'Are there monsters?'

Marfaire squinted her eyes and pointed beyond the veil of water cascading into the pool. There were figures moving on the other side. Then, through the waterfall came a boat, the water parting like a curtain as it passed beneath. A rat was standing at the back of the boat, with a long paddle that it sculled behind. Its fur was wet from the water and gleamed like polished gold.

The Golden Rat stopped mid-pool and called out. 'Who goes there? Name the purpose of your visit.'

Obsidian stepped forward. He let his travelling cape drop to the floor to show his own golden fur. 'I am Obsidian, descendant of Prince Obsidian. I have come to return the *Cursed Night* to its rightful place. The felinrats have been overthrown. With the return of the black diamond, the Golden Rats can rule once again.'

The rat in the boat paddled a little closer. 'And who are the other three travellers?'

Marfaire stepped forward. 'I am Marfaire of the Dockland Rats, Keeper of the map to the City in the Clouds. We have crossed the seven seas. These two ratlings have shown great bravery and saved us from the felinrats. Young Tilbury here tamed the White Death. He has come to return the *Cursed Night* to fulfil a prophecy. He is returning the diamond stolen by Bartholomew.'

The rat was still; the only movement was the circular sculling motion of his paddle keeping him in the middle of the pool. Then he spoke again. 'We know this diamond as the *Eye of Aurun*. If you have the *Eye of Aurun*, then reveal it now.'

Obsidian, pulled the diamond from the silk bag and held it high. 'Here, and I have come to return it to the king.'

The Golden Rat stared at it for some time. 'Wait there,' he said. He paddled back beneath the waterfall and was gone.

Tilbury looked back to the Badlands and shivered. They couldn't go back, and the only way forward was up the sheer rock wall rising above them. And as he looked, he realized there were small steps carved into the rock, and he noticed the scurrying of a rat. It scampered up and up to another point where another rat sat hidden. He watched as they appeared to be talking, then the other rat set off up the cliff, higher and higher until it met another.

'They're sending messengers up the cliff to announce our arrival,' said Nimble-Quick.

Tilbury peered upwards. 'And is that the only way up?

'Yes,' said Obsidian. 'This must be the fabled Ladder to the Sky. It's fiercely guarded. The only route to the City in the Clouds.'

The rockface began to blush pink with the setting sun. Droplets of water from the waterfall caught the light and fell like liquid gold. High above, the clouds cleared a little to show the mountain tops where wisps of snow drifted from the ridge.

A howl rose from behind them again.

'Look, someone's coming back,' said Marfaire.

This time two boats slipped out from under the veil of water, each paddled by a Golden Rat. 'You will rest at the bottom of the Ladder to the Sky until we hear from the king,' said one.

Tilbury, Nimble-Quick and Marfaire were helped aboard one boat and Obsidian aboard another. Tilbury watched the veil of water coming closer and closer. The rainbow seemed to rise above them and disappear as they passed beneath the waterfall. The veil was thin, but the weight of water and the coldness shocked him all the same. The sound of the water echoed in the cave they found themselves in. It was damp inside but a small fire glowed in the centre casting long shadows around the cave walls. It felt safe from the unseen creatures of the night.

'We will wait for the messengers,' said the guard. 'And if the king grants you entry, we will start at first light. Rest now, and eat.'

Tilbury and Nimble-Quick tucked into a plate of dried apricots and sweet flat breads and edged towards the fire, putting their paws as close as possible to feel the heat.

Obsidian sat opposite them on the other side of the fire, his travelling cape wrapped around the bag containing the *Cursed Night*.

Marfaire sat down next to him. 'We have brought you to your home, Obsidian, but the diamond is for Tilbury to return to the City in the Clouds,' she said quietly. 'It is told in the prophecy.'

Tilbury looked across the flames, but Obsidian's face was turned into the shadows.

'It is for me to return it to my people,' said Obsidian, holding the bag closely to his chest.

Nimble-Quick scowled. 'It's for Tilbury to do it. The story of the *Cursed Night* tells that the rat who opens the Gilded Cage is the one to return the diamond to the rightful owners.'

Obsidian glared at her. 'The Golden Rats are the rightful owners. This diamond is part of our story. The *Eye of Aurun* holds great power.' He glanced at the other Golden Rats to check they were not listening, then he lowered his voice. 'I am a noble warrior. Descendant of Prince Obsidian. Why would I let a ratling carry this diamond to my ancestral home?' He turned to face Marfaire.

216

'I will be the one to return it to the king. If you want it, you will have to fight me for it.'

Marfaire sat perfectly still, but the tip of her tail twitched to and fro.

Tilbury felt the heavy pull of the diamond, like a weight around his soul. Its power seemed to swell and fill the small cave and even the flames flickered a little less brightly. He had no wish to hold the *Cursed Night* in his paws. He cleared his throat. 'Maybe we should let Obsidian be the one to carry it. It would be humiliating for him if I carry it into the City in the Clouds. After all, Bartholomew did steal it from the Golden Rats. You said so yourself, Marfaire.'

'Exactly,' whispered Obsidian. 'Tilbury is wise for his years.'

Nimble-Quick flicked a piece of dirt in the fire and gritted her teeth. 'The prophecy said Tilbury must return it, and only him.'

'But I am,' said Tilbury. 'I have brought it safely here. Does it matter who carries it over the threshold?'

Marfaire stood up and paced in circles around the fire. 'Only Tilbury can find the true owner of this diamond, but we must accept the king will want to see it,' she said. She stood in front of Obsidian. 'Tilbury has generously let you present it to the king, but he must be with you when you do so.'

Obsidian stared into the flames, the firelight seeming to make his fur glow like embers. He said nothing but a single whisker twitched.

'You would not be here without him,' said Marfaire, raising her voice such that the other Golden Rats looked around. 'He was the one to defeat the felinrats, not you.'

The guard rats' ears swivelled to hear the conversation.

Marfaire spoke loud enough for the guards to hear. 'Tilbury faced the White Death and saved your life. He has ensured the safe return of the diamond. And he will join you to present the diamond to the king.'

'I agree to it,' snapped Obsidian, glancing at the listening guard rats. He pushed himself back into the shadows, his paws clutching the silk bag carrying the diamond even more tightly.

Marfaire sat beside Tilbury, pushing more twigs and dry grass into the fire. She was silent for a long time, and then as Nimble-Quick was falling into soft slumber, she turned to Tilbury.

'Are you afraid of the *Cursed Night*?' she whispered. 'Is that why you do not wish to carry it?'

Tilbury nodded and trembled. 'I feel its darkness pulling me more strongly than ever before. I'm scared I will fall under its spell, like Bartholomew.'

Marfaire stared into the flames. 'And yet you seem to resist its power.' She poked the fire, sending up sparks that glittered brightly in the darkness. 'Maybe the *Cursed Night* is safer with you. Maybe it is most dangerous with those who desire it most.'

CHAPTER THIRTY-THREE
Medal for a Hero

With the dawn came a messenger who brought news that the king requested the company of the travellers.

And so Marfaire fussed and told Tilbury and Nimble-Quick to dress in their warmest clothes. Nimble-Quick grumbled as they began their climb, feeling hot and sweaty beneath her layers of shirts and long johns, but it wasn't long before the mountain air chilled their tails, and they all felt glad of the winter clothes. One Golden Rat led the way and the other brought up the rear. The climb was so steep that the guards had to point out paw-holds to step onto. Higher and higher they climbed until all around them were swirling white clouds. Tilbury was glad of the clouds because they hid the vast emptiness beneath them. There was nothing between him and the ground but sky.

Up and up they climbed into the wild silence. Once, a bird flew past. It had the widest wingspan of any bird Tilbury had ever seen. It effortlessly soared on the updraughts of air, and he wondered if Bartholomew had once marvelled at these birds too. Sheets of thin ice coated the rocks, making their passage slower, and even the water in the air formed crystals on Tilbury's whiskers. The air was thinner too, and his chest ached with the need to breathe.

'You'll get used to it,' said the guard, watching the new travellers breathing heavily.

'How far now?' panted Nimble-Quick. She was balanced on a precarious ledge.

'Not far,' said the rat. 'The city will be expecting you.'

And they climbed up further, out of the clouds into bright blue sunshine, the City in the Clouds laid out before them.

Tilbury wasn't prepared for the welcome. Silk flags of bright colours fluttered against the clear blue sky. The path into the city was lined with Golden Rats throwing rose petals into the air to greet the travellers. The City in the Clouds dazzled Tilbury. It was hewn from the rock and encrusted with gemstones. It was as beautiful as the myths told about it. It didn't seem possible that it was real. The eastern towers sparkled with sapphires, and the western towers glowed with rubies and gemstones of yellow and orange. The windows and doorways were shimmering with gold.

Obsidian held his head high and his jewel-encrusted dagger even higher as they walked into the city. The ripples of cheers and applause carried Tilbury's weary legs forward. They were led into a large hall where sunlight shone in, through hanging silks, bathing the hall in coloured lights.

An elderly Golden Rat stood before them, his muzzle slightly whiter than the rest of his golden fur. Tilbury guessed he must be high ranking, because he wore medallions of gold around his neck.

'Welcome, warrior and weary travellers,' said the rat. 'I am the king's sage, and we welcome you to our city. Today is the dawn of a new era for the Golden Rats, for the *Eye of Aurun* is returned.' He clasped his hands together and gave a little bow to Obsidian. 'Welcome, returned warrior,' he said, and then he gave a bow to Tilbury. 'I hear you are a young ratling to be honoured for your bravery in the face of a monster.'

Tilbury stared at the floor. He didn't regard the tiger as a monster, but he felt pride spread through him, hearing this rat telling him he was brave.

'Humble too,' said the rat. 'A sign of a true warrior.' He slipped a purple silk ribbon over Tilbury's head which held a small gold medallion. 'The king will hear your tale at a feast in your honour this evening, and you will be written into the book of legends. But for now, you and your travelling companions must be rested and tended to.'

Tilbury, Marfaire and Nimble-Quick were led away separately from Obsidian and into a room that had a large opening looking out over the mountains. Three mattresses lay on the floor with blankets and quilts piled high, and a basket of bread was warming by the fire.

The air felt thin and brittle with ice, and yet a thorned vine clung to the rockface, and a tiny pink flower bloomed at the window. Marfaire reached out to touch it. It seemed impossibly fragile in the high mountain landscape.

'Mountain rose,' said the Golden Rat. 'Known for its endurance and beauty.' The rat put another piece of wood on the fire and the flames burned a little brighter. 'Rest now. I will come back to take you to the Welcome Feast.'

When they were alone, Tilbury walked to the open window cut into the rock. Marfaire came to stand next to him. The mountain tops rose above the sea of clouds. He took a bite of bread and chewed it slowly, savouring its sweet warmth.

'Our journey's end,' sighed Tilbury. 'I can't believe we're actually here in the City in the Clouds. We made it. Obsidian is right. It is the most perfect place in the world. Don't you think so, Marfaire?'

Marfaire turned her head up to watch a bird soaring high above them on the rising thermals. 'It may depend upon your perspective,' she said. 'Sometimes only time and distance can give us that.'

'But we've been given such a welcome,' said Tilbury.

'Have we?' said Marfaire rather abruptly.

Tilbury frowned. Marfaire was not usually so short with him and he wondered if maybe she was tired. He pulled his mattress closer to Nimble-Quick's and sat next to her. 'Marfaire's in a terrible mood,' he whispered. 'The Golden Rats have welcomed us and are kind to us, and she seems ungrateful. They are going to write us into the book of legends.'

Nimble-Quick picked at a scab on her tail. 'I'm tired, Tilbury,' she said. 'I'm going to have a rest.'

Tilbury felt irritation rise inside him. What was wrong with both of them? He tried to push his irritation away and instead ran his paws along the silk ribbon and held the shining golden medallion. It was a medal from the golden warrior rats. He would be written into their legends for returning the *Cursed Night* that had been stolen so long ago. He was brave, he told himself. He was a hero.

He turned his back on Nimble-Quick.

The Golden Rats saw him as a hero, so why couldn't she?

CHAPTER THIRTY-FOUR
Ashes

The sun dipped lower in the sky, turning the snow on the summits to gold. As the stars prickled out in the night sky, the temperature kept falling and Tilbury pulled on the thick padded coat Ma had made him.

A gong sounded and two Golden Rats arrived at their door. One was a warrior dressed in leather armour plated with gold, and the other was a she-rat in a gown of midnight blue silk, dripping in tiny diamonds.

'The king will see you now for the Welcome Feast,' said the warrior rat, to Tilbury.

The she-rat turned to Marfaire and Nimble-Quick, her eyes taking in their well-worn clothes. 'Come, I will take you to the bathhouses where you can wash before the feast.'

Tilbury followed the warrior rat to the large hall. Food was piled high on tables around the edges of the room, and cushions and blankets were spread out across the floor. In full view, with the backdrop of mountains behind, was a golden throne. Tilbury was aware of many eyes watching him.

The sage took Tilbury's paw and steered him to the front with Obsidian.

'You will be honoured to sit with the warriors, clerics and scholars,' said the sage. Tilbury felt very small next to the taller adult rats. He nibbled at a piece of cheese offered to him and looked around at the gathering rats, as conversation rose and fell like waves about him. He looked behind to see the golden she-rat leading Marfaire and Nimble-Quick to the back of the hall. Nimble-Quick spied him and glowered. He wanted to call her over, but music started up and more Golden Rats arrived. The other she-rats came in. Tilbury couldn't help thinking Ma would like to see this. The she-rats wore finery of silk and they were decorated with rings and gemstones. They wore headdresses shimmering with diamonds. Rubies, emeralds and sapphires were stitched into their clothes. Their long gowns were so heavy with the weight of jewels that young she-rats held the hems off the ground. Then came some dancers, younger ratlings, swirling long strands of silk behind them in a kaleidoscope of colour. Tilbury's eyes followed the dancers as he was served warm rice balls and bread stuffed with ripe plums and nuts. And as the sun dipped behind the mountain, the fires and lanterns glowed warmly in the gathering darkness.

Tilbury sat with Obsidian and the warriors. They wore shining gold armour encrusted with diamonds and carried golden bows and quivers of arrows at their sides. A tray with goblets of amber liquid was passed around and held beneath Tilbury's nose. He looked around for Marfaire to see if he should take one.

A golden warrior next to Tilbury nudged him gently. 'Take one, you are a warrior now. You are one of us.'

Tilbury smiled. He was seen as a warrior. His chest swelled with pride. The drink smelled sweet and pungent, and reminded him of the honeysuckle that grew up the chandlery wall. He watched Obsidian drink his in one gulp, slamming the goblet on the tray again. Tilbury did the same. The liquid honey and summer sunshine filled his throat with a heat he didn't expect. He slammed his goblet on the tray too with hiccup and a cough. His head swam a little, but the drink had wrapped him in a warm, fuzzy blanket.

He let his eyes slide around him, looking at the golden warrior rats next to him. Music swirled in the thin air and drew him to them. Maybe he *was* brave enough to be considered one of them. He had tamed a tiger, after all.

Another gong sounded and the sage stood before them. 'Please all rise, for the Golden Warrior King.'

Tilbury was swept up as all rats rose for the king. He strained his neck to see, as the king entered the room escorted by warriors. The king wore a robe lined with white fur. On his head sat a crown of diamonds patterned like the stars against deep blue velvet. He was a young king, with a warm, wide smile and Tilbury felt drawn to him. The king stood before them, then took a seat on the golden throne. All the other rats sat down in silence.

The king held a gold staff in his paw and swept it over his

audience. 'My fellow Golden Rats,' he said. 'Today is a day we have awaited for many, many years. The black diamond, *Aurun's Eye*, has been returned to us, and we will prepare for a great ceremony of its return in the coming days. It will be placed back in the Golden Archway, and when the sun shines through the diamond, we will feel Aurun's gaze upon us once more. His power will return to us. But first, we will hear the tales of these rats who have reunited us with our destiny.' He smiled and indicated for Obsidian to take the floor.

Obsidian stepped forward and bowed to the king and then to the Golden Rats. 'Your Majesty, it is indeed a great honour to be here. I am Obsidian, the descendant of Prince Obsidian who set sail to return the diamond to this kingdom. The thief Bartholomew locked the diamond in a Gilded Cage. We have lived in the Everdark of London, waiting for the moment to bring the diamond home. I have fought many on this journey. I have crossed oceans. I have witnessed the fall of the Palace of the Immortal Emperor.' Obsidian knelt before the king and kissed his feet. 'My ancestor was a faithful brother to yours. I remain your loyal and loving servant.'

A cheer and applause went up.

The king raised his paw for quiet. 'There are not enough words to thank you for what you have done. You will be duly rewarded for your bravery and loyalty. But . . .' he smiled and turned to Tilbury. 'I hear you had a little help from a young ratling.' He indicated for

Tilbury to come forward. 'May we hear your story, for you were the one to unlock the diamond and allow it to be returned.'

Tilbury felt his little legs shaking, but he stood and bowed to the king.

'Tell us how you helped escape from the Palace of the Immortal Emperor,' said the king.

Tilbury felt a little hazy from the drink, but it had loosened his tongue in his mouth a little too.

'We faced the White Death,' said Tilbury. 'A white tiger. A king of cats.'

The crowd gasped and Tilbury enjoyed the reaction and feeling of telling a story.

'It was huge,' he said, standing on tiptoes. 'It could fit ten rats inside its jaws, and still pin ten more down with its claws. And when it roared, even the mountains trembled.' Tilbury opened his mouth to roar, but all that came out was a little burp.

The crowd roared with laughter.

'Go on,' said the king, reclining back in his seat, 'for I am enjoying this story.'

And so, Tilbury enjoyed spinning out his tale as he listened to the Golden Rats drumming their paws on the floor for more.

When he had finished, the sage spoke. 'It is now time for the king to see the *Eye of Aurun*.'

A hushed silence spread across the Golden Rats, and they all craned forward to get a better view.

Tilbury turned to Obsidian and smiled. This was the moment they would present the diamond to the king together, the moment that Tilbury would fulfil the prophecy. But before Tilbury could stop him, Obsidian lifted the diamond out of his bag, knelt before the king and held it out, leaving Tilbury in the cold behind him. Tilbury tried to say something, but his chest felt tight and only a soft squeak came out. Obsidian had broken his promise.

The king took the diamond in his paws, and Tilbury watched him look into the cut surface and study his reflection. Firelight danced, casting eerie shadows on the king's face, concealing his expression in darkness.

The king stood up and raised it above his head. 'The *Eye of Aurun* has returned. My people will be free. We are no longer prisoners in our own kingdom.'

Another cheer rose up from the crowd, and the king placed the diamond on a velvet cushion by his side.

'Sire,' said Obsidian, glancing at Tilbury. 'There is a part of the tale untold. When the diamond was locked in the Gilded Cage, Bartholomew left a metal tube beside it. Master Tilbury has this tube.'

The king's gaze swivelled on Tilbury. 'Come, come,' said the king, holding out his paws.

Tilbury stepped forward. He pulled the metal tube from his pocket and placed it in the king's paws. The king turned it over and over and shook it a little. 'Is there anything inside?'

'There is a parchment, sire,' said Obsidian. 'I believe it has a message written upon it in ratiffi.'

230

The king ran his paws across it. He frowned and turned to Tilbury. 'Do you know how to open this?'

Tilbury nodded. He thought he heard a squeak from the crowd. It sounded like Nimble-Quick, but he could not be sure.

'Then do so,' urged the king, giving it back.

Tilbury put the tube beside the fire to warm until he could barely touch it with his paws, and then slid one tube from the other. He handed the scroll to the king.

The king took the scroll and unfurled it. His face formed a frown as he read the marks scrawled in ink from so long ago. He looked up, his eyes sliding across the audience. Then turned to Tilbury and bent towards him, his voice quiet. 'Have you read this?'

Tilbury shook his head. 'I cannot understand the marks, Your Majesty.'

'And what of Obsidian, what does he say?'

'He hasn't read it yet, Your Majesty. Only you.'

'I see,' said the king, his eyes on Tilbury. He was silent for a moment, then he stood up again. 'We have been blessed by this remarkable, brave ratling with a scroll written by Bartholomew himself. It is my great pleasure to share it with you now.' He cleared his throat before speaking again. '*I Bartholomew, as my last and dying wish, ask that the* Cursed Night *is returned to its true and rightful heir,*' he paused looking around them all, '*to the reigning king of Golden Rats.*'

The crowd cheered.

The king rolled up the scroll and held up his paw for silence. 'The *Eye of Aurun* is returned. Let us show our gratitude to this

231

young ratling who has risked his life for us. And we will in turn give him safe passage home.'

Paws clapped, tails swished and the rats' voices rose with the anthem of their city.

At the end of the anthem, the king leaned forward and held the parchment over the fire. 'History has been rectified,' he said. 'Justice has been done.' And with that, he dropped the scroll into the fire.

Tilbury heard Nimble-Quick cry out loud, but the scroll flared into a flame and spiralled upwards. When it hit the cold air, the scroll disintegrated.

And Bartholomew's last words drifted down, as grey ashes, to the floor.

CHAPTER THIRTY-FIVE
Thoughts Like Treacle

'Now, young ratling,' said the king. 'I have heard from Obsidian of your ingenuity in opening the Gilded Cage. Maybe you could be of assistance to the learned scholars and clerics here. I'm sure Zekali would value your insight, for he has spent his life's work trying to construct the Silk Wing of Bartholomew.'

'The secret of the Silk Wing!' squeaked Tilbury. 'Why, it has been my whole life's desire too.'

The crowd burst into chuckles.

The king smiled broadly. 'Well, cherished Tilbury, I shall ask for you to be taken to Zekali's workshop tomorrow. For you have already shown that age and size are no restriction to success. Indeed, if you help to make the Silk Wing, I shall bestow the medal of highest honour; the *Star of Aurun*, for your loyalty to our people.'

Tilbury bowed low, wonder and pride bursting open in his

heart like a flower bud at the thought of such imagined things. 'It would be my honour,' he said.

Tilbury was given another goblet of honey mead before being taken back to his room. He found that his belongings had been moved and he was in a different room by himself, overlooking the mountain range. A sheaf of plain parchments and ink and quills had been placed on a low table, and even though he had never used such things, he felt important seeing them. His bed was covered in fur and drapes, and roasting chestnuts glowed in the embers of a fire. Tilbury looked at the big soft bed and wished to curl up and sleep.

'Where are Marfaire and my sister?' he asked.

'They are in the next room,' said the Golden Rat. 'This is a room for a scholar. You will need some silence and peace to think.'

'I should like to say good night to them,' said Tilbury.

The Golden Rat nodded and gave Tilbury a candle to light the way.

'Nimble-Quick? Marfaire?' whispered Tilbury. 'Can I come in?'

'Of course,' said Marfaire.

Tilbury slipped through the heavy curtain. Marfaire was heating water in a small kettle over the fire, the smell of peppermint tea rising in the air. Nimble-Quick was warming her paws around a cup, with her back to him.

Tilbury felt suddenly very weary, the honey mead now felt like thick treacle through his thoughts. 'Oh, Nimble-Quick, oh, Marfaire! What an evening.'

'Was it?' said Nimble-Quick, not turning around.

Tilbury sat down next to her. 'Did you not think so, sister?'

She stared into the steam rising up from her cup. 'Does it matter what I think?'

'Of course,' he said. 'But how can you be sad when we have come to the end of our journey? We are now free of the terrible curse.'

'Are we?' said Nimble-Quick, taking a sip of tea.

'What do you mean?' said Tilbury, feeling irritation that she was dampening the spirits of the evening. 'I've returned the *Cursed Night*. I was there with Obsidian to present it to the king.'

'Really?' said Nimble-Quick. 'I only saw Obsidian. You were hidden in his shadow.'

Tilbury clutched the gold medal the sage had given him. 'I was there. I've kept the promise. I've fulfilled the prophecy.'

Nimble-Quick spun around to look at him. 'How do you know? What makes you so sure the king is the rightful owner?'

Tilbury frowned. He rarely saw his sister so angry. 'The king read out the scroll, the words of the prophecy. It said the *Cursed Night* must be returned to him.'

'How do you know that's what it said?' snapped Nimble-Quick. 'Who else read it?'

'Nimble-Quick! Are you saying the king is a liar?'

Nimble-Quick narrowed her eyes at him. 'I'm asking if you think the king is telling the truth?'

Tilbury shook his head. 'Why would he lie? The *Cursed Night* belongs here. Where else would it belong? Who else would it belong to? The Golden Rats are going to give us safe passage home.

Is that not what you want? Didn't you hear what the king said? He said we are heroes.'

'No,' said Nimble-Quick, taking a step towards him. 'He said only *you* are the hero.'

'He enjoyed my story,' said Tilbury. 'Didn't you hear them? They were laughing.'

'They weren't laughing *with* you, little brother,' snapped Nimble-Quick. 'They were laughing *at* you. You were the court jester.'

Nimble-Quick's words stung. Tilbury blinked back tears. 'That isn't true. You're just jealous. Jealous that they wanted me to tell the story, jealous that they want to show me the Silk Wing.'

'I'm not jealous,' snapped Nimble-Quick. 'I'm angry. Marfaire and I weren't mentioned by Obsidian, by you, or by any of the Golden Rats,' she said, pressing her face against his.

'Yes you were,' said Tilbury trying to reel back his mind to the evening.

'No, we weren't,' said Nimble-Quick. She folded her paws over her chest. 'And the thing that makes me really angry is that you didn't even notice at all.'

'What are you talking about, Nimble-Quick?' said Tilbury, who now wished he'd gone straight to bed.

'Did you even notice where we sat?' asked Nimble-Quick. 'No, you didn't, did you? You were having too much fun. Well, we sat at the back with she-rats and ratlings. All he-rats sat at the front.'

'What of it?' said Tilbury.

'We were written out of the story,' said Nimble-Quick, pressing her paw into Tilbury's chest.

'No, you weren't,' said Tilbury, although his mind could not recall either Obsidian or himself mentioning Marfaire or Nimble-Quick.

'She-rats had to stay at the back and be served last, didn't you notice?'

'Maybe it's the custom here,' said Tilbury.

Nimble-Quick stood up and walked away from him. 'Oh, and that just makes it right, does it? There are no she-rat clerics, no she-rat scholars and no she-rat warriors.'

Tilbury's mind felt fogged, and he was no match for Nimble-Quick in a battle of words. He thought of the golden she-rats and their beautiful clothes dripping in jewels. His mind tumbled back to Obsidian's comments to Ma. 'They worship their wives,' said Tilbury. 'They protect them.'

Nimble-Quick slashed her tail through the air and knocked Tilbury from his feet. He fell on his back and she was on top of him, pinning him down. 'I don't need protecting,' she snarled. 'I came on this journey to protect you. I can look after myself. I don't need you at all.'

Tilbury wriggled free and kicked her away. 'Well, I don't need you either.'

He stormed back to his room, pulled off his cape and curled up in the soft bed of feathers, enveloping him with warmth. He had never been in such a comfortable bed, but he couldn't sleep. He twisted and turned and as he did, his thoughts shifted and curled over themselves like tangled, angry snakes.

Tilbury thought of the king dropping the scroll into the flames, and how Bartholomew's words had turned to ash. What had they said? Bartholomew's thoughts were now dust, blowing on the wind. But what even was a thought? Written in ink, a thought could travel in time from the past to the future. It was of ink, but it was not ink. It was something intangible, something precious, and something that could so easily be destroyed.

He thought of Nimble-Quick too. She was just jealous, he told himself, jealous because she didn't get the attention for once. But he felt something else, a feeling he'd never had before. He couldn't get comfortable, despite the soft bed. He curled himself in a tight ball, wishing he could start the evening all over again. He had made a fool of himself this night, led to believe he was a warrior by a king. He had thought he was someone important as he spoke to the king, but now he realized he was nobody at all.

He didn't even have Nimble-Quick to hold on to in the darkness.

And for the first time on their journey, he felt utterly alone and very, very small.

CHAPTER THIRTY-SIX
Zekali

Tilbury woke to rainbows spinning on the walls of his room as the breeze turned crystals in the morning light. The bed was too comfortable, and Tilbury pulled the blanket around him. His toes and tail were deliciously warm. Only the tip of his nose stuck out. And that nose could smell the plate of sweet almond bread and a pot of peppermint tea that had been left at the foot of his bed. He hadn't heard anyone come into the room and put it there, and the thought unsettled him of someone being in the room watching him sleep.

He thought of finding Marfaire and Nimble-Quick, but he still felt cross with Nimble-Quick. She'd still be cross with him too, so he took the plate of bread and curled back in the bed, careful not to spill crumbs on the clean sheets.

'Hello, Master Tilbury.'

Tilbury turned around to see Marfaire in the doorway holding her cup of peppermint tea.

'Are you quite well this morning?' she asked.

'I am,' said Tilbury, trying to hide the plate so that Marfaire wouldn't see he was eating breakfast in bed. 'Is Nimble-Quick still mad at me?'

'A little,' she said.

'She's just jealous,' Tilbury mumbled.

'Maybe,' said Marfaire. 'Though her jealousy may be justified. It can be hard to see yourself written out of a story you were part of.'

'What does it matter now?' sniffed Tilbury. 'We should be happy. We've returned the *Cursed Night* to the rightful owners and fulfilled the prophecy. We can go home. Isn't all this worth celebrating?'

Marfaire shrugged. 'What if this is not the end of the story? What if there is yet more to be told?'

'How can there be? Bartholomew stole the *Cursed Night* and now it has been returned.'

'What about the words of the prophecy?' said Marfaire. She repeated some of the words passed from Keeper to Keeper. '*Only there, in the deepest darkness, can a light shine on the truth and set my soul free.*'

Tilbury scratched his head. 'But Marfaire, even you said you do not know what this means. Maybe we have been through dark times and now found the truth.'

Marfaire sipped her tea, the hot steam hiding her face. 'Are we free, Tilbury?'

'Oh, Marfaire, this is the most beautiful place I have ever seen.' Tilbury twisted his tail in his paws. 'This is paradise.'

'Whose paradise, Tilbury?' said Marfaire. 'Who looks after this paradise? Who brings the food, who plumps your pillow?'

Thoughts tangled in Tilbury's mind. 'But Marfaire . . .'

His words and thoughts were interrupted by a Golden Rat walking through the door. 'Greetings, Master Tilbury. Zekali would like to see you.'

Tilbury stood up, the plate and crumbs falling about him.

'Come.' The Golden Rat smiled. 'For there is great expectation from a descendant of Bartholomew.'

Tilbury followed the Golden Rat. He looked back to see Marfaire staring out to the mountains. Maybe he should ask if she and Nimble-Quick could come too, but Nimble-Quick's words still stung. She'd said she didn't need him. Well fine, he didn't need her either. He would see Zekali and talk about the Silk Wing by himself.

Tilbury was taken a little further up the mountain, where there was a long, flat ledge before the mountain rose up steeply again. A scholar came walking out from a cave to meet Tilbury. He was an old rat. His golden fur had faded to pale apricot and he walked with a stoop, but Tilbury could see an intensity and sparkle in his eyes.

'Greetings, I am Zekali. We did not have time to talk last night. But it is my honour to meet you. Why, you are a direct descendant of Bartholomew and I can see you possess his curious mind.'

Tilbury puffed his chest out in pride. At home, his endless curiosity had been the bane of Ma's life, but here it was celebrated.

Zekali pointed to the long, flat rock with his paw. 'And this is the very runway that Bartholomew took off from with the diamond nearly two hundred years ago. Can you imagine it? I have thought of it every day, ever since I was a young ratling. I imagine that beautiful machine taking off into the air. Oh, I should like to see it in my lifetime.'

'I should too,' said Tilbury.

Zekali beamed. 'Come,' he said. 'Let me show you my workshop, my emporium of wonder and delight.'

So, Tilbury followed Zekali into the cave, and indeed he stopped in wonder. Light came in from holes in the cliff face to show a workshop with desks and tables. There were neat piles of nuts and bolts and fine wire. The floor was covered in wood shavings, and in the corner of the cave a furnace burned with white-hot flames. Everywhere about him were contraptions and machines in various stages of development.

'This is where I make my dreams a reality.' Zekali beamed.

And Tilbury beamed too. It reminded him of the chandlery back home in Tilbury Docks, a place of endless engineering possibilities.

'Now this,' said Zekali, pulling on a long rope, 'this is my new pulley system to help haul the harvest up from the orchards. It takes a week for the Sand Rats to carry food up from the valleys, and sometimes the food is already spoiled or picked off by ravens and eagles. My pulley system will haul food up in less than a day.'

'Who are the Sand Rats?' asked Tilbury.

Zekali gave him a curious smile. 'The workers. How else do you think we get food up here? Surely you've seen them serving your drinks last night and bringing your breakfast.'

Tilbury tried to recall seeing the rats that had offered him food. But he shook his head.

'Well, that's a good thing,' said Zekali, seeing Tilbury's blank expression. 'The king likes the Sand Rats to be as discreet as possible.'

'Where are the orchards?' asked Tilbury.

Zekali led him to the wide-open window. 'Down there, far, far below, on the other side of the lake. This valley is hidden on the other side of the mountain from the Badlands and the Palace of the Immortal Emperor. If we hadn't had this valley, we would have starved.'

Tilbury looked into the valley. The lake was the colour of the sky, and little boats with bright sails were skimming across the water, going to and from rich pastures and orchards on the other side. He could see the Sand Rats moving up and down the mountain from a pontoon below, carrying sacks. Some were carrying sacks bigger than themselves.

'My pulley system will be much more efficient,' said Zekali.

But Tilbury was only half listening. 'Do they mind?' he asked.

'Do they mind what?' said Zekali.

'Do they mind carrying all that food up and down for you?'

Zekali pulled at a whisker. 'Well now, I don't suppose they do. I've never asked. But it's not for them to mind, because it's their job. Besides, they are well looked after with enough food and drink and a safe place to sleep.' He frowned. 'Sometimes there are a few troublemakers.'

'What happens to them?' asked Tilbury.

'We let them go,' said Zekali. 'If they don't want to stay, they are free to go.'

'But where?' said Tilbury, his mind racing with questions.

'We let them go free into the Badlands.'

'Into the Badlands?'

'Yes,' said Zekali. 'It's their choice.'

'But no one survives the Badlands alone,' said Tilbury.

'Exactly,' said Zekali, sounding a little impatient. 'That is why they should do as they are told. They have a choice.'

'What are the Sand Rats like?' asked Tilbury, his mind curious about these rats he had not even noticed.

Zekali sighed. 'I like them well enough as a group, but it is not for us to mix. It is said they do not have our intellect.' He paused. 'Though there was one ratling who seemed bright enough, and she was even a she-ratling. Her parents sailed the boats across the lake. She helped me here, for a while. She could work all sorts of stuff, and she could read too. Her mother had taught her. But her mother was trouble. The little ratling became very disturbed after her mother and father were released to the Badlands.'

'She lost her ma and pa?' said Tilbury.

Zekali leaned forward. 'I blame them. It was their choice, leaving a small ratling alone. They were a bad influence and taught her to disrespect the Golden Rats. She used to look the warrior rats in the eye.' He shook his head. 'It is not for the Sand Rats to look us in the eye, especially a she-rat. It is a great insult. They should know their place. She stirred up other young Sand Rats to make trouble.'

'She wasn't sent to the Badlands too?' gasped Tilbury.

'No, she was just a ratling. I hear she was sent to the orchards. She has time to learn to adjust her ways. Though I have my doubts.' He lowered his voice. 'She is a seventh seventh-born after all. It is a pity she had to go, for she was useful to me and a clever little thing.'

'My sister is clever too,' said Tilbury.

Zekali laughed. 'Well, be careful not to let her get above herself. There is nothing more troublesome than a clever she-rat with an opinion. But let us not waste time with idle talk. Let me show you what I have been working on my whole life.'

With a flourish, he pulled back a cotton sheet to reveal a construction of beauty and design that took Tilbury's breath away. The sheet rippled to the ground and Tilbury found himself looking at what appeared to be a large elongated silver egg. It was standing on three wheels, one wheel at the more pointed end and two at the back. There was an open cockpit with three red leather seats; one in the front and two behind it. But it was the metal coils on each side of the 'egg' that fascinated Tilbury. He looked inside the cockpit and could see they were attached, via axles, to a propeller at the pointed end of the 'egg'.

'It's a clockwork engine,' said Tilbury.

'Ingenious, isn't it,' said Zekali. 'The metal coils are wound up and that turns the propeller. So Bartholomew could wind up two coils separately to keep the propeller constantly spinning and the Silk Wing moving forward.'

Tilbury looked at him. 'But how do you know this is Bartholomew's design?'

Zekali's eyes sparkled. 'When I was a ratling, my father let me read in the Room of Ratiffi where we keep our parchments. And one day, when I was not much older than you, I found a piece of silk hidden in an old binding. The silk showed the plans for the body of the Silk Wing. I have been obsessed since that day. But the plan only showed the body and not the wings. The silk was ripped in two and I have not been able to find the other half.'

Tilbury clutched at the scarf around his neck. 'But I have the other half.'

Zekali just stared at him. 'Is this true?'

Tilbury nodded.

'And can you remember the design?'

Tilbury's heart quickened. He slipped the scarf from his neck. 'I have it right here.'

Zekali's whiskers trembled and he had to sit down on a stool. He reached into his pocket and pulled out a faded leather purse, and from that, he extracted a long piece of yellowed silk. He lay his half next to Tilbury's and they matched perfectly. 'Oh, Master Tilbury, I do not have much longer in this world, but I do believe my dream could come true.' He grasped Tilbury by the paw. 'We can see the Silk Wing fly again. Let us make it so.'

And so, Tilbury and Zekali began work at once. Zekali fired up his furnace to melt the metal needed to make the frame of the wing. Tilbury knew how to make the frame and the steering mechanics. But the strength and shape of the wing itself would be in the design and the stitching of silk.

And Tilbury knew he couldn't do it by himself. He didn't know how to stitch the silk so that it did not rip under pressure, or how to shape it, allowing the flow of air to lift the wing.

They couldn't do this without his sister.

He knew they needed Nimble-Quick.

CHAPTER THIRTY-SEVEN
Aeronautical Design

'I'm not wearing it,' snarled Nimble-Quick.

Tilbury arrived back to find Nimble-Quick and Marfaire being dressed by one of the golden she-rats. Marfaire was dressed in a shimmering silver smock.

Nimble-Quick was being given a sky-blue smock sparkling with sapphires and tourmaline.

'But it's an honour,' said the golden she-rat. 'Don't you want to look beautiful for your brother?'

'I'm not his possession,' snapped Nimble-Quick. 'I don't care how I look.'

'You will want to look your finest for the ceremony when the *Eye of Aurun* is returned to its rightful place in the Golden Archway. You cannot go the ceremony without wearing it.'

Nimble-Quick folded her paws over her chest and scowled. 'Fine. I won't go then.'

The golden she-rat smiled, although her tail tip twitched irritably. 'I will leave it here for you to try on in your own time. The ceremony will be held in three days, at noon.'

Tilbury watched the she-rat leave the room and then turned to see Nimble-Quick glaring at him.

'Oh! Master Tilbury has decided to bestow his fine company upon us,' Nimble-Quick snapped. She tossed the dress on the floor.

Tilbury picked it up and ran his paws on the fine silk embroidered with jewels. 'Why don't you want to wear it?' he asked. 'It's beautiful. Ma would like it.'

'Ma would hate it,' said Nimble-Quick.

'But it's beautiful,' said Tilbury. 'Ma would love the beadwork with the jewels.'

'Can't you see what's wrong with it?' snapped Nimble-Quick. 'At home, Dockland Rats come to Ma to make them clothes, because Ma's clothes let them show who they are. These clothes show wives as possessions, as living hoardings. She-rats are just decoration here.'

Tilbury sat down on the mattress. He was thinking about the Sand Rat that Zekali had spoken of. The Golden Rats had seen the young she-rat as trouble. Maybe the Golden Rats would see Nimble-Quick as trouble too and send her to the orchards, or even worse, the Badlands. Tilbury looked up at her. 'Maybe it's best to do as they ask, until after the ceremony, when we get to go home.'

'No way,' snapped Nimble-Quick. 'I'd rather not go to the ceremony. Besides, you'll be up there receiving a medal instead of us.'

248

Tilbury took Nimble-Quick's paws in his own. 'At the ceremony I'm going to say that I'm taking the medal for you both as well. I'll call you up to join me.'

Nimble-Quick looked into Tilbury's eyes. 'Do you mean it?'

'Of course,' said Tilbury. He stared at his feet. 'I'm sorry, Nimble-Quick. We wouldn't be here if it weren't for you and Marfaire.'

Nimble-Quick softened. 'I'm still not wearing the dress. The Golden Rats have no she-rat scholars or clerics or warriors. It's just not fair.'

'So, prove them wrong,' said Tilbury, looking up. 'Oh, Nimble-Quick, I have the most exciting news! Zekali has the other half of the plans to the Silk Wing. Please agree to wear the dress at the ceremony, and I'll persuade Zekali to let you make the Silk Wing with us. I can't do it without you. We need to prove that you are the one to make the Silk Wing fly.'

'I've brought my sister,' said Tilbury to Zekali as they entered the workshop together

Zekali pulled at his long whiskers and didn't acknowledge her. 'I'll have no she-rat's tittle-tattle disturbing us. There is serious work to be done. We only have three days to complete the Silk Wing for the ceremony. She can't be here. She'll have to go.'

Tilbury sighed. 'Then I will have to go too. We won't be able to make this fly without her. Only Nimble-Quick understands the tensioning of silk and thread.'

'Well, she can do her needlework and then go,' said Zekali.

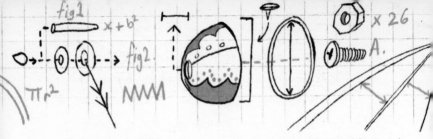

'I prefer to call it aeronautical design,' said Nimble-Quick. 'Unless we have lift, we will never be able to fly.'

Zekali turned to look at her for the first time and Nimble-Quick stared fiercely back. His eyes darted between Tilbury and Nimble-Quick and he could see Tilbury would not stay without her. 'Very well, I will accept her support as a technician.'

'We accept her as a fellow engineer,' said Tilbury, 'or we do not work at all.'

Zekali paced up and down. 'But it is most unusual. I for one, do not mind, but the other scholars will not accept it and will stop her. For your sake and mine I would not mention it.'

Tilbury shook his head. 'We won't, until the Silk Wing is built. But when it is finished the three of us shall be credited with the success of flight of the Silk Wing.'

'Very well,' said Zekali, looking between them. 'I agree.'

Nimble-Quick lashed her tail. 'If you go back on your word, we won't teach you how to fly. You would plummet to the ground on your first flight without us.'

Zekali glared at her. 'There is no need for such an aggressive tone with me.'

Nimble-Quick glared back. 'How else can I have my voice heard?'

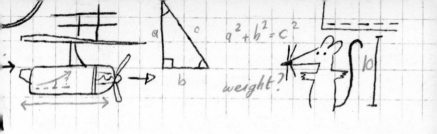

And so, Zekali and Nimble-Quick worked in frosty silence, re-creating Bartholomew's Silk Wing. Tilbury worked on the design of the metal frame and Nimble-Quick took measurements and used chalk to mark the lines and pleats on the rolls of silk. She used smooth shiny silk for the upper wing and rough raw silk for the underwing, to slow the air passing beneath the wing to create lift.

Nimble-Quick was not only clever in aeronautical design but she chose a palette of colours such that the Silk Wing would be beautiful. 'Science should be beautiful,' she said, 'for then it shall impose upon the heart as well as the mind.'

The day before the ceremony, the king came to view the work. He walked a circle around the Silk Wing, marvelling at the arrowhead design of the wing. 'Tell me, Zekali, will the Silk Wing be ready to fly tomorrow after the ceremony?'

'Yes, sire,' said Zekali. 'We have been working on it day and night.' He stood back to admire the Silk Wing. 'It is done,' he said. 'My life's work is done.'

The king pulled at his long whiskers. 'Tell me, who will fly the Silk Wing on its first flight?'

'I will,' said Zekali, 'with Master Tilbury.'

Nimble-Quick coughed loudly.

'Your Majesty, my sister must join us too,' said Tilbury, 'for she is part of the success of the Silk Wing.'

The king turned to look at Tilbury. 'Your sister?'

Tilbury felt his paws tremble, but he held his voice steady. 'Without her, we could not fly.'

The king turned to Zekali. 'Is this true?'

Zekali stared at the floor, unsure of what to say. 'We will not know the answer to that until we try.'

The king looked between them all. 'Then the three of you shall fly.'

Tilbury's paws twitched with excitement as he and Nimble-Quick walked back to their rooms.

'We're actually going to fly the Silk Wing,' said Tilbury.

Nimble-Quick beamed. 'I know.' She turned to Tilbury. 'Thank you for standing up for me.'

Tilbury smiled. 'I couldn't fly without you, Nimble-Quick.'

'Oh, Tilbury, do you remember how we used to play in the chandlery and dream of finding the plans to the Silk Wing? And now look at us. Here we are.'

'Home seems so far away, doesn't it,' said Tilbury. 'I can't wait to get back.'

Nimble-Quick was quiet for a moment. 'I'm not sure I want to go back.'

'What do you mean?'

'Well, I want to see Ma and Pa, of course,' said Nimble-Quick. 'But now I've seen some of the world, I'm not sure I want to just stay in the Docklands. There is so much more to explore.'

Tilbury said nothing, but felt his little heart ache, for he could not understand how you could love someone so much and yet want different things.

'Come on,' said Nimble-Quick. 'We need a good night's sleep for the ceremony tomorrow.'

Tilbury followed, but then stopped. 'Look, Nimble-Quick,' he said, pointing through the window. 'That's where the *Eye of Aurun* will be placed tomorrow, hanging from the Golden Archway. We have fulfilled the prophecy. We have returned the *Cursed Night*.'

Nimble-Quick turned to look down at the wide plaza. Scaffolding had been built around a tall golden archway so that it framed the mountains. 'Our adventure is almost over,' she said.

'Almost,' said Tilbury, his eyes shining brightly. 'But tomorrow, we fly.'

CHAPTER THIRTY-EIGHT
The Ceremony

Tilbury found it hard to sleep. In his mind he was practising flying the Silk Wing, adjusting the frame, and tilting it to the wind.

'Good morning, Master Tilbury,' said a Golden Rat who was standing at the foot of his bed. 'The ceremony will commence soon. Please get dressed and join us on the plaza.'

Tilbury glanced at his reflection in the water bowl as he washed his whiskers. Today, he would be receiving the Star of Aurun from the king, and he would call both Marfaire and Nimble-Quick to join him. They were part of this story and belonged in the retelling of it too. He would insist that Nimble-Quick and Marfaire were written into the legends.

'Are you ready?' asked Nimble-Quick, pushing her head around the door. 'It's time to go.'

So, Tilbury followed Marfaire and Nimble-Quick to the open plaza where many Golden Rats were already gathering. Silk flags in a rainbow of colours rippled in the breeze. Marfaire and Nimble-Quick were dressed in fine jewelled clothes. Nimble-Quick wore a frown of irritation, but when Tilbury looked across at her, she lifted the hem of her dress to show she was wearing the sky-blue bird-suit she had made, beneath. Tilbury smiled at her silent protest.

Sand Rats scuttled about with plates of food and trays of rich sweet coffee. Tilbury noticed them now, moving quickly and discreetly in the shadows. He helped himself to stuffed dates and honey fritters. The plaza was circular in shape, the Golden Archway where the *Eye of Aurun* would be returned rising up from the centre. The king's throne had been placed in front of the archway and the seats for the warriors, scholars and clerics had been arranged in a semicircle around the king.

Tilbury could see Zekali talking with the other scholars, and he worked his way through the crowd to join him. Zekali smiled, but it was a formal smile, not the boyish enthusiasm he had shown on the first day in the workshop.

One tall scholar leaned forward. 'We are looking forward to the flight of the Silk Wing today.'

Tilbury smiled. 'I am too –'

But another scholar interrupted. 'It is through the extraordinary ingenuity of Zekali that this has been made possible.'

Tilbury glanced at Zekali, but Zekali just nodded and accepted the compliment without drawing Tilbury into the conversation.

Tilbury wanted to say how he and Nimble-Quick had designed the wing from the original plans, but a horn sounded, and all the

rats began to take their places for the ceremony.

Tilbury was unsure where to sit. Would he sit with the scholars, or with the warriors like before? Zekali had already sat down, and he could not see any seat saved for him. Obsidian was talking to two other warrior rats, but he couldn't see a seat beside him either. He didn't want to push his way forward, so he sat on the floor rugs behind the scholars, craning his head to see the throne of the king and the *Cursed Night* glittering darkly on a cushion beside it. He glanced back to see Marfaire and Nimble-Quick with the other she-rats at the back of the crowd.

Pipers began to play, and a soft drum roll became louder and louder, and all the Golden Rats stood up as the king walked in followed by the sage.

The king stood in front of the throne with a backdrop of mountains behind him. The peaks were magnificent in the glittering whites and sharp ice blues of late morning. The shadows were shortening and before long, the sun would shine through the golden archway where the *Eye of Aurun* would be returned.

The king sat down, and the rest of the Golden Rats sat too, the scholars and clerics leading from the front. Only the sage remained standing. He unfurled a scroll and cleared his throat. He bowed to the king and the warriors, and then to the scholars and clerics. 'Your Majesty, warriors, scholars and clerics,' he said in a loud, clear voice. 'We are gathered here today to celebrate the return of the diamond, the *Eye of Aurun*. We lost our power when it was stolen from us on a cursed night two hundred years ago, but we have

it safe in our keeping again. With its return comes our strength and the knowledge of the Silk Wing. We will be invincible to our enemies. For under *Aurun's Eye*, we will prosper. This moment is pivotal in our history, and the king calls upon the Royal Clerics to write down this moment for future generations. We must celebrate and acknowledge those who have helped return the diamond and brought freedom to this kingdom. We pay homage to one brave rat in particular, the one who tamed the White Death.'

Tilbury felt his heart swell. He would play a part in the history of this city. And he would make sure he said that Marfaire and Nimble-Quick would share the medal. Their names would become part of the legends too.

The sage continued, 'The king wishes to bestow the highest honour to this rat, for he has brought about the fall of the Immortal Emperor and won our freedom. This rat has travelled across treacherous seas, and risked his own life. He will be awarded the Star of Aurun, the medal of greatest bravery.'

Tilbury felt his whiskers quiver. He wondered how to accept such a medal. Did one bow, or take it, or wait for it to be given?

'And we now call forward this brave warrior,' said the sage, raising his voice with the drama. 'Please rise . . .'

Tilbury clasped his paws together, waiting for his name to be announced.

The sage gave a little bow. '. . . Please rise . . . Obsidian.'

Tilbury took a sharp intake of breath. He looked around but other Golden Rats were standing up and clapping their paws together and banging their feet on the floor. Tilbury felt as if the ground had fallen away from him. He tried to look between the jostling rats to see Obsidian walking towards the sage and bowing to the king.

'Wait!' Tilbury squeaked. 'Wait, but I tamed the White Death. Marfaire and my sister defeated the felinrats.' But no one heard him above the foot thumping and cheering. No one heard him at all.

Tilbury felt confusion, then hurt and anger rose up inside him. He had been the one to tame the tiger. Nimble-Quick had opened the cage and they couldn't have made the journey without Marfaire. Obsidian would be dead if it hadn't been for them. But the whole story had been changed. First Nimble-Quick and Marfaire had been written out of the story and now he had too.

He now understood how Nimble-Quick had felt, and he felt shame and frustration at himself for not standing up for her at the time. The felinrats had ruled with fear, he thought, but the Golden Rats ruled with words. Maybe silencing someone's voice was the most powerful weapon of all. And not speaking up for someone else eventually silenced your own.

Tilbury glanced back to look for Marfaire and Nimble-Quick, but they were lost behind the Golden Rats clapping and cheering.

Obsidian was walking towards the king, in his full finery and armour, the jewel-encrusted dagger at his side. The sun shone through his fur so that he seemed like polished gold, haloed by a rim of light.

It surprised Tilbury to see tiny flakes of snow beginning to fall, dusting the ground. He looked up at dark clouds that had formed above him, and he wondered if they might not be able to fly today. A sudden squall spun the fallen snow in whirls across the ground.

Tilbury clenched his little paws. Everything was happening so quickly. He tried to calm himself, forcing his worries into the base of his tail. He breathed in and out and watched as Obsidian knelt in front of the king.

'Obsidian,' said the sage. 'The king welcomes and recognizes you as his humble loving servant.'

The Golden Rats chattered their teeth in approval. But only Tilbury noticed that Obsidian clutched the hilt of his dagger a little too tightly. Only Tilbury saw the dark glitter in Obsidian's eyes.

The king bent forward to put the ribbon holding the medal around Obsidian's neck, and as he did so, Obsidian rose, pulling his dagger from its sheath and plunging it deep into the king's chest.

Black cloud shadows raced across the plaza, as the king slumped back onto his throne.

A deep silence descended across the watching rats.

Darkness had come to the Sky-Mountains.

The king of the City in the Clouds was dead.

CHAPTER THIRTY-NINE
Rightful King

Obsidian grabbed the diamond and faced the crowd. 'I am Obsidian, the heir of Prince Obsidian,' he roared. 'For too long you have been ruled by a weak king. I have returned to lead you out of this darkness. I have tamed the White Death. I have defeated the felinrats. I am the one to restore the City in the Clouds to its rightful glory.' He leaped up the scaffolding around the archway and hung the diamond from the golden chain. 'I have returned the *Eye of Aurun*. I am now your rightful king.'

The silence continued. Only the wind whistling around the plaza could be heard. No one moved. A shaft of sunlight broke through the clouds, shining right through the *Eye of Aurun*, showing its glittering darkness.

The sage got to his feet and turned to the Golden Rats. His eyes flashed across the warriors and scholars. His tail swished from side to side. 'Today is an auspicious day,' he said, his voice shaking. 'For we knew there would come a time to restore our kingdom. Prince Obsidian was brave enough to set sail to seek the stolen diamond, and his descendant has returned it to us. We must recognize Obsidian as the rightful reigning king to take us to power and prosperity. We shall become a mighty kingdom once more.' He bowed low to Obsidian. 'Your Majesty, may your greatness deliver us from evil.'

There was much muttering and anxious shuffling amongst the other rats. The warrior rats were the first to bow down, followed by the scholars and clerics.

Tilbury shrank back, feeling the nervousness of the others.

'All praise for the new king,' cried the Warrior General.

The Golden Rats began stamping their feet, the beat becoming faster and faster and louder and louder. Tilbury felt the sound inside him as if it were the drumming of his heart. This change in loyalty seemed as fast as the change in the weather. Sharp needles of sleet struck him, and a wind howled down the valley. A storm was upon them and rats held on to each other as chairs and rugs were whipped into the sky.

Obsidian stood beneath the archway, holding his dagger high above him. 'We have been oppressed for too long. The descendants of Prince Obsidian were kept in the Everdark of the city of London.' His eyes sought out Tilbury and he pointed at him with his blade. 'We were forced to live in the filth and grime by the very rats that walk amongst us now.'

Tilbury shrank back, but he had nowhere to hide from all the eyes that turned to him.

Obsidian spat out the words. 'These rats stole our past and stole our dignity. I will not let them steal our future.'

A low hiss rose higher and Tilbury pushed his way through the crowd to find Marfaire and Nimble-Quick. He grasped Nimble-Quick's paw.

'Take them to the dungeons,' roared Obsidian. 'Their punishment is to live out the rest of their lives in darkness. Justice shall be done.'

The crowd cheered and jeered. Tilbury, Marfaire and Nimble-Quick found themselves being escorted out of the plaza and then down a dark passageway.

Down, down, down, led by a guard who held the stub of a candle to light the way. He pushed them into a room and clanged the door shut. The door was made from solid iron bars and he locked it with a large iron key that was tied to his belt with a long chain. He stared at them through the bars, then turned and walked away with the candle, leaving them in pitch-darkness.

Tilbury clung to Marfaire and Nimble-Quick.

Their dreams of returning home had been swept away as suddenly as the storm that swept through the city.

Tilbury wrapped his tail around Nimble-Quick and Marfaire.

It was cold and musty. The floor was hard rock.

Marfaire held them both with her paws. 'Are you hurt?' she whispered. Her voice echoed as if they were in a large space.

'I'm OK,' whispered Tilbury.

'Me too,' said Nimble-Quick.

Tilbury's eyes ached with the darkness. He began to think he had never been anywhere where there was no light at all. Even in the sewer there had been the seeping glow of electric lights, and the chimney flues filtered light from either end. But here the darkness was so solid that it seemed the rest of the world had ceased existing.

Tilbury felt Nimble-Quick's whiskers bristling against him.

'Let's explore,' she said. 'There might be a way out.'

The three of them crept forward, feeling with their paws and whiskers. The found they were in a vast room that was more like a cave with solid rock walls. It was impossible to tell the height of the ceiling. There was only the door they had been pushed through, which was firmly locked with one of the large keys on the guard's belt.

'It's empty in here,' whispered Tilbury.

Somewhere on the other side of the room there was a scuttle and a pitter-patter of feet. Nimble-Quick and Tilbury held their breath.

'Who's there?' asked Marfaire.

There was no answer, but Tilbury felt another presence in the cave and pressed closer to Nimble-Quick.

'I'm cold,' whispered Nimble-Quick.

'Let's stay close,' said Marfaire, wrapping her tail around theirs.

Tilbury dozed in an uncomfortable sleep, his ears twitching for the sound of the other presence in the cave. He was woken by heavy footsteps and a light approaching.

The guard arrived and pushed a stub of candle through the bars. 'Light and heat,' he said gruffly. 'Make the most if it. One stub per day.'

Then he left a loaf of stale bread on the ground next to the candle and threw a crust into the far corner of the cave. A scuttling sound could be heard and then the chewing of the crust being eaten. Tilbury peered into the shadows, but somehow the light from the candle made the corners of the cave even darker.

'There's a flagon of water and a bucket for slops,' said the guard. 'I'll be back tomorrow.' Then he turned and left, his footsteps receding up the passageway.

The candle sputtered and burned low and gave only a little light and heat. Nimble-Quick ripped off the dress of jewels and flung it to the ground, stamping the jewels into the dirt. It was only then that Tilbury remembered she was wearing her sky-blue bird-suit beneath. Flying in the chandlery seemed oh so long ago.

The scuttling sound came again, nearer this time.

Marfaire held up the candle, looking to the corners of the room. 'Hello? Who's there? We mean you no harm.'

Tilbury could just make out a small figure wrapped in blankets.

'Would you like some of our bread?' asked Marfaire, taking a step closer. 'You can share our candlelight.'

But the figure shuffled away into the shadows.

Tilbury and Nimble-Quick sat around the candle, feeling its warmth.

'How has it come to this?' said Tilbury. 'We have returned the *Cursed Night* and freed our people from the curse, but we have not freed ourselves. And how will they know? Are we to perish here in this darkness? Why would Obsidian do that when we have helped him? He gave a golden oath to my father for our safe return.'

'Obsidian is ruthless,' said Nimble-Quick. 'He killed the king. The *Cursed Night* has power over him. The oath is empty words. He has what he wants, and we are nothing to him.'

'Then maybe the terrible curse has gone from the Dockland Rats to the Golden Rats,' said Tilbury. 'Maybe the curse goes with the owners of the *Cursed Night*.'

'Maybe,' said Marfaire. 'Or maybe we do not know the whole story yet.'

Nimble-Quick sat in the light of the flickering candle. She licked her paw and traced marks in the dust.

'What are you doing?' asked Tilbury.

'I'm making the ink marks that were on the scroll that the king burned,' said Nimble-Quick. 'I wonder what it really said. Maybe he was not telling the truth.'

'Are you sure you can remember them?' asked Tilbury.

Nimble-Quick nodded. 'I remember it exactly, like a map in my mind.' She drew the marks and sat back, as if somehow the message would magically reveal itself.

The candle sputtered, the hot wax spitting on the ground.

'I don't want it to be dark again,' said Tilbury with a shudder. He held his paws to the flickering light, trying to gain every last bit of warmth. He didn't hear soft paws behind him, but he heard sharp intake of breath.

'Who wrote this?' said a voice behind them. The voice was full of suspicion and hate.

Tilbury, Nimble-Quick and Marfaire turned to see a young ratling staring at the marks on the ground. The ratling was a Sand Rat. She was thin, with matted fur and a scabby tail showing beneath a threadbare blanket.

'Who wrote this?' snarled the ratling again.

'I did,' said Nimble-Quick.

The ratling looked up. Despite her unkempt appearance, she had fierce bright eyes. 'And who are you?'

'We have come across the seven seas,' said Nimble-Quick. 'We have come to return the *Cursed Night*, stolen by Bartholomew, to its rightful home.'

Tilbury nodded. 'We have fulfilled the prophecy and returned it to the Golden Rats.'

The ratling gave a hollow laugh and pointed to the marks in the dirt. 'Have you actually read this?'

'We don't know how,' said Marfaire.

'This is a confession of a liar and a cheat,' spat the ratling. 'The diamond doesn't belong to the Golden Rats. They are thieves, just like Bartholomew. But Bartholomew was the greatest thief of all, for he stole hope, when hope was the very last thing we had.'

CHAPTER FORTY
Pawprint in the Sand

'What do the marks say?' asked Marfaire. 'Please tell us, so that we can know Bartholomew's last words.'

The ratling cleared her throat, and her eyes blazed with rage. *'This Cursed Night carries my deep shame for I, Bartholomew, succumbed to its power. I betrayed the rightful owners and shed their blood for my greed. I ask the bearer of this scroll to atone my sins and return the diamond to the Sand Rats. For I am deeply sorry.'*

'The Sand Rats are the rightful owners?' said Tilbury, wide-eyed.

'Of course we are,' snarled the ratling. 'We were the ones forced by the Golden Rats to dig the diamond from the bare earth. The City in the Clouds is built from our labour. From our blood.' She pushed her face close to Tilbury's. 'Bartholomew's name is dirt to us. He promised to take us and the diamond to our ancestral home in the Diamond Mines, if we helped him to escape.'

'Bartholomew had help?' said Tilbury, who had always wondered how he had found his way out from the dungeons.

'Yes,' said the ratling. 'Sand Rats that worked in the dungeons disguised Bartholomew as one of their own and slipped him past the guards.'

'But Bartholomew betrayed them?' whispered Nimble-Quick.

'Yes,' snarled the ratling. 'Bartholomew took the diamond and escaped on the Silk Wing by himself.'

She picked up the stub of candle and held it high. On the wall beside them, Tilbury could see ratiffi engraved into the rock itself.

'What does this say?' said Marfaire, tracing her paw across the rock.

'It's Bartholomew's promise to take us home,' said the ratling sourly. 'A promise he broke. And any Sand Rats that helped him were put to death. Many of us died because of him.'

The flame sputtered and died and plunged them into darkness.

And even though Tilbury could no longer see the marks on the wall, the truth burned brightly. The *Cursed Night* did not belong to the Golden Rats. The prophecy had not been fulfilled. The diamond had to be given back to the rats who were forced to dig it from the ground. The *Cursed Night* had to be returned to the Sand Rats of the Diamond Mines.

Nimble-Quick held Tilbury's paw and recited the lines from the prophecy. '*A warrior to find a truth we cannot see . . .*' she said.

'Oh Marfaire,' said Tilbury. 'This is what Bartholomew meant in his last words, the secret to his mother.'

'Yes,' said Marfaire. 'Bartholomew left his promise on the wall for you to find: *only there, in the deepest darkness, can a light shine on the truth and set my soul free.'*

'He was too ashamed to admit his truth to the Dockland Rats,' whispered Nimble-Quick.

'He wanted to be seen as a hero,' said Tilbury, feeling a twinge of guilt, for he too had wanted this himself.

'He was a coward,' spat the ratling.

'What can we do?' whispered Tilbury.

'There is nothing we can do,' said the ratling, bitterly. 'There is no way out. There is no one to save us now.'

'Where are the Diamond Mines?' asked Nimble-Quick.

'At the end of the Diamond River, where it meets the sea,' said the ratling. 'There lies my homeland, and the homeland of all the Sand Rats. The Golden Rats once ruled us and made us dig for diamonds. When there were no diamonds left to be found they forced us back to the City in the Clouds to serve them here. But some Sand Rats fought for their freedom.'

'What happened to them?' asked Tilbury.

The ratling sighed. 'We don't know. Many believe they returned to the place of the old diamond mine. Ma told me that if we ever got the chance, we should try to find it. Ma said freedom is the most precious thing. It must be fought for and never taken for granted.'

'Then we must search for the diamond mine and return the *Cursed Night*,' said Nimble-Quick. 'And we can return you to your people too.'

Tilbury sank his head on to his chest. He was glad the others couldn't see him. This journey seemed impossible. How could they get away? How could they retrieve the *Cursed Night* from the Golden Archway with the guards standing beneath it? He just wanted to be home, with Ma and Pa. But they were ever so far away. And he would have to live in the darkness of the dungeon until he died, never to feel Ma's paws around him again. He sniffed as a tear ran down a whisker.

'Tilbury?' whispered Nimble-Quick.

'I want Ma,' sniffed Tilbury, 'and Pa.'

'Me too,' said Nimble-Quick, putting her paws around him and entwining her tail with his.

'I want my Ma and Pa too,' whispered the ratling. 'But they're gone. They were sent to the Badlands.'

'You're Zekali's assistant, aren't you?' whispered Tilbury.

The ratling ground her teeth with anger. 'Zekali used my skills. But he is a coward. He got scared when the Golden Rats found out that Ma taught me to read. Reading is forbidden for Sand Rats. We are not meant to think.'

Tilbury remembered how Zekali had taken the credit for the Silk Wing.

'What's your name?' asked Marfaire.

The ratling was quiet for a moment. 'Our names are held secret between all Sand Rats, because it is the only thing that the Golden Rats cannot own.'

'Well, we are glad of your company,' said Marfaire. 'And maybe when we have some light, you could teach us to read too.'

Thoughts and worries filled Tilbury's head. Would they live here for ever and ever? Would he be able to send a message to Ma

272

and Pa? He tried to force his worries down into his tail, but the darkness and silence enveloped him, and all he could hear was the whooshing of blood in his own ears.

Time passed and Tilbury counted five times that the guard had come with a stub of candle. Had it been five whole days in the dungeon? Had Zekali already tried to fly the Silk Wing by himself?

On the sixth time the guard came down with a stub of candle, he unlocked the door with his iron key and ordered Tilbury out. Tilbury rubbed his eyes as he walked into the blinding sunlight. The guard had hold of his cape and he marched him to Zekali's workshop where Obsidian was waiting for him. Obsidian was dressed in the king's fur-lined robes and a large plume of feathers rose from a golden crown.

Tilbury felt an unexpected anger surge inside him. 'You lied to us,' he shouted, swinging his paws at Obsidian. 'You promised my pa you'd return us home.'

The guard tightened his grip on Tilbury, but Obsidian waved his paw. 'Let him go. He has work to do here.'

The guard released Tilbury and went to stand by the furnace, warming his paws by the flames.

Zekali came into the workshop, nervously clutching his tail.

Obsidian kept his gaze on Tilbury. 'Zekali says you understand the mechanics of the Silk Wing.'

Tilbury said nothing but nodded. He stared down, pushing his toes into the soft dirt.

'Then you must teach him how to fly,' said Obsidian. 'You will fly the Silk Wing tomorrow.'

Tilbury swallowed hard. 'No,' he said. 'You betrayed us.'

'If you do not do as I ask, I will kill the old maid,' Obsidian snarled. 'And if you try to escape on the Silk Wing, I will kill your sister.'

Tilbury's mind somersaulted. He could see no way out. He didn't want to teach Zekali how to fly, and then be sent back down to the dungeon. He stared down at his feet, seeing the imprint of them in the sand. Is this all that would be left of him, he thought, his pawprint? He wondered if he could scoop it up and send it to Ma, as a reminder of him. She would know his pawprint anywhere. His pawprint was unique, different from Nimble-Quick's or Marfaire's or any other rat's, like a key to who he was.

With this thought in his head, an idea filled his mind as he stared at his pawprint. He wasn't even aware he was being spoken to until Obsidian shoved him in the chest.

'Are you listening?' Obsidian snarled.

Tilbury looked up at him.

'You are to fly the Silk Wing tomorrow,' said Obsidian. 'Just you and Zekali.'

'Yes,' said Tilbury, thinking fast. 'But we had tensioned the wires for the weight of three of us, for Zekali, Nimble-Quick and me. I will need to change the tension on the wires supporting the wing.'

'Then do it now,' said Obsidian, watching him.

Tilbury walked across the workshop, and as he came close to the guard he pretended to trip, knocking the guard off his stool.

The guard fell, his eyes wide in surprise, and he sprawled on his back. Tilbury fell forward on top of him, and in the chaos he stamped on the key that hung from the guard's belt, pushing it into the ground, making a perfect imprint of it in the soft, damp sand.

The guard struggled up. 'Get off,' he spluttered, and Tilbury scuttled away from him.

Obsidian scowled at the guard. 'Pay attention,' he snapped. Then he turned to Tilbury. 'The Silk Wing will fly tomorrow at noon.'

Tilbury waited for Obsidian to leave, keeping an eye on the guard who settled himself on a piece of sacking by the entrance to the workshop. 'I have to strengthen the frame,' said Tilbury to Zekali. 'I want to put more solder on the metal joints.'

Zekali nodded. He seemed wary of Tilbury, and Tilbury guessed it was because any trust between them had been lost.

Tilbury started smelting metal in a crucible in the hot, white flames of the furnace and his thoughts burned with the injustice in the City in the Clouds. The guard swiftly got bored and nodded off, and when Zekali left Tilbury alone for a moment, Tilbury took the crucible and poured the molten metal into the imprint the key had made in the dirt. The liquid metal hissed and turned black as it hit the cold, damp sand. When the metal cooled and solidified, Tilbury picked up the newly made key, filed the rough edges and tucked it inside his pocket.

'I've finished,' called Tilbury when Zekali returned.

Zekali nodded. 'Tomorrow the Silk Wing shall fly once more.

My life's work will be done.' He turned to the snoozing guard. 'Wake up,' he said irritably. 'You can return the ratling now.'

The guard spluttered awake, got to his feet and grabbed Tilbury by the scruff of the neck. 'Right, let's get you back.'

The sun dipped low as the guard led him back to the dungeon. He opened the door to the cell and pushed Tilbury through, leaving them with a tiny stub of candle.

Marfaire, Nimble-Quick and the sand ratling crowded around him.

He could feel their questions in the silence.

'We escape tonight,' whispered Tilbury. 'All four of us.'

'But how?' said Nimble-Quick.

Tilbury then reached into his pocket and pulled out the key. 'I only hope it works.'

Nimble-Quick marvelled at the key. She took it to the door, slipped it into the lock, turning it slowly not to make any noise. The lock slid open. 'Oh, little brother,' whispered Nimble-Quick in astonishment. 'You're a genius.'

'Well done, Master Tilbury,' said Marfaire. 'But how are we to escape from the City in the Clouds?'

Tilbury broke into a wide grin. 'The same way Bartholomew escaped. By the Silk Wing, of course. We'll fly by moonlight.'

CHAPTER FORTY-ONE
Moonflight

The ratling looked at Tilbury. 'Are you really taking me with you?'

'Of course,' he said. 'We couldn't leave you here.'

'My name is Rose,' she whispered. 'Ma called me her wild mountain rose.'

Marfaire smiled. 'It is a very fitting name. For the wild rose blooms in the harshest of times. Your ma would be proud.'

Rose sniffed. 'Thank you.'

Nimble-Quick was pacing up and down. 'But how do we know when to leave? We do not know if it is day or night down here.'

'The sun was setting when I was brought back,' said Tilbury, 'so I guess that this candle will burn for a while longer. When it burns low we make our escape. We must lock the door again just in case the guard returns.'

Nimble-Quick nodded. 'And we must use this time to teach Marfaire and Rose how to help us fly.'

So Tilbury and Nimble-Quick talked through the take-off procedure several times. They all sat together as if they were sitting in the cockpit of the Silk Wing and Tilbury described how to wind up the clockwork engines and how to steer by leaning and shifting their weight.

'What about the diamond?' said Nimble-Quick.

'It's heavily guarded in the Golden Archway,' said Tilbury. 'I don't see how we can get it.'

'We have to try,' said Nimble-Quick. 'Don't we, Marfaire?'

Marfaire was silent for a moment. 'There has been much blood shed over this diamond. I do not wish to see any more.'

When the candle began to sputter wax, Marfaire stood up. 'I think it's time to go.'

Tilbury nodded. He unlocked the door, and they all crept forward along the corridor and up the steps. The guard was sitting on the ground at the entrance to the dungeons, snoring quietly beside the glowing embers of a small fire, safe in the belief the prisoners were locked up.

The moon had risen high in the sky and shone brightly in the indigo sky. It lit up the clouds such that they seemed to glow with their own light. Tilbury led Marfaire, Nimble-Quick and Rose through the city, the plumes of their breath rising up into the still, cold air. They crept beneath open windows where the gentle snoring of sleeping Golden Rats drifted into the night. With each step, Tilbury expected a Golden Rat to spy them and call the alarm. There were guards patrolling the Golden Archway and the *Eye of Aurun*. The scaffolding had been taken away and it was

278

so heavily guarded that Tilbury could not see how they could take the diamond with them. He felt bitter disappointment. If they couldn't return the diamond to the Sand Rats, then they couldn't fulfil the prophecy. They would have failed at the final hurdle, and Tilbury felt it was all his fault. Although maybe it was enough to escape themselves.

At last, they reached the steps to Zekali's workshop. It was dark inside except for the light from the furnace. Tilbury pushed his head inside the workshop and listened, but it was silent, and Tilbury guessed Zekali was out.

But he was wrong.

'Tilbury?' It was Zekali. He had been sleeping next to the Silk Wing. He lit a candle and held it up. 'Tilbury, what are you doing here?'

Tilbury thought of finding an excuse, but the candle's light pooled on Marfaire, Nimble-Quick and then Rose.

'The sand ratling!' Zekali gasped. 'What is she doing here?'

'Escaping,' spat Nimble-Quick. 'With us.'

'No, no, no!' stuttered Zekali in horror. He backed away. 'I'm going to call the guards!'

Marfaire snatched a sharp chisel, leaping forward and holding it at his chest. 'Move and you die.'

Zekali shook his head. 'You are not a killer.' Then he turned and ran, shouting for the guards at the top of his voice.

'Make haste,' said Marfaire.

But Tilbury paused, reaching out for two pieces of silk that lay on Zekali's desk and wrapping them around his neck.

'Come on,' called Nimble-Quick, wheeling the Silk Wing out onto the runway. Tilbury climbed into the cockpit and Nimble-Quick climbed in behind him and started pulling the tension on the wing above. Marfaire and Rose squeezed into the seat beside Nimble-Quick, wound the coils of the clockwork engine tightly and set them ready to release and spin the propeller.

'Ready?' cried Nimble-Quick.

'Ready,' they all called, and Tilbury released the spring and the propeller started to whizz faster and faster, then he released the brake and the Silk Wing lurched forward, rolling across the runway towards the edge of the cliff.

He could hear Zekali shouting behind him.

They picked up speed as they hurtled down the runway, the thin air whistling through their fur. Tilbury released the second spring coil to move the propeller faster and they shot forward, the edge of the cliff rapidly approaching. Would they fly? Were the four of them too heavy for the Silk Wing? There was no turning back now. Tilbury had never travelled so fast. His whiskers were pressed flat against his face, and it felt as if a great weight was crushing his chest. His eyes streamed with water and he tried to speak, but only a gargle came out. Faster and faster and faster. The wheels roared and rumbled beneath them, and then there was silence, as the Silk Wing shot off the cliff edge and into the night.

Tilbury closed his eyes, expecting to plummet to the ground.

But instead, the Silk Wing embraced the gentle breeze and flew like a bird, up, up and up into the sky, silhouetted by a brilliant, bright white moon.

CHAPTER FORTY-TWO
Go Well

The updraughts carried them high above the city.

'Look, Tilbury, look!' cried Nimble-Quick.

Tilbury opened his eyes to see the clouds spread out below them. They looked like big, soft, fluffy feather pillows. Mountain peaks pierced through them and the snow dazzled in the bright moonlight.

Below, guards were shouting and pointing at the Silk Wing. Tilbury could see Obsidian running into the plaza, whipping his tail in anger and thrusting his sword upwards as if he were trying to rip them from the sky.

'Which way do we go?' called Tilbury.

'Follow the river,' said Rose, leaning forward and pointing to a silver strip of river reflecting in the moonlight. 'The Diamond River will take us to the Diamond Mines by the sea.'

'What about the *Cursed Night*?' said Nimble-Quick.

Tilbury shook his head grimly. 'We'll have to leave it.'

Nimble-Quick leaned forward and held Tilbury by the shoulders. 'We have a chance to get it,' she said. She stood up on her seat and opened the wings of the bird suit.

'No!' cried Tilbury. 'It's too risky.'

'We have to get the diamond,' said Nimble-Quick. She pointed in the direction of the river, where it cut between two mountain peaks. 'I will fly to the *Cursed Night*, then fly back and meet you by the gap in the mountains.'

'No –' said Tilbury.

But it was too late to stop her. Nimble-Quick launched from the Silk Wing. Tilbury watched as she glided in a wide circle over the city. The pale blue silk of her bird-suit shimmered in the moon-light and she used her tail to steer. The Golden Rats looked up to see her soar out over the cliff edge, and then back again towards the archway. She swooped down, faster and faster, aiming straight for the diamond. Obsidian screeched in anger and Golden Rats swarmed forward but Nimble-Quick flew through the archway, ripping the diamond from the chain it was hanging from. She shot over the precipice, stuffing the diamond down the front of the bird-suit then spreading her paws again to open the wings of the bird-suit wide.

Tilbury tipped the Silk Wing into a dive and headed to the gap in the mountains where they would meet. Arrows from the Golden Rats streaked through the air, and Tilbury watched one pierce right through the outstretched silk of Nimble-Quick's bird-suit. It ripped through the fabric, slashing it between her right front paw and her hind foot. She could no longer soar and began to tumble downwards. Down, down, down she fell. The puffy clouds were not soft pillows, but just thin, wet air, and she disappeared through them towards the valley below. Tilbury pushed the Silk Wing into a vertical dive too, and they were both plunging straight down, right into the opaque whiteness of the clouds. Tilbury couldn't see ahead at all and he hoped he would not fly straight into her. They came out of the base of the cloud, the forest rushing towards them. Nimble-Quick was just ahead of them as they fell towards the forested floor of the Badlands, the sheer cliff-face a blur beside them. She spread her paws wide, trying to slow her fall.

'Wind the propeller,' Tilbury yelled to Rose, and she tightened the coils again and the propellers spun even faster, closing the gap between them and Nimble-Quick.

Marfaire reached out and hauled Nimble-Quick into the cockpit, then Tilbury pulled the controls to lift the nose of the Silk Wing into the air. They were travelling too fast. Tilbury pulled up just in time to scrape the treetops, and with a shearing crack, the wheels ripped off from underneath the Silk Wing.

Rose was furiously winding up the propeller to gain more speed, and Tilbury pulled the joystick lever back to pull the nose of the Silk Wing into the sky, but the air was thin and there was no breeze to catch in the steep valley between the mountains. They flew, skimming the treetops and then up the side of the mountain above deep powder snow. Jagged rocks rose up ahead of them, a barrier against the midnight sky.

'We won't make it,' cried Tilbury.

Nimble-Quick tried to adjust the tension in the lines holding the Silk Wing to the cockpit, and Rose kept the propeller spinning, but the Silk Wing was in line with the rocks and not gaining height.

'I can't pull her up,' cried Tilbury, his paws tight around the joystick. 'We're going to crash!'

Marfaire leaned forward, placing her paw on Tilbury's shoulder for a brief moment. 'My dearest Tilbury,' she said. 'This farewell is shorter than I wish it to be. But you no longer need me. And the Silk Wing needs to be lighter to fly. Go well, my friend. It has been an honour knowing you.'

'Marfaire!' cried Tilbury. 'No!'

But Marfaire leaped from the Silk Wing, and as she did so, it found new speed and shot upwards towards the sky. Tilbury glanced back, but the bright glare from moonlight on snow was blinding and he could see no trace of her at all. Marfaire, his mentor, the rat who had taught him to believe in himself and to be brave and wise, had gone.

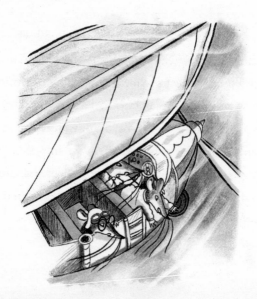

CHAPTER FORTY-THREE

The Diamond Mine

The Silk Wing skimmed the jagged rocks and an updraught from the mountain peak snatched them into a turbulent vortex of air, and it was all Tilbury could do to keep them flying straight. The swirling currents smoothed out and they found themselves rising up, up and up above the mountain range, above the clouds and high above the world.

'We have to go back for Marfaire,' said Nimble-Quick.

'It's impossible. There is nowhere to land,' said Tilbury.

'But Tilbury . . .' began Nimble-Quick. But her voice faltered, for she knew the truth that neither dared say, that they could not rescue Marfaire, and that she would not want them to. This was her choice, and she had wanted them to go on.

As the Silk Wing caught fresh mountain winds, Rose didn't need to wind the propeller quite so often and the three young rats could breathe more easily.

Nimble-Quick took the *Cursed Night* from inside her bird-suit and slipped it into Tilbury's rucksack. 'You must carry it again,' she said gravely.

Tilbury hefted the rucksack, feeling the weight of the diamond inside him. He missed Marfaire with all his heart and soul. He missed her fierce wisdom, but most of all he knew he would miss her kindness and her trust, for she had not doubted him, even when he had doubted himself the most of all. The *Cursed Night* felt heavier than ever, and somehow the need to return it to the Sand Rats was more important than anything if they were to free themselves from the curse.

And so the Silk Wing flew high above the glittering Diamond River, following its path to the sea and to the diamond mine, where the *Cursed Night* had been dug from the earth so long ago.

As the eastern sky began to lighten, and the first rays of sun flared into the sky, Tilbury felt hope soar too, that soon he would return the *Cursed Night* and fulfil the prophecy.

Soon, they would be free.

Tilbury followed the river, away from the mountains, across the plains and over farmland and human cities. As the sun rose in the sky, rising thermals of air lifted the Silk Wing higher and the three young rats could sit back and let it soar. And now Tilbury had time to marvel at this flying machine, its design and beauty, and he wished he could talk with Bartholomew. The Dockland Rats hailed Bartholomew as an eccentric genius and a troubled hero. *And maybe that was how he wanted to be remembered*, Tilbury thought, *because no one wants to be the villain of their own story.* But Bartholomew had hidden his deep shame in his own lifetime, unable to tell even his own mother the truth. He had rewritten his own story.

'Look,' said Rose, leaning forward. 'There! I can see the sea.'

Tilbury peered at the horizon, and a strip of sea reflected the sunlight. Noon had passed and the layers of air were cooling. The Silk Wing could not gain as much height on the thermals.

Nimble-Quick leaned forward. 'That must be the diamond mine,' she said, pointing to a deep, wide man-made crater in the ground. The humans had long gone, and from high up all they could see was an open mine, overgrown with grasses and shrubs.

Tilbury circled the mine and they all looked down, trying to see any signs of life.

'Do you think anyone lives down there?' asked Nimble-Quick.

Rose stared down but said nothing. Maybe her homeland was empty. Maybe the descendants of the Sand Rats had gone.

The river fanned out into a broad delta with networks of smaller rivers and islands as it opened into the sea. Tall dark clouds were forming in the distance, their underbellies swelled with rain.

'We'll have to land soon,' said Tilbury. 'A storm is coming.'

'The riverbank looks flat enough,' said Nimble-Quick, pointing to a wide stretch of sand to the west of the diamond mine.

'You'll have to hold on,' said Tilbury. 'We've got no wheels.'

Tilbury brought the Silk Wing in a wide circle and straightened up, aiming for the riverbank. Rose stopped the propeller and they glided down, and soon the Silk Wing was level with the tops of the grasses along the riverbank.

'Hold on,' cried Tilbury as the Silk Wing made contact with the hard ground. They bumped twice, the Silk Wing rising into the air and bouncing back down, then they hit a rock, and the Silk Wing whirled though the air.

The world spun around Tilbury: sand and grass and sky in a twirling blur. He heard the ripping tear of the silk and the twang of the tension wires snapping, as the Silk Wing fell apart around him.

Pain shot through him, as it splintered into pieces.

It came to a stop with a sickening, stomach-lurching thud, and Tilbury found himself flying through the air.

He felt his body slam into the hard ground, and then he didn't feel anything at all.

CHAPTER FORTY-FOUR

Guardians of the Oath

'Tilbury?'

Tilbury opened his eyes and Nimble-Quick's face blurred in and out of focus.

'Tilbury. It's me, Nimble-Quick.'

'Is Ma here?'

Nimble-Quick put a gentle paw on Tilbury. 'We're not home yet.'

Rose came to stand beside her. 'We're with the Sand Rats in the diamond mine.'

Tilbury struggled to sit up. He could see they were in a small cave with sandy walls that glowed warmly in soft candlelight. He tried to stand, but pain seared through his right leg and when he looked down it was wrapped in bandages with a wooden splint.

'Your leg's broken,' said Rose. She handed him some hot tea. 'Here, drink this, the Sand Rats say it will help with the pain.'

'The *Cursed Night*?' said Tilbury, looking for his bag. 'Is it safe?'

'It's here,' said Nimble-Quick. She leaned forward. 'Oh, Tilbury, none of us are safe. The diamond has brought its curse with us.'

'How long have I been asleep?' said Tilbury, feeling an unquenchable thirst despite the tea.

'Three days,' said Nimble-Quick. 'The Sand Rats want to call a council to rid us of the curse.'

A Sand Rat came into the cave. He was an Elder rat, wearing a white smock and carrying two long sticks in his paws. His whiskers were white and curled in tight spirals.

'Greetings, Master Tilbury,' said the Sand Rat. 'I am one of the healers. It is good to see you in the land of the living.' He passed the sticks to Tilbury. 'Here, to help you walk while your bones make friends with each other again.'

Nimble-Quick and Rose helped Tilbury to his feet, and he leaned on the sticks and tried a few hops across the cave.

The Sand Rat watched him and nodded. 'I would like to give you more time, but time is something we do not have.'

Another Sand Rat came into the cave. She was tall, wearing sand-coloured leather armour, with a sword at her side and a horn slung across her shoulder. She stared at Tilbury. 'He's awake. But is he ready?'

The healer Sand Rat nodded. 'He is ready.'

'Good,' said the other Sand Rat. 'Then let's make haste. I'll call for the hearing.'

Nimble-Quick and Rose helped Tilbury and they followed the Sand Rats out of the cave. They were standing on a steep slope within the vast crater of the diamond mine. Trees and grasses grew from the slopes of the mine and Tilbury could see lots of burrows and passageways leading off from the sides of the crater deep into the earth. The bottom of the crater was wide and flat, with white stones placed in concentric circles, creating a ripple pattern.

The warrior Sand Rat stopped and put the horn to her mouth, and a clear single note carried across the mine. Tilbury could see other Sand Rats emerging from holes and burrows, and soon the sandy paths between the long grasses and trees were full of Sand Rats heading downhill. He noticed that they all carried swords and knives, and wore tough leather armour.

'This way,' said the warrior Sand Rat.

Tilbury found it hard to walk with the sticks and so Nimble-Quick and Rose carried him between them, using the sticks as a seat he could sit upon.

'How's the Silk Wing?' asked Tilbury, already knowing the answer and feeling a tight knot in his chest.

'It's broken beyond repair,' said Nimble-Quick.

'But we have returned the *Cursed Night*,' said Tilbury, forcing a smile.

Nimble-Quick did not smile back. 'It's not that simple.'

Tilbury stared at her. 'Aren't these the descendants of Sand Rats of the Diamond Mines? Did we get it wrong?'

'They are the descendants,' said Rose. 'They are the rats Ma said we should find.'

'I don't understand,' said Tilbury. 'Surely our journey is at its end.'

But he had no more chance to talk as he, Nimble-Quick and Rose were led to the very centre of the circle of sand. Another Elder Sand Rat came to join them and brought Tilbury's rucksack. The Elder wore a sword and shield at her side.

'I am Meliah, one of the Guardians of the Oath,' said the Sand Rat. She handed Tilbury his rucksack. 'I believe this belongs to you.'

Tilbury took the rucksack, feeling the heavy weight of the diamond inside. 'NO –' began Tilbury, but Meliah put her paw up.

'Please,' said Meliah. 'We will hear your story, but we must wait while all the Sand Rats are seated.'

Sand Rats poured down from the slopes of the mine and took their seats on the white stones. There were Sand Rats of all ages and they sat attentively, their ears swivelling towards Tilbury, Nimble-Quick and Rose.

'Friends,' said Meliah. 'Thank you for answering the call, for today is a day that has been long foretold and will test the oath our ancestors asked of us.'

Grasshoppers chirped from the long grasses and seed pods popped in the heat, but all the rats sat still, waiting.

'We are here to greet these three visitors and hear their story,' said Meliah. She turned to Tilbury. 'Please, tell us how you came to be here and why.'

Tilbury turned to all the faces looking at him. He took a deep breath, not quite knowing where to start. He decided to begin at the beginning. 'My name is Tilbury Twitch-Whiskers, the seventh seventh-born of Mr and Mrs Twitch-Whiskers. The Great Bartholomew once stole a diamond, the *Cursed Night*, from the Golden Rats. But he knew the true owners were the rats who were forced to dig it from the bare earth. Their freedoms were stolen. I am here with my sister, Nimble-Quick, to lift an ancient curse on our people. For only when the diamond is returned to you, can we be truly free.' He lifted the diamond from the rucksack and heard a collective intake of breath from all the rats. He laid the diamond at the feet of Meliah and bowed. 'We return the diamond to the Sand Rats of the Diamond Mines. You are truly the rightful owners.'

Meliah shook her head. 'But, Master Tilbury, we do not wish to have it.'

Tilbury frowned. 'But it belongs to you.'

Meliah picked the diamond up in her paws.

'Don't look at it!' said Tilbury. 'For it contains the curse. Its power will possess you and will reveal the deepest darkest reaches of your soul.'

But Meliah looked into the surface of the diamond, shrugged her shoulders and gave a wry smile. She then threw it to another rat to look. The other rat looked at his own reflection, chuckled and passed it on, each rat looking at the cut surface, the sound of soft laughter rising up around them.

Tilbury felt a knot in his chest, and he clenched and unclenched his paws, feeling hurt and anger swell inside him. He tried to push those feelings down into his tail, but it was impossible, they rose and overwhelmed him in tide of frustration and grief. 'How dare you!' he shouted. 'How dare you laugh. I have travelled oceans for you. I have left my family for you. I have almost lost my sister for you, and all you do is laugh. We have returned the diamond to you, and all you do is mock us. I wish we hadn't bothered.'

Meliah stepped forward, her paws out to Tilbury. 'Oh, Tilbury, please forgive us. We recognize you have had quite a journey. But you have to understand that it's your journey, your story, not ours.'

'Don't you want the diamond back?' said Tilbury, glaring at them.

'No, Master Tilbury,' said Meliah. 'We do not.'

Tilbury stared at them in stunned silence.

Nimble-Quick spoke up. 'You mean to say we have brought it all this way, and you really don't want it?'

'No,' said Meliah firmly. 'We do not.'

'But it holds a curse and a prophecy,' said Tilbury. 'Many rats have died for it.'

'It is true that many rats have fought and died for it,' said Meliah. And this time there was no hint of a smile, only sadness. 'For we recognize its power. Rats have lied and killed for it. They have let it possess their minds and forsaken friends and family for it. In their search for it, they have forgotten how to live. In their desire for it, they have forgotten how to love.'

Tilbury shook his head. 'But surely you want it? Your ancestors dug it from the earth with their bare paws. It's a diamond, the most valuable jewel in the world.'

'Who puts that value on it?' asked Meliah.

There was a hushed silence waiting for Tilbury to answer.

But it was Rose who answered.

'We do,' said Rose quietly. She looked at Meliah. 'Now I see it for what it is.'

Tilbury shook his head. 'I don't understand.'

Meliah lifted up a pawful of sand. 'What if we put value on each grain of sand?'

'But sand is everywhere. A diamond is rare,' said Tilbury. 'Especially this size.'

'What does it matter?' said Meliah.

'But it's a diamond,' said Tilbury.

Meliah nodded. 'Indeed. It's a diamond. A diamond dug from the earth like any other rock. It's a bit prettier than other rocks. It sparkles a little more. The value we give it is of our own making. The stories we tell about it hold our own hopes and fears. But the diamond itself holds neither a curse nor a prophecy.'

Nimble-Quick picked up the *Cursed Night* and held it in her paws. She stared into its surface and nodded.

'It's a rock, isn't it,' she said. 'Nothing more, nothing less.

'That's all it is.

'Just a rock.'

CHAPTER FORTY-FIVE
Return of the Cursed Night

'What shall I do with it?' said Tilbury.

'That's up to you,' said Meliah. 'But you cannot leave it here.'

'Why not?' said Tilbury.

'Because it brings death and destruction,' said Meliah. 'We swore an oath that we would not seek or hoard these rocks that other rats desire. If any rat wishes to do so, they are allowed to leave and live as they choose. But here, we will live in peace but be prepared to fight for our freedom.'

'Maybe it's safe here. No one will know if you keep it,' said Tilbury.

Meliah shook her head. 'It is too late. Already we have been visited by rats from across the seven seas looking for you. They arrived at Felinport and they came here with their army and ransacked our homes. They will come again, especially as they will have heard of the Silk Wing flying high in the sky.'

'Who are they?' asked Tilbury, fearing he already knew the answer.

'They are from your land,' said Meliah. 'The leader says his name is Yersinia.'

Tilbury felt sick in his stomach. 'We will fight them with you,' he said.

'We fight only for our lives and our freedom,' said Meliah. 'We will not fight over this rock from the ground.'

'So what do I do with it?' said Tilbury.

Meliah smiled. 'You could give it to Yersinia.'

Tilbury looked at Nimble-Quick. 'But give it up so easily?'

Nimble-Quick shook her head. 'But the Dockland Rats will fight for it again. The fighting will not end.'

'You cannot control what others think of the diamond and what they do,' said Meliah. 'You can only control your own thoughts and actions.'

'But –' said Tilbury.

His words were cut off as a horn blasted three times in urgent succession.

All the rats stood up and looked at the rim of the crater where the sentry rat stood with her horn.

'Soon we will be under attack,' said Meliah. 'We must make haste to the top of the mine and see who is coming.'

Tilbury let Nimble-Quick and Rose carry him up. Far below, two boats were sailing towards the water's edge. They were not human boats, but rat-sized boats with sails similar to the ones Tilbury had seen on the mountain lake. As they drew near, Tilbury could see Obsidian in the prow of one boat. On the other boat stood Yersinia, his sword raised. Tilbury thought he could see Elberry, his oldest brother, with the Tower Guard. The boats were cresting through the water, racing each other to the shore.

'The Tower Guard and the Golden Rats!' said Tilbury quietly. 'They are coming for the diamond. They are coming for me. When will this end?'

'Give them the *Cursed Night* to fight over,' snarled Nimble-Quick. 'I'm done with it.'

'There must be another way,' said Tilbury. He looked down to the shore. 'I need to get down there and draw them away,' he said. 'I need to sail away from here.' He turned to Meliah. 'Is there a way down avoiding the Yersinia and the Golden Rats?'

Meliah nodded. She called to several Sand Rat guards. 'Take Tilbury through the old tunnels.'

'I'm coming too,' said Nimble-Quick. 'I'm not leaving you.'

Rose stepped froward. 'Me too.'

Tilbury turned to her. 'No. You are with your own kind.'

Rose shook her head. 'Have you ever sailed a boat?'

Tilbury said nothing.

'Then you need me,' she said. 'I sailed them with my ma and pa across the lake to the orchards in the City in the Clouds.'

'You'll need both of us,' said Nimble-Quick. 'You can't walk by yourself. You need us to help carry you.'

Tilbury couldn't bring himself to look at the *Cursed Night*, even though he knew it was just a rock. He slipped it back in his rucksack and let himself be carried along by Rose and Nimble-Quick, following the guards along a passageway and down into deep, deep tunnels.

'Take care,' said the guard, scurrying ahead with a small oil lamp. The path was slippery and steep and smoothed from many tiny feet over the years. At last Tilbury could see a tiny pinpoint of light that became bigger and bigger and brighter and brighter, until he could see it was the opening to the tunnel. They walked out into bright, bright sunshine.

The two boats were moored at the water's edge and they were empty. Tilbury looked up the slope of the mine to see the Tower Guard and the Golden Rats racing each other to the top, Obsidian and Yersinia out in front.

'That one,' said Rose, pointing to the smallest boat. 'It has the fastest design.'

And while Rose and Nimble-Quick prepared the boat, Tilbury took the *Cursed Night* from his rucksack and raised it up high. The guard blew on his horn and both Yersinia and Obsidian turned to look down at the boats.

'I have it,' shouted Tilbury. 'If you want it you will have to get me first.'

'Come on!' yelled Nimble-Quick, seeing the Tower Guards and the Golden Rats running back down towards the shoreline. She helped Tilbury inside and Rose cast off. She let the sails out and the wind snapped them taut and soon the little boat was riding out into the surf, froth and foam flying past them.

Tilbury was glad of Rose's skill with the boat. She steered them into the furling waves, telling Nimble-Quick how to trim the sails. Nimble-Quick learned quickly too, and Tilbury marvelled that the curved sails of the boat were not so dissimilar to the shape of the Silk Wing. They ploughed through the waves, each crest threatening to break and take them tumbling back to the shore. But soon they were beyond the rolling waves and sailing out over the pale blue of the reef to the indigo of the deep ocean.

Tilbury looked behind to see Yersinia and Obsidian scrambling over each other into the remaining boat. They launched into the sea, rising up and down through the waves, chasing after Tilbury.

'Where are we heading?' called Rose.

Tilbury pointed out into the ocean.

'How long will we run for?' said Nimble-Quick. 'They will never stop hunting us down.'

'A bit further,' said Tilbury.

The midday sun burned down, and the sharp wind fell, such that their little boat began to slow. Tilbury turned to see both Obsidian and Yersinia getting the oars out, quarrelling and ordering each other to row faster.

'They're going to catch us up,' cried Nimble-Quick.

'It's time,' said Tilbury. 'Rose. Stop the boat and turn to face them.'

Rose glanced at Tilbury and turned the boat, letting the sails flap loose. Tilbury heaved himself on to the prow of the boat and looked at Yersinia and Obsidian who were racing towards him.

Both boats were beyond the shelf of the reef. Beneath them the ocean fell away into the deepest blue, into the fathomless, dark depths.

Tilbury grasped the diamond in his paws and held it out over the water. 'Stop,' called Tilbury. 'Come no closer.'

Yersinia and Obsidian turned around and stopped rowing, both fixed on the diamond held precariously above the waves.

Yersinia held his up his paw. 'Master Tilbury,' he said. His eyes glittered darkly, watching the diamond. 'Less haste. I'm sure we can come to a deal, for we are both Dockland Rats. In return for the diamond, I can make you lord and master of the Docklands of London.'

Obsidian pushed his way forward. 'Tilbury, you know the diamond is rightfully mine. If you throw the diamond in the sea the curse shall follow you and your family for eternity.'

'I do not want it,' said Tilbury.

'Then give it to me,' snarled Yersinia.

'No, to me,' said Obsidian.

'Then you can fight each other for it,' said Tilbury. 'Here!' he said. 'Catch.'

He swung his paw back and hurled the *Cursed Night* up high. It spun and twisted as it flew in an arc, glittering in the sunlight.

Tilbury couldn't help glancing at it one last time, before it plunged beneath the waves. In that split second, he caught sight of his reflection in its cut surface. He saw a rat searching for the truth. But this time, there was no terrified rat looking back at him, but his own clear-eyed, steady gaze. Behind the bright eyes and nervous twitchy nose, he saw a brave warrior, a brother, and a true friend, perfect in all his imperfections.

And Tilbury Twitch-Whiskers, a seventh seventh-born, smiled the widest smile, because in that moment, he had truly seen into the deepest reaches of his bright and beautiful soul.

EPILOGUE

It is a truth universally acknowledged that all rats enjoy a good story, even if the stories are embroidered with half-truths and embellished with exaggeration. And for the Dockland Rats, there is nothing more satisfying than sitting around a fire on a cold winter's night, roasting chestnuts and listening to tales by candlelight.

Tilbury finished his story and took a sip of blackberry wine.

'But, Pa, you haven't finished,' said Tilbury's oldest daughter, the first-born of his first litter. 'What happened to Obsidian and Yersinia?'

'Obsidian and Yersinia wanted that diamond so badly that they both dived down after it, clutching each other and fighting and biting and scratching as they went,' said Tilbury to his wide-eyed ratlings. 'Down, down, down . . . to the bottom of the sea. Maybe they found the diamond and maybe they didn't. But they were never seen again. And since then, the Dockland Rats have given up their hoardings of jewels and life is much finer for it. They are kinder, too. For much wealth can bring greed, jealously and want for more.'

'But what about your brother Elberry?' said Tilbury's second son from his third litter.

'Ah, poor Elberry,' said Tilbury. 'The diamond still possesses his mind, such is its power. He is still out there, digging into the sand of the Diamond River, hoping to find more diamonds there. He has become a prisoner of his own making, putting value on something that has so little worth.'

'And what about Marfaire?' said Tilbury's daughter from his fourth litter.

Tilbury smiled. 'Well now, I have heard from Nimble-Quick that there are tales of a white she-rat that rides a white tiger in the high mountain kingdoms. And I have heard it said that they are the greatest of friends.'

Tilbury's daughter from his sixth litter sighed. 'Why didn't Nimble-Quick stay here in the Docklands too?'

'She has always loved adventure,' said Tilbury. He ran his paws along the two silk scarves around his neck. 'We did make the Silk Wing together again from Bartholomew's original plans. We made it here in the chandlery basement. She has travelled around the world, across the seven seas, the great mountains and vast ice-sheets. I always look forward to her stories when she visits, but she is always happiest following where the winds take her.' Tilbury helped himself to a large piece of cheese and settled back into the orange furry tummy of Marmalade Paws. 'Whereas, like

Marmalade, I never really wanted to leave the chandlery basement of Tilbury Docks. It is an emporium of wonder, containing everything I could possibly want to know. He smiled at all his children and their bright eyes looked back at him. 'And now it contains all the riches I could possibly ever want to have.'

'But, Pa,' said Tilbury's third-born from his fourth litter. 'You told us that stories change with the teller. Would Nimble-Quick's story about the *Cursed Night* be different from your own?'

'That's a good question,' said Tilbury, 'for everyone has their own version of a story to tell.' He paused. 'We are made of stories; they shape us and tell us who we are. But we must honour those who share our story, tell their truth and let their light shine too.'

'Tell us about Rose,' said Tilbury's first-born son of his seventh litter. He looked up shyly. 'We want to know what happened to Rose?'

Tilbury smiled. 'You know this story,' he said, and chuckled. 'Why, you wouldn't be here to listen if it hadn't been for her. I have travelled far across the world, to learn that greed can destroy you. It will take away all that matters most.' He pulled Rose towards him and kissed her on the top of her head. 'The most valuable thing is often right under our noses.'

'But, Ma,' said their son. 'Didn't you want to stay with the Sand Rats in the Diamond Mines? You spent so long trying to find where you belonged.'

Rose tweaked her son's whisker. 'I have often wondered where home really is. Was my home in the City in the Clouds with my family there? Or was my home in the ancestral lands of the Sand

Rats? I only ever felt I half belonged to either place.' She sighed and held Tilbury's paw. 'I have never felt more at home than when I am with your pa. Home is not a place. Home is a feeling. It's where the heart is.'

Tilbury's youngest son twitched his tail and big tears filled his eyes, for this was the first time he had heard Pa tell the story of his remarkable life.

'What is it, Barty?' said Tilbury.

'Oh, Pa,' said Barty. 'I am named after Bartholomew, but now I hear he was no hero. He was a liar and a thief. Maybe I will become like him too.'

Tilbury pulled his youngest son closer. 'Indeed, Bartholomew was a thief, but he tried to put things right. That's what counts. In the end, he was true to himself. And now we are telling the truth of his story.'

'But I'm your seventh seventh-born,' said Bartholomew, 'and I'm afraid, for it's said that a seventh seventh-born in want of adventure does not last very long in the world. Maybe there is a curse upon me too.'

'There is no more a curse on a seventh seventh-born, than on the diamond that I threw into the sea,' said Tilbury. 'Do not be trapped by others' fears and superstitions. Your precious life is yours and yours alone. To live, you must seek the truth and learn to tell your own story.'